NEVER TO RETURN

European
Women
Writers
Series

ESTHER TUSQUETS

PARA NO VOLVER

Translated and with an
afterword by
Barbara F. Ichiishi

NEVER TO RETURN

University of Nebraska Press, Lincoln and London

Publication of this translation was assisted by a
grant from the Program
for Cultural Cooperation
between Spain's Ministry
of Education and Culture
and United States' Uni-
versities. Originally published as *Para no volver*
by Editorial Lumen, S. A.,
Barcelona, 1985.
⊖ Library of Congress
Cataloging-in-Publication
Data. Tusquets, Esther.
[Para no volver, English]
Never to return / Esther
Tusquets : translated
with an afterword
by Barbara F. Ichiishi.
p. cm. (European
women writer series)
Includes biblio-
graphical references.
ISBN 0-8032-4433-9
(cloth : alk. paper)
ISBN 0-8032-9438-7
(pbk. : alk. paper)
I. Ichiishi, Barbara F.
(Barbara Franklin),
1948–   . II. Title.
III. Series.
PQ6670.U8P37.13
1999   863'.64—dc21
98-53764 CIP

Contents

Never to Return   1

Afterword   173

Glossary   189

Youth, divine treasure,
now you're leaving, never to return . . .

THIS NAGGING IRRITATION, THIS SIMMERING RAGE brought on by so many things over the last few months. It must be that she's growing old, this time for real, not like at the age of seventeen or twenty when fantasizing about being old and world-weary was simply one more form of playful affectation ("For Elena, who at the age of seventeen feels like an old woman," the sacred cow of Spanish letters, the greatest novelist since the generation of '98, had written in her autograph album), or at the age of thirty or even forty, because it's clear that she hadn't felt anything very special upon passing the threshold of forty, maybe because everyone around her was going through it along with her or had already gone through it two or three or five years earlier, one unexpected advantage of having long ago chosen friends older than oneself, and Julio continued treating her, as always, like a little girl ("An overgrown, silly little girl who can't resist mothering you," she had joked with him just a few months before), and besides, when Elena turned forty she must have been caught up in one of her peculiar obsessions (impossible now to recall which one), suffering and rejoicing and struggling over something that had little or nothing to do with the real world, nor with her age, or at least that's how it seemed to Elena, although she couldn't be too sure about it, because maybe she *had* gotten something after all out of those two months of psychoanalysis, and it was among other things, the almost constant habit of turning things around, of asking the minute an idea crossed your mind if it couldn't just as well be the opposite, the notion that two contrary assertions were not necessarily mutually exclusive but rather could perhaps coexist in

3

a dense amalgam of truth and falsehood, the suspicion, which existed prior to analysis, it's true, but which might have intensified over its course, that one could without letup be playing dirty tricks on oneself – weren't there individuals who, to Elena's amazement, cheated themselves playing solitaire? So easy, moreover, to detect these failings in others, so evident from the outside what was happening to others, so obvious ("The analyst spends his time pointing out the obvious," she had protested crossly at one stormy session, and the guy, imperturbable, with that wooden look that was starting to get on her nerves, "Couldn't it be because the analysand spends his time denying the obvious?" and "My face wouldn't bother you if you were lying down on the couch," so that yes, he did want her once and for all stretched out on the couch and him behind her back, despite the fact that at the outset – so later it perhaps became difficult to correct – in a display of express heterodoxy, he had allowed her to adopt whatever position she preferred, so Elena sat with her legs crossed in lotus position, her back against the angle of the wall, facing the Wizard head on from the farthest corner of the room). So obvious, then, what was happening, only one didn't hit upon it oneself, or one couldn't allow oneself to recognize it, and this was one of her long-standing doubts about psychoanalysis, because what dosage of truth could each individual stand without it blowing up in his face and breaking him in two, body and soul? what happened when you confronted a human being – through psychoanalysis or some equivalent kind of experience, the nature of which she could not imagine – with a reality that he had made great efforts to deny to himself for ever and ever, since he first developed the faculty to reason? and how could the analyst for his part precisely measure the potency of the fire he was playing with, the dosage at which the medicine would perhaps turn into a lethal poison? And at one of the first sessions, when she still didn't know the half of it, Elena had begun to tell the joke (with the annoyance, considered absurd by the Wizard but to her insurmountable, of not knowing whether he already knew it, if she was like an idiot telling the guy a story he already knew, and not having the nerve to ask him, because she had already learned that she'd only receive silence in answer, or if he was feeling especially benevolent, the assurance that the fact that he had or had not previously heard the content of a joke the woman told would in no way impede the favorable course of the analysis), the joke, then, about the poor devil who went to consult a psychiatrist, and of course, she admitted obediently, a psychiatrist was not the same as a psychoanalyst (allusions to psychiatry, like any complacent reference to religion and, she would discover later, to feminism, caused the wooden face's expression to darken for a few seconds: it was strange how a wooden face without the slightest muscular contraction could darken), how could you compare those individuals, the psychiatrists, conceited and dangerous, who went around handing out potions and lavishing intrusive advice, and who occupied, the Impassive One had pronounced, with that air of solemnity that the overwhelming profusion of his silences lent to each of his interventions, "an impossible space." Someone, then, some poor guy went to consult a psychiatrist, explaining distressed and terrified that he had a crocodile under his bed, and begging the doctor to free him from this uncomfortable hallucination, and the psychiatrist actually did cure him, except that afterward, some days or weeks later, the crocodile without any more nonsense ate him up. You can be sure the psychiatrist prescribed colorful sugar-coated pills (they had at their disposal, as Elena well knew, drugs for everything, or for almost anything, including drugs to neutralize the image of the crocodile lurking under the bed), he must have administered kind words, and even some soothingly paternal pats on the back, while in contrast a psychoanalyst, a more genuine and experienced wizard, would have urged him to confront all alone, without any pills whatsoever and hence unarmed, the psychic reality of

5

the crocodile and all its possible origins and associations, because, let's see, what did the patient associate the image of the crocodile with? did his mama scold him when he was little for crying crocodile's tears, did his nanny or governess threaten to take him to the zoo so the crocodile would gobble him up if he ever again wet his bed? but one way or another, whether through the intervention of psychiatrists or psychoanalysts, it seemed to Elena that such poor fellows inevitably ended up being eaten by the crocodile who was waiting patiently under the bed, although maybe it *was* to their advantage after all, she conceded sarcastically, that those who had been analyzed had a more complete un-derstanding of what to be devoured meant. And what did one do, Mr. Wizard – she continued her harangue from the couch-stage, on days when she felt in a better mood or less darkly depressed – with the patient whom no one in the world loved, with the analysand who was really, for family and strangers alike, an authentic disaster, who was dull and stupid, had a shitty character, a huge rear end, an almost total lack of kindliness and charm? what happened to them, and they were without number ("Do you imagine yourself among them?" had inquired wily Wooden Face, always ready to put salt on the wound and think badly of his patients, "Why don't you tell me about the crocodile you do or do not have under your own bed?" and she had admitted that yes, sometimes she did fantasize herself to be among them, although she didn't have too clear an idea – and that's why she was there – of what could be her particular crocodile), what did you do, then, with the multitudes who had long before taken the wrong turn and could not go back, and did not even know at what bend in the road they had gone astray? with all those who had devoted themselves to a cause that was, more than lost, misguided – lost causes at least had a certain charm – to an endeavor in which they would never succeed and yet for which it was now impos-sible to substitute another? In short, what would happen, Mr. Wizard, if you placed before their eyes that implacable mirror and obliged them to contemplate themselves in it, and even forced them to recognize themselves, that dreadful mirror which almost all of us, with model tenacity and discretion, have strived day by day to remove or at least blur? "You are playing with fire, Stranger" – had the Impassive One seen the film? – and the Stranger, undaunted, he too poker face or wooden face, infinitely wise and contemptuous: "What else would I play with?" bewitching Elena, sitting there like a ninny in a seat in the darkened theater, so shamefully in love with risk and adventure – it would have been truly magnificent to be able to sidle up to the Stranger with the long snakelike body of Bacall, in a tight-fitting suit, eyebrow raised, and declare her solidarity and love in a brief, unforgettable phrase – and then suddenly overcome with fear, with the huge and urgent need to ignore all fires and run to the bed and get under it and not find the slightest trace of any crocodile whatsoever.

This nagging irritation, that boundless rage – it might come from aging, or simply be the other side of the bitter pill of depression, which leaves one exhausted, defenseless, without the strength to so much as lift a finger, go get a glass of water, make it to the next corner, and at the same time excitable and testy as a powder keg – as she finds herself obliged to repeat for the hundredth time, without the salesgirl understanding or even listening, that what she wants is six frames of exactly the same size, fifty by sixty-two centimeters, "Make a note of it, Miss," and centered in the six equal frames the six prints which, it's quite apparent, are not equal in size, and the employee with her broad flat face, as though she lacked one dimension, and her thin hair turned into Brillo by a bad-quality dye – would things be different if she looked like Bacall? – knits her brow and focuses all her attention on this difficult problem and stubbornly insists that she also has to record, one by one, the dimensions of each of the six prints, the length and width of the six. And yes, it must be due to her age or to depression, this urge to grab her by the shoulders and shake her, as the girl goes on measuring and taking notes, and then, after an interminable pause, concentrates still harder and picks up her calculator – and what the devil is she trying to calculate, what rule of three or cube root is she seeking, when it would have been much simpler once and for all to listen to her? – and Elena repeats again, teeth clenched so as not to scream, "six prints of different sizes, each of the six centered in six equal frames," and the salesgirl interrupts triumphantly, "But then the borders won't be equal!" no, of course not, it's very clear that the borders won't be equal, and that doesn't matter to Elena and there's nothing to make note of or calculate, it's enough to jot down carefully the size of the frames, and the girl again frowns, at the height of confusion, and concludes that, in any case, it's better for her to take down all the measurements, and Elena thinks, as a homicidal rage creeps from the tail of her spine up to the nape of her neck: "I'm going to kill her if she uses that damned calculator one more time, if she takes down one more figure I'll kill her, I'll drag her by her steel wool hair, I'll pull it out by the handful, I'll slap her in the face, I'll kick her, I'll make her swallow in a horrid death rattle that pencil and notebook and that blasted calculator." All the while conscious of the absurdity of the situation, the enormity of her anger, Lord what would the papers say: "The wife of one of our most distinguished movie directors, whose latest film, by the way, is going to have its Broadway début in the coming days, attempts to assassinate without plausible motive the salesgirl of a prestigious downtown art gallery . . ." There's no history, of course, although . . . "perhaps the explanation for such deviant behavior lies in a sudden fit of madness, given the fact that the assailant has on various occasions consulted a psychiatrist, and is currently undergoing analysis (no, it would be 'psychoanalysis,' because the terms 'analyst' and 'analysand' are part of the jargon of the initiated, who also always talk about the unconscious rather than the subconscious, the latter term used by the common people

8

and badly informed journalists) with an eminent professor from the University of Rosario . . ." Maybe they'd even print a photo of Wooden Face in the papers, but joking apart, what would her colleagues in the production company think? what would she tell Julio when he called, amazed and incredulous, from New York? and how would she explain it to the Wizard at tomorrow's session? "What do you associate the salesgirl's face with?" he'd ask suspiciously, although in a bored and neutral tone of voice, as though going around murdering salesgirls-with-steel-wool-hair were an everyday occurrence, and then, "Doesn't it occur to you that these uncontrollable fits of anger, which you've described to me on various occasions and which are totally out of proportion to the trivial incidents that set them off, may have deeper roots, may be closely linked to your depression?" Yes, of course they could have something or a lot to do with her depression, something or a lot to do with her age, and Eduardo might even have been right when he pronounced, shaking his index finger at her admonishingly, with regard to Elena or other people or himself: "These irrational outbursts directed against individuals you don't give a damn about only occur when one is walking around feeling very unloved or very screwed up." So that, when the employee finishes taking notes, raises the notebook close to her nearsighted eyes, nibbles again at the tip of her pencil, picks up her calculator once more and starts saying, "So the first print . . . ," Elena, so as not to kill her, gathers up the engravings, stuffs them any which way into her briefcase, stands up and leaves the gallery so fast that the girl has no time to react, and by the time her boss reaches Elena she's already at the door and doesn't have to explain. "There comes a time in one's life, perhaps around the age of fifty, when one is excused from having to go on tolerating certain doses of human imbecility," she could have told him, "and all the more so when they come from art gallery employees with badly dyed hair and two-dimensional faces who don't even remotely resemble Lauren Bacall," although it's much

9

better that she didn't have time to say it, because if she had she would later have suffered such an attack of shame that to her dying day she would not have dared return to that gallery to view a fucking exhibition.

The Wizard lets her in with a competent, professional air ("serious as a dog in a boat," her Argentine friends would say, one of the many unusual expressions that amuse her and that she often adopts as her own), he briskly shakes her hand, makes way and follows her along the dark corridor (both of them, not just today but always, a little stiff, slightly uncomfortable, with that forced naturalness one assumes in the corridors of houses of assignation, the same impossible ease, although she'd better not inform the Impassive One of this association because there's no telling where it might lead them), to his office, a small interior room, the window of which, Elena imagines, opens onto the elevator shaft and the inner courtyard – she sometimes hears sounds and voices, which makes her automatically lower her own – with a desk, a Kennedy-style rocking chair for the Wizard, a couch for the patients, two small armchairs that get lost on either side of the desk, where they sat only on the first two or three days before agreeing that Elena would indeed begin treatment, whereupon he moved to the rocker and she to the couch, and some shelves on which she has seen the books grow and multiply in an almost miraculous proliferation from one session to the next, so already there is room for only a few more and they are pushing toward the edge, where they are on the point of knocking off the ceramic jug she had bought the Stranger at the very outset, en route from the house by the shore to one of the first sessions, at a time when Elena still did not know the most basic rules of the game – to be sure, she had read Freud with delight during her college years, but that was a long time ago, and besides, she doesn't find in Papa Freud a hint of those rigid tics, those schematic methods, that set of rules seemingly devised by Puritans or Mormons – and that's why it had bothered her a little, bothered, not hurt her, because they were still in the prehistory of the analysis and she had not yet fallen into the trap hook, line and sinker, that the guy took it with a neutral air, without thanking her or smiling, total impassivity, so Elena had said, "It's folk art pottery from La Bisbal; do you like it?" and she wasn't sure if even at that point he had talked or smiled, although perhaps he did mutter "Yes, thank you" while placing the jug at one end of the desk, and by the following session it had been shifted to one of the bookcases, and the fact that it had been stationed there, that it had won a place in the sanctuary, had been interpreted by Elena as a real sign of acceptance, however minimal, a recognition on the part of the Stranger of the slightest underground current of understanding or affection. At least she had the jug before her during the sessions – in that initial stage when she didn't even hint at the idea of lying down, but rather sat with her legs crossed on the couch in the corner where the latter was lodged – and its presence lent the room – so empty, so aseptic – a minimal degree of familiarity and warmth. Elena came close to attributing to the jug the secret powers of a talisman, and would seek it out bewildered in search of shelter and support, when she and the analyst – and this began very soon, when they had barely emerged from the prehistory – faced off with fury, like cat and dog, although to tell the truth there was probably no fury at all on his part, just the serious air of a dog in a boat, and she was a cornered cat belly up, clawing and hissing, and in moments of red-hot anger, when so much free-floating aggression, such disproportionate rage (maybe Eduardo was right that it all came from being badly screwed up, what did the Wizard think? and the Wizard smiled slightly, and traced a vague arabesque in the air with his hand) focused fleetingly on a single point, on that stuck-up guy who seemed sure of possessing the whole truth – damn he must be pedantic and overbearing in his real life – that guy who possibly spoke with God every night and who came to symbolize for a few moments or a few hours everything Elena most feared and detested in the outside world. At these moments, then, the woman directed her gaze toward the jug, situated at the other end of the bookcase invaded by the huge carcinogenic growth of the books, and she promised herself, "The day when it's unseated, the day I enter this office and the jug is no longer there, I'll put an end to this stupid game," because she needed this boast, which she herself did not believe, which she least of all believed, to continue feeding the illusion, from day to day dying out, that it was entirely up to her whether or not to abandon the sessions and terminate the psychoanalysis: in fact, it would simply be a matter of not showing up for an appointment, of being at that very hour – five o'clock sharp in the afternoon – somewhere else, engaged in some other activity, with other people. So Elena made luncheon dates that would inevitably stretch on and on, she left to spend the day at the house by the shore, she arranged meetings for that hour that would later be impossible to cancel or postpone, she interposed between herself and this place – the little room with the rocker and the couch – every distance, every imaginable obstacle, and yet, until now such scheming had been to no avail, because without knowing exactly how or why, the luncheon abruptly ended, the work problems were resolved in record time, the throughway was unexpectedly empty, so there was Elena charging full speed ahead, foot all the way down on the accelerator, or jumping in the first taxi, hardly aware of what she was doing, and all she knew was that at ten minutes to five she found herself on that precise corner of that very street (the only one in the whole city where she was not supposed to be), and there was even time to gulp down a cup of scalding coffee at the bar next door. What occurred, then, was very similar to something Elena remembered from an old children's film – in this case she could bet the Impassive One hadn't seen it – where the tie binding the dog Lassie to the boy who was her owner, and whom she awaited every day at the close of school – it wasn't clear to Elena that school got out at five in the afternoon, but it might well have been that hour – was so strong that, when through human intervention – not the boy's, of course – the dog was moved to a place hundreds or thousands of miles away, at that hour she felt an extreme restlessness, an intense nostalgia, a restlessness and nostalgia that impelled her time and again to set forth, braving all kinds of risks, taxing her strength and endurance to the limit, even abandoning the kind folk who had taken her in and really loved her, to arrive one day at last (the Wizard could well imagine how Elena as a girl used to weep at this point in the story) at the door of the schoolhouse, at five o'clock sharp in the afternoon, and rush into the boy's arms in an endless, stirring embrace (with the single proviso that in Lassie's case it was a pure and simple question of love, whereas what Elena felt for the Wizard was not so simple or univocal). So to end the analysis it would have sufficed, it might still be enough (although the woman was feeling day by day more insecure), to make a phone call, or not even that, to send him a brief note with a check for what she owed for the month's sessions, and the guy dubbed Wooden Face, Poker Face would have sat there frozen in his rocker – of course this formed part of the master plan and was anticipated in the Manual of the Perfect Psychoanalyst – he would not have allowed himself a single dirty look, nor taken a single step to detain or follow her, he would not have picked up the phone to give or demand an explanation, he would not even have stood up, as indeed he did not get up on the day when they fought – or when Elena fought with him, with something that was less than the shadow of a phantom – and the woman declared they were through and filled out a check then and there for the approximate amount and put it on the desk and left, without anyone following her, without anyone trying to hold her back, without the Impassive One so much as opening his mouth, to the door, the stairway, the street, her face burning like a red-hot coal and spouting tears of impotent rage, because at the very moment she slammed the door and started down the stairs, she realized she had taken a step that she would not later be able to sustain – it was then that she discovered, with alarm, that she had fallen into an extremely well-designed trap from which she could not extricate herself, she realized she had set up a dependency relationship that made all those she had experienced up to now, with parents, spouse, children, lovers, friends, seem like child's play – and she stopped the car by the first phone booth and called him, and she heard the Wizard's voice at the other end of the line, and Elena asked, "What are we going to do now?" as though the question implicated them both equally (when the Wizard had already explained at one of the first sessions – before the woman fell face down in the trap and discovered how dangerous that game could be – that the analyst-patient relationship was of necessity asymmetrical, but at that point Elena had not understood what he meant, nor had she felt a need to ask or insist) and it wasn't basically her problem, and Poker Face, maybe in a slightly more cordial and less aseptic tone than usual, perhaps with a speck of compassion (and her desire to arouse his compassion and revel in it humiliated her more than anything else), "Come back, if you like, and we'll talk about it," as though the woman were still in a position to choose what she did or did not want to do, and she quickly answering "yes," dashing back to the house in a heat, leaving the car double-parked on the street, entering the office crawling on all fours, creeping along the walls, belly dragging on the floor and tail wagging, like a puppy who has wet the carpet and is scared of being punished, a wretched little puppy who needs to ingratiate herself – it's a matter of life or death – with her master, the only thing missing was to start barking or rush to lick his shoes, so whispering in a voice that pretends to be ironic but breaks on the first words, almost hoping that on this occasion he's distracted and not listening to her (something that can easily happen on other days, but not today

14

with all the ruckus she has raised), "I'll be your lordship's dog," without explaining that it's a quote from Lorca, and then during the time remaining, which luckily isn't much, enduring all the rigor of what she calls the punishment sessions (not the least trace, she must have dreamt it, of the touch of warmth of his voice on the phone): didn't it occur to Elena that her violent, wholly inappropriate reaction, with the "we're through" and subsequent door slamming, had a lot in common with the reaction of an enraged lover? and she biting the dust, tail invisible now between the legs, yes, yes it did seem that way to her, yes there was a lot in common, and he relentless, determined to carry through to the end: wasn't this a decidedly infantile way to behave? and Elena, about to grab him by the throat or throw herself off the balcony (which wasn't a balcony, only a sad window overlooking an inner courtyard so by throwing herself off she would only have managed to break a leg), yes, yes it was infantile behavior, yes she was acting like an idiot child, but why? did the Wizard know why? what was there about psychoanalysis that drove her almost inevitably to behave like a stupid little girl?

So today the Wizard has again let her in, a day after the incident at the art gallery that could have but did not end in homicide, he has made way as usual and followed her along the dark corridor – where they never exchange a single word – and has sat down in his rocker, while Elena confirms with a glance that the blessed jug is still in its place, takes off her sandals, undoing the complicated laces – which always gives her a terrible time, clumsy as she is and to top it off nervous with the other boldly and patiently looking on, and which to make matters worse she feels obliged to justify or comment on – she gets settled cross-legged on the couch and begins to tell in a joking tone (it's anyone's guess why on some days she feels pretty good, even with light, sporadic waves of euphoria, whereas on others, most days, she feels so sad, so frightened, so ill, so sure that the crocodile that is hiding under the bed is

15

sooner or later going to eat her up), so she tells Wooden
Face the anecdote about the art gallery and the six unequal
prints that were to be framed in six equal frames, and she
tells it in an amusing way, expecting the Impassive One
to suddenly burst out laughing or at least for his eyes to
light up in friendly complicity (because behind the solemn,
almost liturgical mask he wears at all hours in the sanctuary,
behind the numerous obstacles interposed, the barrier of
his hands interlaced before his mouth, his bristly tricolored
beard, his thick glasses for myopia, at times the Wizard's
eyes light up with warmth and amusement – at others with
emotion – which would perhaps seem very bad to Papa
Freud, but which, along with the jug's sojourn on the
bookshelf, is one of the very few reasons why Elena, before
falling face down in the trap and its closing behind her
back, had put in an appearance four times a week at this
office), but now there's no twinkle at all in the Wizard's
eyes, the Impassive One looks at her distracted, you can't
even tell if he sees her, he yawns, takes off his glasses, passes
a hand over his face, puts them on the desk, slowly lights
a cigarette (without offering her one, without giving her a
light when Elena takes one of her own out of her purse), so
the Wizard visibly demonstrates that he's bored, that her
chatter does not interest him, that the two are miserably
wasting their time, and then Elena starts shifting nervously
from one topic to the next, from the salesgirl-with-steel-
wool-hair to her own inexplicable aggression, and from
there to the problem of aging, anxiety over the passing
of time, so bound up with the certainty of dying – it seems
to her that the conflict does not lie in the death drive, but
in death itself, a reality that human beings could not, apart
from religion, and with or without analysis, understand or
assimilate – and then Elena tells him about the past, about
her sons when they were still little boys and wanted time
and again to sleep in bed with their parents, and they
showed up at all hours, barefoot and in pajamas, sleepy-
eyed, on the lookout for the slightest sign of tolerance or

resignation that would allow them to discreetly climb in and by nudging with the rump make a place for themselves between the two of them, and this usually occurred on nights when Julio was away but also occasionally when he was there, so they were all crowded together in disarray, Julio grumbling in his sleep and turning his back, the two boys still half asleep giving her a kiss on the cheek and holding her hand – one hand for each child, how did mothers manage who had three? – and even the dog and a teddy bear and a toy truck, Jorge sometimes even hid his sheriff's revolver under the pillow, and as much as Elena joined in Julio's protests the next morning and lodged her own futile, shocked complaints, the truth was that at heart she liked it – why would she have allowed it to go on for so long if she didn't? – she liked sleeping that way as much as or more than the kids (like gypsies, her mother would have declared, without understanding it at all), all of them promiscuously scrambled together, because ever since she was a little girl it had saddened her that the end of the day meant they had to separate and each one sleep in his own bed, especially after the bingeing and partying of adolescence (that's why she almost always asked Andrea at least to stay over, and they prepared a folding bed in her room and whiled away the remainder of the night in lucubrations and secrets), when her friends went back to their own homes and left the house dreary and what's worse turned upside down, with so many half-empty bottles, plates with leftover sweets and snacks, records mixed up and out of their jackets, ashtrays, never enough, full to overflowing, and that unpleasant stench of things that are over, of dead realities, and Elena would have liked a thousand times more, it would have seemed to her more normal and sensible, that they all get wrapped up in blankets and sleep on the sofas and the carpet, before the dying embers in the fireplace – that too heightened the feeling of things ending – so the arrival of night would not imply – as it had for many years and especially before meeting Andrea – the

17

onset of loneliness, and the truth is that since then she has never gotten accustomed, and at this point probably never will, to sleeping alone at home or in a hotel room – who knows which is worse – and in fact she doesn't like one bit sleeping alone these days – it's been two nights since Julio left for New York – very childish about this too, right? an idiot child, an absurd woman who hasn't managed, who can't manage, to age correctly, on the brink of menopause without ever having advanced beyond adolescence, without having grown into an adult woman. And Elena is telling the Wizard all this in a light, almost worldly tone, the tone she might adopt sitting around the table after dinner with friends, half joking and hoping to make him laugh, but the Wizard is smoking, his gaze lost high above in the direction of the ceiling, and he again passes his hand over his face, exerting pressure at those points where his glasses must bother him, after which he again hides behind that barricade, which today is effective because Elena can't even tell which way he's looking, and conscientiously and methodically cracks his knuckles: the Wizard gives no response, asks no question, makes no comment. He has left her alone on the couch, drowning in the rough stormy ocean of her own words, sinking into that thick swampy sea, clumsily waving her arms in the air so as not to entirely lose her footing, more and more depressed and anxious – more aggressive too, although she might not be willing to admit it – unable to pretend any longer, throwing the Impassive One irate, despairing looks, give me a hand, bastard, can't you see that if you don't I'm certainly going to drown? – "The wife of one of our most distinguished movie directors, whose latest film, etc., has mysteriously perished by drowning, buried under the rushing sea of her own words" – and the Wizard is perfectly aware of what's happening, he knows exactly what the woman is going through, and yet he remains silent, because this is another of what she calls the punishment sessions – at times, like today, she hasn't a frigging clue why she is being so cruelly punished – so she remains there, cringing in the farthest corner of the couch, tail between her legs, ears drooping, with those wretched eyes of a meek dog, his lordship's dog, whom they're brutally whipping with harsh lashes of silence, until Elena can't stand it any longer, because the entire room has been inundated and submerged in that silence, which has overflowed its narrow banks and is starting to flood the other rooms of the house and the elevator shaft, this sorcerer's apprentice undoubtedly capable of annihilating the world, and the ceramic jug sways on the shelf without being touched, as though it were undergoing the shock of an earthquake, a mini-earthquake that at the moment affects only that spot, and the air has gotten thick and dense and refuses to pass down Elena's throat to her lungs, and she's suffocating and can't stand it any longer, and has lost all semblance of self-control and sophistication (what's happening to her now could not take place at the coffee table or a bar or anywhere else), and she does something that she's already done on two occasions and had sworn never to repeat, Elena begs him in her worst idiot-child, retarded-little-girl voice, "Please say something, anything, don't leave me here jabbering on all alone like a complete moron!" because she knows that if the session ends without the Impassive One's having broken his silence, she's going to leave there, like other times, all done in, and she'll be in an awful state during the hours intervening until the next session, like a dog who's been abused by her master, a ridiculous dog who alternately or simultaneously hates and loves a cruel master whom she never understands but upon whom she hopelessly depends, and she also thinks that everything that transpires within the four walls of this office makes no sense, at least not to her, it's a silly perverse game, pure childishness, but a game so well constructed, so clever – or she so dense – that it's managed to ensnare her in its plot and now Elena, like it or not, is taking part (a crazy chess game, she thinks, in which I have no king). And so she pleads with him, flushed with anger and shame, "Say something please, anything

19

at all, I feel so absurd chattering on here alone without anyone answering and maybe without anyone listening!" and finally she lies down on the couch, docile and defeated she lies down on the couch, because she knows this is how the Unflappable One, the Great Silent One, wants her, stretched out on the couch and him behind her back, and it's possible, not certain, of course, and not immediate – that would in some sense be to give in, for him in turn to enter the dynamics of the game, a game that he perhaps controls from outside but in which he definitely does not take part, that would be too childish, the two of them behaving like silly little kids – but yes perhaps later, when a little time has passed, it's possible that the Wizard, in view of the surrender or goodwill of the patient, Elena's surrender – not unconditional, no, not forever, and of this too they're both aware – would allow himself to break the rule of silence and utter, in his aseptic tone (a tone of voice so neutral that it scarcely betrays the Argentine accent: a voice from nowhere, a phantom voice), some phrase, without any particular significance – what's important is that he talk, not what he might say – which an Elena returned to life from the depths of the swamp, an Elena who can again thrust the air into her lungs, will immediately transform into a verdict – of acquittal – from the oracle.

How strange the paths taken by our feelings and our emotions, Elena says to herself, and it's odd, or maybe ironic and even cruel – except cruel on the part of whom? didn't her trouble and anxiety exist prior to the start of psychoanalysis? doesn't the analysis at most confine itself to bringing out something that was already there? "I think I've discovered what the game consists in," she commented to the Wizard, who of course did not open his mouth, at a fairly recent session, "it's as though you were doing a very very long arithmetic problem, and you went over it a thousand times but it always came out wrong, because if for example you add five and six and get fourteen, it doesn't help to go over and over it since you'll always err at the same point, and the analyst could be someone from outside who makes us suspect that five plus six are not necessarily fourteen" – so it's ironic and even cruel – although it could not have happened otherwise – that this heap of contradictions and inexplicable emotional reactions, which do not even remotely pass through the screen of the intellect and of which she was hardly aware, has overwhelmed her precisely now, at the start of this beautiful September – autumn has always been her favorite season – when she is about to turn fifty and when by sheer coincidence they have all left her alone at home, and perhaps, she admits, she had been left alone for a few days at other times in the past, but she hadn't even noticed, and it's ludicrous – although this too could not have happened otherwise – that of all people this has happened to her, who has always bragged so much about her own consistency, perhaps the sole virtue she had been sure of possessing, her one and only source of swollen pride – because despite what some might think, she has never even felt sure of her own intelligence – the certainty that her thoughts and words and deeds constituted a monolithic block with almost no fissures, and that she had, through strength of will and backed by a series of decisions, charted a life course in which chance was relegated to the most remote corners of the attic, or the unconscious – Lord she must have pontificated bull, with wrinkled nose, knit brow, and shaking an index finger absurdly at others in warning, like a little country schoolmarm! – so intolerant, she now realizes, of all those who, admit it or not, aware of it or not, psychoanalyzed or not, live from day to day, allowing others or the wheel of fortune to decide their fate from without and badly, clumsily dragging along a heavy load of multiple and irreconcilable contradictions. And now the monolithic block of her unquestionable consistency – it's no longer certain that it had no fissures – has been blown to bits, the countless particles dispersed at random to thousands of light years of space, dynamited by something that must have lodged there, at the precise center of her being, from time immemorial, and that analysis will perhaps, she isn't sure, help her to surmise, but there's no analysis in the world capable of reuniting the scattered parts into a harmonious whole, Elena now fears, sad and distressed, sitting in the almost empty hall, a movie theater for re-runs and double features, one of those outlying neighbor-hood theaters she had never been to before – or maybe she had, also thousands of years ago, everything seems to have taken place thousands of years before, with her high school friends at the start of vacation after the exams, wild and rowdy, talking out loud, making bad jokes about the film, chewing sunflower seeds, so eager to display their youth, to become protagonists and call attention to themselves, secretly wishing the usher would throw them out of the the-ater in response to the complaints of the other viewers – but where nowadays she often takes refuge after leaving the analytic session, when she finds herself in the middle of the street at six in the afternoon, the sky still aglow with a blazing summer sun, aggressive and masculine, and she cannot overcome the inertia that keeps her from picking up the phone and trying to locate a friend who is not at work, nor can she bring herself to go back to an empty house, because Julio left for New York four or five days ago, and since the kids have more permanently left home she finds the solitude there unbearable, so Elena takes refuge in some movie theater – hopefully not one of those she went to with her high school friends, but one she has never been to – to huddle among strangers, secretly sheltered in their midst, and cry softly in the darkness, because she often cries now, more often than during any earlier period of her life, since something inside her has exploded and the pieces have been catapulted to the far ends of the universe, and no one or nothing, not even psychoanalysis, can retrieve, much less reassemble them, and the same blast has at the same time, it seems, opened an enormous channel for tears, so Elena cries at all hours and for the most foolish reasons, she cries pell-mell tears accumulated and not shed, tears that were awaiting the moment when the containing dike would break, as it has, she cries because the hunters have killed Bambi's mama and he calls out to her sad and helpless through the wide reaches of the forest, or because Jane and Boy have been tricked once again (they must not be any smarter or sharper than the employee of the art gallery, always falling into such traps) by evil men from civilization, who unbeknownst to them are about to betray Tarzan, or because the slave army has reached the coast and the ships are not there that were supposed to carry them to a land of freedom and they are going to be destroyed in a final battle at sea, or because Umberto D's dog refuses to commit suicide with his master and bolts terrified from his arms, although that way of crying is not entirely new to Elena, because even as a little girl, instead of crying over real life, real events, she would cry buckets over imaginary scenes, she sobbed like a ninny over tragedies that unfolded on the stage or screen, or over scenes narrated in books – under the dining room table, with almost no light, reading for the thousandth time *The Little Mermaid* or the final pages of *Peter Pan* – as though reality had to be transformed into a story to fully touch her sensibility, and what's worse, she would cry just as much over the coarsest, cheapest melo-dramas, and to top it off the most excessively reactionary, she sobbed over stories that at the same time turned her stomach with disgust, and how strange it is to cry one's heart out over a tragedy that is discredited by one's reason and intelligence and ideology, and this alone was enough to prove that particles of emotion and feeling do not pass through the sieve of reason, the rigorous selection process of the mind, and Papa Freud – who is not directly to blame for the wrongs inflicted on patients by his disciples of the eighties, whether or not they are from Rosario – might have been right that these feelings that are in and of themselves inexplicable are just the external result, the symptom of something whose roots go deep into the unconscious, so you don't have to go searching for them among the stars in the far reaches of the cosmos. So recently Elena cries at any time of the day or night and for no or almost no apparent reason, over trifles which during other periods of her life she would not even have noticed, usually she cries without even realizing she is crying, and she takes refuge in movie theaters, more in search of a complicitous darkness, to feel herself sheltered among strangers who are watching the movie along with her, than in search of a pretext – which she does not need – for tears, and although the process must have started a long time ago, the first time she became aware of the damage, the first time she considered herself sick was the middle of the summer, in mid-August, when after making a hasty retreat from Germany she found the house strangely empty, with an emptiness that seemed to her different, more final, more irrevocable, because Pablo had settled in that horrid provincial city in southern Germany which she fled from aghast but where he seems to feel happy and at home, married to that little girl who seems to have stepped right out of a cartoon, sent direct from Disneyland in a pink box with cellophane ribbons – maybe if she had agreed to take him there as a child they would have forestalled the subsequent disaster . . . a little figurine from Walt Disney or *The Wizard of Oz*, with blond hair, very blue eyes, porcelain skin, who makes her appearance bright and early, just after awakening, in a raspberry-colored robe, brushes her long golden hair before the mirror – without asking if she is or is not the fairest of them all, without leaving behind her bonnet so the little shepherd boy will have to chase after it – and sings delectable Schubert lieder while boiling water for coffee and the apartment gradually fills with the luscious aroma of toast for breakfast (which Elena for the first time finds revolting), until Pablo makes his entrance, freshly shaved, smelling of eau de cologne, showing off his newest smile, leather briefcase under the arm, and still standing gulps down the buttered bread and burns himself on the *café con leche* (he who at home

24

had always refused to eat breakfast and for years declared himself incapable of consuming a morsel at such hours), and then gives the little cartoon character a kiss on the mouth – the busy, flushed little mouse with a raspberry ribbon at the end of her tail, the blinking bunny with curly lashes, Judy Garland in some appalling good-girl role that embodies the American dream? – a pat on the swollen belly and a fatherly reminder not to wear herself out or bustle about too much, not to lift any weight, not to catch the flu in the corridors of the courthouse, and all that's missing is the punch line to have a perfect TV commercial, and Elena cannot recall that scene repeated every morning – although on most days she stayed in bed in order to avoid seeing it, and because she has never been an early riser, so rather than seeing she heard and imagined it – without feeling annoyed and offended, so to escape this and other equally innocent, sugar-coated scenes of affection she had fled from Germany, fearing that one fine day the little cartoon character would give birth – without anesthesia, of course, in a beatific delivery without pain, which Pablo, who used to faint at the mere smell of medicine and couldn't get past the lobby of hospitals and clinics, would watch moved and supportive and participatory from the foot of the bed – and immediately begin playing the role of the perfect mama in Technicolor, those awful doll mothers they sometimes award on television, a mama determined from the start to get the Oscar for being the best mother of the year, and it goes without saying, the best friend of her children, and Elena wondered if it had been necessary to go to such trouble for such poor results, if they needed the permissive upbringing, the progressive secondary school, the studies abroad and a European fiancée with a doctorate in law, if it meant anything at all that she had continued working at the court or that they had lived together for the first two or three years without getting married, and she also wondered what crime or error she and Julio had committed that their elder son would pick a girl like that to share his life with

("And doesn't something occur to you?" asks wily Wooden Face at this point, and Elena, on the verge of getting angry, "Nothing occurs to me, but I'm sure I know what occurs to you," and he almost laughing and disarming with his almost-laugh the almost-anger of the woman, "And may I ask what occurs to you that's occurring to me?" and then, serious, "Why does Pablo's wife make you so furious, when you assure me that she has always treated you well, and above all, why do you feel personally offended by Pablo's choice?"), and around the time she got back from Germany, cutting in half the four weeks she was supposed to spend there, Jorge was already packing his bags, he was just waiting for her return to say goodbye, and he was delighted to be going back earlier than planned, because they had renewed his grant, the grant they never renewed for anyone much less a foreigner, and the academic year was about to start at the University of Rome and he had to prepare his classes, and the truth was he could no longer suppress his impatience to return to the laboratory, where the reproduction of some flies that were serving as guinea pigs (they had chosen flies because of the speed with which they reproduce) was expected to confirm the fundamental law he had intuited long before in his studies and that should revolutionize, if proved, an entire field of biology, and he was even worried about how the flies had managed to continue reproducing without him, in his absence, so her elder son, Elena concluded her harangue to the Wizard, had abandoned her for a little cartoon character out of Disneyland and the second for a swarm of fornicating flies. And Elena was laughing as she started telling the Impassive One about her children, as she laughed when she repeated it to herself, because it would be really ridiculous and out of place to make a fuss about things she had always known, like the fact that children leave home one day and take their own paths, which are not necessarily parallel to those taken by her and Julio (although she certainly could not have imagined that Pablo would choose the path he had

26

chosen), she had known from the outset that motherhood constitutes just one stage, one part of a woman's life, but the blasted particles of emotion, irrevocably scattered in space, were stronger than all reason – Elena would not, could not attend to reason – and the woman discovered in astonishment that rivers of tears were pouring down her cheeks, without her being able to stop them, without even knowing at what exact moment she had started to weep. And that was what had happened the day of her first meeting with the Wizard, when she sought out that den of phantoms, this infamous sanctuary, because she was feeling terribly ill – no, not just sad or unhappy or distressed, like many times in the past: now she was feeling really ill – and someone (she couldn't remember who, it might have been Julio or some friend, because Elena remembered only vaguely and with blank spaces everything that had happened that summer) had called and set up an appointment and put the address in her hands, and she went without having too clear an idea what she was going to find – she could have ended up with something else, she often tells him, saucy and defiant, to see if she can shake him up, out of his silence and immobility, she could have ended up with a mini-course in yoga, with some meditation exercises, or even worse, with one of those behaviorist doctors who made him so nervous – without the slightest intention to go into psychoanalysis, with him or with anybody, because the one thing she knew was that she was in a bad way and she didn't want to go on like that and on this occasion she needed a kind of help that neither Julio nor her friends nor her children could provide, nor did she decide to begin analysis with the Wizard – she sometimes responds to his coquettish question – because of having seen in him anything special, in fact she did not even *see* him during the first few days, if they had asked her to describe him they would have put her on the spot: a thin Argentine from Rosario, with glasses and a multicolored beard, or maybe not even that. And even on the first day, having just arrived

27

from Germany and bade farewell to Jorge the day before, she had told the Wizard about her children, told him the little story about the Disney doll and about the flies (how could anyone in all seriousness imagine, despite this being what the Wizard would suggest in subsequent sessions, that she could be jealous of a cartoon character straight from Disneyland and a throng of turned-on flies that were frantically fornicating to allow a new biological theory to be established at their expense?), and the Impassive One had gazed at her slyly, shrugging a little, without uttering a syllable, and then and there Elena learned that the Great Witch Doctors of the Tribe, like the hermits of earlier eras, have taken an oath of silence: he had not spoken more than six or seven sentences, not counting the "hello" and the "good afternoon," during the first six or seven sessions, and at times she could not stand the stupidity of talking on and on to a guy who never answered and in the worst case was not even listening, because it was quite possible he was thinking of other things (for example, about the chess problem that was set up on a table in the waiting room, and it was pretty weird for starters to be in analysis with an individual who played chess with himself between sessions, and was most likely planning the strategy of his next move while Elena reeled off that stream of words from the couch!), although the silence did not take on the guise of a powerful, deadly weapon until two or three weeks into the analysis – no more – when the woman fell face down in the trap that had been prepared for her and established with the Wizard a type of dependency relationship beyond anything she could have imagined, as a result of which everything that happened in the sanctuary began to be a matter of life or death, and on one of those transitional days between the prehistory and the history of the analysis, Elena entered the office like a shot and climbed on the couch without starting the complicated process of untying her sandals, and rattled off in one breath – as though it were a speech prepared in advance at home, when in fact it

28

had welled up unexpectedly the moment she entered the room – that Julio had a lover and he had taken her with him to New York, she thought, and the whole thing didn't matter to her, and she had said the last in a defiant tone, certain he was not going to believe her, certain he would immediately ask, painstaking as ever and serious as a dog in a boat, why she hadn't told him about it until today and why she seemed so upset if the story did not bother her, and wasn't it something of a coincidence that she would be upset to such a degree, and in a similar way, by her elder son's wife, her second son's work, and now her husband's possible lover? But contrary to her expectation, the Wizard had not uttered a word, he had confined himself to observing her, from a very remote point lost somewhere in the jungle of his nearsighted eyes, through which at times she could see moving striped felines and golden leopards – in pursuit of what? – his eyes barricaded behind the thick lenses of his glasses, and these behind the bristly beard and the beard behind the interlaced hands, and the day she told him that Julio had a lover and had perhaps taken her with him, was the first when Elena spent the second part of the session lying on the couch, to escape the indifferent stare of the Impassive One, the Lone Ranger of the Pampas, fixed on her, or in the worst case not on her but on what was behind her, on the other side of her body which might, without Elena's noticing in time, have become transparent, so the Wizard might very well not be on the lookout for anything special but simply be observing the white wall behind the couch, and it was for this reason, to avoid the humiliation of constantly spying out the effect of our words on a mute listener, or perhaps a deaf-mute, that she had finally caved in, had lain down before him with her back turned, as the woman imagined the Wizard had wanted from the start, and a long silence ensued – just the to-and-fro motion of one of the Stranger's legs swinging on the other, rhythmically revealing the tip of the foot sheathed in a beige shoe – which she had broken to insist that at bottom it did not matter to her that Julio was having another affair, as the earlier ones had not mattered – which were not so great in number, one could not in fairness say her husband was such a womanizer – it would be senseless at this point to be jealous or offended, and then, after another interminable silence, as though she were discovering gunpowder, as though she were offering the Wizard a supreme concession, she had acknowledged that maybe something did not have to make sense in order to exist, it simply was, and then the Wizard-Trainer, perhaps to reward her goodwill and disposition, the double goodwill demonstrated by lying down on the couch and expressing an idea so contrary to her usual way of thinking (it was at these moments that Elena felt like a ridiculous little trained dog – not even his lordship's dog – who walks on two legs displaying a little bow on her tail, or like a trained seal who ascends a set of stairs and even manages to balance a ball on its nose, in reward for which the trainer supplies biscuits and fresh sardines throughout the circus act), had suggested, "Maybe it's not Julio that matters, don't you think it may be a question of a wound your narcissism cannot endure?" and Elena, "You mean that it's not a question of love, but of vanity? Do you think that, if for so many years it did not matter to me and now it does seem to matter, it's because with the passing of time, I'm feeling more insecure?" as she thinks it may well be true that jealousy is grounded in self-love rather than in love for the other, and then she had whispered, unable to recall where the quote came from, who had said it or where she had read it, "Jealousy is the self-love of the flesh," and he, speaking for the second time during the session, which implied such excess that Elena felt alarmed, "Narcissism always begins with the body," and then, another quote whose source she could not remember, "The deepest thing is the skin," and Elena never did find out where the quotes came from, if they were quotes, and did not completely understand what the two meant, although even if she had it didn't really matter much to her to know where narcissism began or whether the wound she was suffering from was or was not narcissistic, and the crucial thing, she insisted, was not that Julio had a lover, what made this situation serious and different was that, while on other occasions it hadn't mattered, this time it had somehow affected her, perhaps because she had in fact aged or because the boys had in a more definitive way left home, or because – perhaps for the first time, the first time in almost thirty years – she felt unsure of Julio's love, that perfect relationship which, to the amazement of friends and strangers alike, the two had constructed between them, she was jealous for the first time because she suspected that to make Julio come back, who was living out the greatest, most spectacular triumph of his career with a girl who was not her, it might no longer be enough to whistle (and if the Wizard hadn't seen the Bogart films, he could shove it).

The one thing she knew for sure was that now, during this autumn prelude in which she was going to turn fifty and in which they had left her alone, Elena wept over any trifle and without even knowing why she was crying, and maybe she was crying over herself, over the passage of time, over youth now irrevocably lost (if he wanted literary quotes, she had said in that now distant session, Woolf acknowledged in her diary that after going through the fifties one could no longer delude oneself, there was no way to get around the unavoidable and devastating fact that one had grown old), or over the long time – more than half her life – shared with Julio, a time with its plusses and minuses, its tantrums and tempests, its passionate phases and phases of relative indifference, but during which they continued to share the conviction (did they still today? and if not, at what moment had the collapse occurred, without Elena's noticing it, at what moment had the world come crashing down on their heads without their even realizing it?) that together they were building a rare and exceptional relationship, far superior to what they witnessed all around them, such foolish and conceited couples, who showed off their perfect understanding and happiness as if they were showing friends and neighbors a new-model car or a sophisticated Hollywood-style refrigerator, or over the splendid years when the children filled and overflowed the house – and it's possible that at the time she was not aware of it, but now she knows how splendid they were – impossible, then, to know the cause of her tears (unless Papa Freud lends her a hand), which may be due to all the causes listed above or to only one or even to another or others not identified or classified, the one thing she knows for sure is that her eyes fill with tears at the most unexpected moments, for instance, when she enters the bedrooms that belonged to the kids – which she keeps as they were, because the house is very large so she doesn't need them and because Elena doesn't like to change anything, so you still find Pablo's workbench, Jorge's drawings and electric train, the walls covered with posters, not at all alike, because the boys' tastes could not have been more different – she dissolves in tears while driving the car aimlessly around the city or on the highway that runs south along the sea, or while walking the city streets, again with no destination – until she finally bought herself, another lunacy, a pair of enormous dark sunglasses like Garbo's, to mask and hide from other passersby the spectacle of her weeping. And upon leaving the psychoanalytic session, four times a week at only six in the afternoon, with a late-summer sun shining aggressively in the sky, not daring to return to the now empty house, and lacking the will and desire to enter a phone booth and attempt to locate some friend, she often took refuge in a local movie theater, she huddled in the darkness, sunk way down in the seat, knees up and resting on the back of the seat ahead – almost a fetal position, the Wizard would have pronounced, if by chance he had seen her and had not been half-blind and mute – and gave free rein to her newfound passion for crying: she cried nonstop, sobbing her heart out, whether or not tears were called for by events unfolding on the screen, because who, among Elena's friends and associates, could be sitting in a local double-feature movie theater in the middle of the afternoon? until one day she was caught by surprise by the words "The End" at an adventure film (at the last minute Tarzan had saved Jane and Boy from a tribe of Pygmy cannibals – who had taken them prisoner because of their dimwittedness – riding on the most potent male of the entire elephant herd and arriving at the village when they were about to be put to a horrid death, so in the end the only ones who died were the bad guy and a few natives you didn't have to worry about), so the ending caught her unawares looking like a Magdalene, eyes red and swollen – she wasn't going to wear sunglasses in a movie theater – a soaking handkerchief in hand that could not mop up another tear, and right there, just in the row behind, was a group of friends – rather than friends, Elena would have clarified, acquaintances, people they saw time and again without its ever developing into a real friendship – and she would have found the encounter, instead of annoying and embarrassing, funny, if it were not for the fact that in the eyes of those people, in their pretending not to see her until bumping into her at the exit, in their words of greeting, by anyone's estimation overly cordial and gushing, you could read like in an open book that they pitied her, with all the ill will in the world they pitied her, because Elena, poor thing, was going through such a hard time, the poor thing had aged so much lately, and to top it off, poor Elena, it was obvious that Julio was deceiving her with another woman.

Perhaps that's one of the reasons for her depression and her sadness: it comes in part from realizing how little the world has changed for the better, how little those of her generation have succeeded in changing the world. "Or how much you yourselves have changed for the worse?" the Wizard suggests, or maybe Elena herself suggests, making him speak through her lips, in an attempt to guess the words that he sometimes voices and more often does not, so at the

sessions she often feels as though there's a shadowy presence behind her – when she has lain down on the couch
like a good little girl – swaying on the rocker, swinging a
foot the only visible part of which is the tip of a beige shoe
rhythmically appearing and disappearing, good leather,
certainly Italian – "Are you still there?" Elena asks abruptly
from time to time, as though, like a new Cheshire cat, the
Wizard could suddenly vanish into thin air, leaving behind
instead of the smile, the tip of a shoe, and it *does* seem a
little ridiculous to go on telling whatever comes to mind
to a shoe – and Elena playing the roles of the two of them
in turn: so I say this and then you'll say that and then I'll
reply . . . until the Impassive One loses his patience – fed
up with being made to say what he doesn't say, fed up with
this theatrical performance, with only one character and
likewise a single spectator, into which Elena sometimes,
most of the time, converts the couch, a couch-stage the
Wizard called it on one occasion, with her playing thereon
all the roles of the farce – and finally he opens his mouth
and lets out a few words, which Elena sometimes instantly
transforms into a verdict from the oracle, but which on
many other occasions, strange to say, she interrupts or simply does not hear, so that after complaining so bitterly about
the muteness or oath of silence of the Supreme Sorcerer
of the Pampas, she later finds herself in the middle of the
street, trying in vain to remember what he said or what
he started to say without her letting him finish, and then
she laments what she considers an irrevocable loss, and of
course she does not have the nerve to pick up the phone
and tell him, "Today you said something that seems to me
important, but I wasn't listening so I didn't hear it," so she
brings it up at the next session, and suggests that maybe
her erratic deafness is due to the fact that she's afraid to
hear what he may have to say, and it occurs to her at that
very moment, although this she keeps to herself, that in
reality she's not very interested in the Wizard's words, in
their meaning, he might just as well recite Hail Marys or

34

read out the names and numbers in a telephone book, and though at times she confesses this to the Impassive One, at other times, knowing that he will pronounce, tired of such extreme stubbornness, "What you want, the only thing that matters to you, is to get a rise out of me," and knowing likewise that she does not have valid arguments to refute this, she remains silent, she discreetly remains silent. How little, then, the world has changed for the better, how little they have managed to change the world, how much (the Wizard is right about this) they themselves have changed for the worse – because they have not changed to become like the ideal role models they had chosen in their adolescence and youth, but rather to become more and more like the role models of the previous generation, it's dreadful how as the years go by we come to resemble, even physically, our parents – although it may also be true that she has changed only a little, much less than the others – one advantage at least, it now occurs to her, of never having attained adulthood, of not having matured properly, of parading around the mentality of an idiot child and the absurd sentimentality of an adolescent – Elena herself, like so many of her college classmates and friends, born during the first year of the civil war, on a morning when the Germans were bombing the city, and the midwife, out of fear, lack of transportation, carelessness, could not get there in time, she arrived when the baby had already been born, hence inopportune even in the moment of being born, a first indication that she would later do so many things backward or out of turn (and now it's the woman who's offering her trainer a biscuit or a fresh sardine, because she thinks that what she is relating qualifies – since the Oedipus and castration complexes have not shown up anywhere – as the type of guilty confession that he considers to be "good material" for the analysis, although they are stories so well known from time immemorial, so often repeated, so adulterated with self-pity and the worst literature – she'd be better off for once to finish a story or a book of poems – that she doesn't know if any sense can be made of it, but she is speaking now in a slower, more serious tone of voice, while thinking, "I am playing the part of myself psychoanalyzing myself," a monologue consisting of equal parts of truth and sham, and how hard it is to distinguish and separate one from the other!), so Elena, like all of her generation, like almost all her friends, growing up under the Francoism of the forties and fifties (which had little to do with the subsequent Francoism that they must have found – and of course the Impassive One does not ask who, apart from himself, is included in this plural – upon their arrival, and in any case, how did it occur to them to drop anchor precisely here, to flee one military dictatorship only to fall into another? or had the Generalissimo already died by the time they arrived? yes, yes the Wizard had arrived in Spain after the death of Franco, and for once he has answered a direct question from Elena, one ship sunk in the naval war game, one pawn less on the chessboard, or perhaps two vessels have been sunk at once, two pawns eliminated in one stroke, because not only has the woman managed to rouse him from his dumbness, make him break his oath of silence, but she has also gleaned a fact about his private life, the real life that runs its course outside the sanctuary, and this – in the complex, candid and dangerous game invented by Elena, a private game that is uniquely and exclusively hers, a game she plays in secret, within the other grand game invented by Papa Freud and reproduced as best he can by the Wizard – amounts to a double prize, and the danger lay in the fact that the guy, as on so many other occasions, might not have answered, in which case the woman's entire fleet would have gone under, or her queen been placed in check: not her king, because Elena is playing a game in which she has no king, so she can never win, and, as the Wizard pointed out one day, neither can she lose, how can you checkmate a king who is not, as he should be, on the battlefield? so it seemed the game could have no possible end), a Francoism, moreover – and this is crucial – that they experienced from the winning side, a Francoism seen from the perspective of the victors, she and her childhood friends the offspring of those who had won the civil war, and had bet on Germany's triumph in the world war, and of course had imposed their law, except that Elena, like others, from a very early age had flashes of suspicion, voiceless intuitions, brief moments of clairvoyance, the vague foreboding that they were not living in the best of all possible worlds, that some or many people somewhere – at times nearby, at times right at their side – were being made to pay the price for so many privileges, and that something was out of line in that chiaroscuro of winners and losers, good and bad, that they taught her at home and at school, although at home the views of her parents, siblings, friends differed widely from those of the servants, and as a girl Elena learned a great deal in the ironing room or the kitchen, and then in high school a teacher, the same one who, in response to a veiled and bashful question from one of the boys, had slowly gotten out of his chair, gone up to the blackboard and explained to them, with the aid of some diagrams and sketches, the very simple and innocent and totally innocuous mysteries of sexuality, thereby helping to dispel so many idle phantoms, the same one who, when a classmate declared that Catalan was not a language but a dialect (a belief Elena also shared but prudently kept to herself), had replied that whoever said that was a stupid ignoramus, and had not even batted an eye, had only shrugged slightly, when the student informed him that the presumed stupid ignoramus was none other than his father – and most of our fathers, Elena had thought, again without unsealing her lips – the only teacher with whom you could discuss the movies, talk about the news reported by the press, and even question it and learn to read between the lines – in fact, the only thing you could not do with him was to learn Latin, because he had been assigned this discipline by decree since nobody was qualified to teach it and the short straw fell to him, and on the first day he

37

confessed to them that he didn't know a word of Latin, so they read the manual together and made out the best they could – the same teacher, then, one day had begun discussing the essence and significance of the Paris of the fifties, a mythical Paris (which had nothing to do with the also mythical Paris of her parents and grandparents) full of crazy artists, inspired bohemians and heroes of the Resistance, where every day students and intellectuals invented something new and different, and you could see Sartre and Simone eating croissants at Les Deux Magots or the Flore, or buying a newspaper at the corner kiosk, and the songs of Boris Vian flew through the Latin Quarter, and Gréco was singing in picturesque bars and cafés, so Elena already knew about her before they brought her to Barcelona – the contradictions of the Spain of the fifties, she insists, had no limits – to sing in the swankiest nightclub in the city before the cream of the bourgeoisie, at astronomical prices, and Elena, always astride two worlds, always out of place and not knowing exactly where she belonged – throughout her life it had been much easier to figure out where she did not belong – had attended the late-evening recital, after the opera, with her parents, Andrea, Eduardo, her parents' friends, not their own friends, since around that time the three of them had made new friends and these would not even consider going to an elegant – pseudoelegant, to make matters worse – and expensive locale, where they required dark suit and tie, and Elena wore – she can't remember it without feeling a touch of nostalgia and another touch of shame – a splendid floor-length gown of white tulle dotted with silver, with a very full skirt, more or less the gown one imagines Cinderella wearing to the ball, with her very blond hair, much blonder than it is now, gathered into a chignon and fastened with a silver ribbon, to go with the silver high-heeled shoes that she could not and still has not learned to walk in, and the pearl necklace they had given her for her coming-out and a little white fox skin cape, the full-dress uniform for true-blue upper-middle-class girls,

38

did the Wizard get the picture? and Andrea had worn an emerald green gown that left one shoulder and the back naked – which was quite daring in the Spain of the fifties and on such a young girl – and she wore her long straight hair down, and was, that night perhaps more than others, incredibly beautiful, and Gréco had performed (a Gréco who was different from the graceful charming girl with beautiful eyes and protruding cheekbones and a certain feline air who would later prevail, and even more unlike the great sophisticated cat she has now become, a Gréco before plastic surgery, a wild cat who took refuge on the rooftops and refused to eat out of anyone's hand, a Gréco with a long nose and slender frame, swathed in a simple black gown that clung to her body), so Gréco had performed that night with a devil-may-care ease that was deliberately crude – later Elena learned that she too had been born into the bourgeoisie, another little good girl who had no choice but to learn brazenness and a low-life manner elsewhere – and she had sung with force and passion songs the lyrics of which the audience surely could not understand – Gréco's French was very different from the French they used on their periodic trips to Paris, that of the shops along the Champs Elysées, the Opera quarter, the expensive restaurants, the evening shows for wealthy tourists: a different language for a different Paris – but if they had by chance understood, they would have applauded with the same enthusiasm, for the bourgeoisie of this city was impervious – perhaps more so than that of other countries, because it was not for nothing that they had won a three-year civil war and thereby multiplied a thousandfold their power and privileges – to that kind of experience, which they devoured and digested without pain and later defecated with equal ease, without having absorbed or learned anything, that is to say they had applauded a lot, had made some foolish, pedantic comments, and had gone home satisfied, but for Elena, Andrea and a few others it had been an unforgettable evening, because Gréco's songs were inextricably bound

39

up with the characters of Sartre, overcome with nausea or rejoicing over the liberating discovery that God had died or had never existed, or those of Camus, agonizing to a greater or lesser degree over the human condition and human folly, all of these books – not only the existentialist, but also the Marxist and the supposedly pornographic – purchased in the back room of some bookstore, or slipped under the counter by the book dealer, or bought from a fellow student at the university who imported them no one knew whence or how and in this way defrayed the costs of his education, or smuggled across the border at the very bottom of the most innocent-looking suitcases: Marxism and eroticism, *Ruedo Ibérico* and *Playboy*, so closely allied in Franco's repressive regime that it later became very hard for Elena – and in a sense the difficulty persists to this day – to distinguish between eroticism and pornography and to go along with the feminists' radical rejection of the latter (feminism, like psychiatry and religion, invariably makes the Wizard frown, does he fear illicit competition for the souls of his female patients? or is it all due to obscure and complex personal motives, sunk deep in the unconscious? because let's see, what does the Wizard associate pornography and feminism with? and the Wizard reminds her for the hundredth time that it's not he but she who is being psychoanalyzed), because it does indeed seem to Elena that the feminists are right when they affirm that, while the most liberated eroticism, enhanced by multiple perversions – what would eroticism be without perversion? – and enriched with throngs of ghosts – what would sexuality be without them? – can provide a salutary shock and thus be creative, in contrast pornography, far from liberating sexuality, seeks to harness it within an order, and it's really the limit for them to create for us a universal scheme of sexuality and pressure us into accepting some crude, obscene perversions and dull, lifeless prototypical phantoms. Books then, Elena continues to explain, bought in the back room of left-wing bookstores or in the homes of other students, or smuggled in suitcases from Perpignan, because during the years when almost everything here was banned, Perpignan had fleetingly been transformed into a beacon, a city of light, a tiny but much closer subsidiary of that Paris which for us Catalans of the fifties and sixties was the only capital, as it had been and continued to be for our parents, and had been earlier for our grandparents and great-grandparents, but as it would no longer be for our children: Jorge once commented that the period in which she grew up must have been strange and stimulating, it must have been amusing to have to buy the most innocuous books in back rooms and to have to travel to Perpignan to read a decent newspaper and get some idea of what was happening in the world, and above all what was happening in Spain, and Elena had been puzzled and shocked by the unforeseen possibility that someone, in this case her own son, would take it into his head to try to reclaim, through nostalgia and the picturesque, what she knew to be unreclaimable, and if she had not managed to transmit to her sons a correct image of what those years were like, it would be much more difficult to communicate it to the Wizard, almost impossible to make him grasp not only certain facts but an atmosphere so different from the one he must have breathed on the other side of the ocean, and she suddenly suspects that it would have been better to go through analysis with someone from her own country, and above all with a woman – though Elena knows, admit it or not and reprehensible as it may seem to her, that there did not and does not exist the slightest possibility of establishing a relationship with another woman even remotely like the one she has established in spite of her-self with the Wizard, nor the slightest possibility of telling the same or similar stories to another woman, not due to lack of trust, but simply because, much as she hates to admit it, she would not be inclined to do so – and although Elena has not uttered a word to this effect, the Wizard, who at times seems like a blooming idiot and at times like an absentminded professor, but at other times appears to read her mind, assures her that it has no bearing on the course of the analysis whether or not he knew the Spain of the fifties, and the woman thinks that the Wizard is probably right and that the analytic process may have little or nothing to do with understanding the historical context (maybe psychoanalysis has little to do with *any* kind of understanding since, Elena is beginning to realize, it is not a question whether the Stranger does or does not understand her, understanding is not what she can hope to get from him, and on the other hand, is this really what analysis is all about? what the hell is she doing in the sanctuary of the false gods – in any case no falser than others – except to blindly respond to a call she does not comprehend, as his lordship's dog responds to his master's whistle?), so maybe the Stranger is right, but if this is the case, and if what counts is the progress of the analysis, it would be much better – the woman suggests – instead of the two of them frantically running around looking for a needle in a haystack where no one has lost a needle, an absurd phantasmal Oedipus and castration complex in which she does not believe (why should she believe in a hypothesis that has not been proved – a hypothesis of that kind can never be proved, the Impassive One protests in his worst class-know-it-all tone of voice – and Elena corrects herself, in an unprovable hypothesis that denigrates her, that condemns her to being a second-class citizen? would she by any chance accept the intellectual superiority of the white race if she were black, would she subscribe to the doctrines of Nazism if she were Jewish? Elena's masochism does not go that far, Mr. Wizard, and as for all those women professionals in the clique, those women analysts with whom she could not have gone through analysis are all in some sense subservient and masochistic), so instead of going over and over a sad childhood, or one that she remembers as sad, a troubled adolescence – what adolescence isn't? – youthful dreams, individual and collective, some realized, most coming to nothing, instead of harping on an absent father, an overly

brilliant and unloving mother, the not very long list of
men she had loved, really loved, with body and soul, at
a given moment, but whom at another moment, whether
precise or indeterminate, she had invariably stopped loving, except in the case of Julio, which may have begun as
just another love affair – only with greater intensity – but
which then took shape in such a way that the two of them,
Julio and she, believed it was going to be different, that
this time it was going to be forever (Julio declared, Julio
pronounced, as proud of this as of any of his other cre-
ations, that what was not possible was to love the same
individual for years and years with the same kind of love, but
that it was possible – and this was what they had done – to
experience with the same person over time various creative and stimulating kinds of love), that relationship which
they believed to be eternal and is perhaps now breaking
apart, instead of going over and over the story of her
absent elder son, settled in the Germany of order, of sophisticated but nonetheless brutal repression, progress and
consumption, the poor guy contentedly living with that
little cartoon character whom he mistakes for a flesh and
blood woman, and her younger son, also gone, studying
the incessant copulations of some obscene flies who do not
even remotely imagine that they are thereby contributing
to the development of science, and surrounded, although
he has not yet established permanent relations with any
of them, with spectacular women – Ethiopians with deep-
set eyes and interminable legs, rather pallid but statuesque
Swedes, adolescent girls from Harlem established as models
for the most famous and sought-after photographers and
publicity agents – her two sons, then, far away and to top it
off selecting companions who do not appear to be real, but
rather cover girls for different style magazines – *El Hogar
y la Moda* and *Playboy*, for example – who are of course
totally different from Elena herself, from Andrea, from
her friends, from the women who have frequented the
house since they were children (and on this point she

refuses to blame herself: the part that she played in this nonsense her sons can examine with their analyst of the moment, in the event that they some day go into psychoanalysis), instead of going over and over why she has never completed one of the many books she has started, has never made up her mind to publish them (it cannot be solely due to the fact that Julio and the kids and the work at the production company have always seemed more important to her and always taken precedence over her writing, and even if that were the case, one would have to ask the reason why), instead of going over all of these questions ad infinitum and without much success, wouldn't it be more beneficial, she suggests, to what the Wizard calls "the analytic process" or "the favorable course of the analysis," to use as material (he too calls it this), as a more fruitful quarry, the stranger and more inexplicable fact, also crazier, more deeply rooted in the unconscious, of the absurd and ferocious dependency relationship she has established with her analyst, this force she cannot comprehend and which carries her four times a week – tail wagging, ears drooping, belly dragging on the ground, in her eyes that fear mixed with love and spun with hate, which only dogs can feel before that cruel master whom they do not understand – at a fixed hour – and what's worse it's five in the afternoon, the terrible five in the afternoon – to a place where she is frustrated without letup, and where she does not even know for sure what she is hoping to find?

She does not even know why she proposed it, Elena starts explaining to the Wizard eight days after Julio's departure without her for the Americas, eight days she has let go by waiting – as though she did not know the rules of the game and the behavior of this or perhaps of all supreme sorcerers of the tribe – for him to ask, impossible that he would not be surprised and curious why, after talking so much about the trip, even exploring the possibility of making up before or afterward some of the sessions she would

44

miss (without the Impassive One's giving a categorical response, of course, but hinting that perhaps, they'd see when
the time came, something could be worked out), she had
remained in Barcelona, and had spent the previous two
sessions talking about the salesgirl at the art gallery, her two
sons, about anything except the one thing that completely
absorbed her interest, and only now, at the third session,
does she start telling him (hating him because the Impassive One has not helped her along, has not opened the way
to confessions so she has to say it straight out) that she does
not even know why she said it, why she even suggested the
possibility, maybe it was just talk for the sake of talking – that
talk for the sake of talking which in other people makes
her nervous and for which she has taken Andrea to task
throughout thirty long years of friendship – although she
has already learned from the Wizard, or from Papa Freud
himself incarnate in him, that things are virtually never
done or said or come to pass by chance, chance in large
part supplanted not by decisions consciously made and
sustained through sheer tenacity and willpower, as she had
wished to believe, but rather by the dark, stormy and uncontrollable forces of the unconscious. Perhaps she suggested
it to him merely as a coy flirtation, to hear Julio assure
her that, as always in the past but perhaps now more than
ever, since the trip signified – symbolized – the pinnacle
of a career (many years earlier, well over twenty, he had
embraced her in the middle of Times Square, had picked
her up and spun her around, had kissed her on the lips
and declared that *that* was success and everything else just
nonsense, success was to have one's movie open in New
York, forget Spanish film festivals sponsored and promoted
by the Cinemathèque, the Museum of Modern Art or the
Casa de España: success was to see the posters for one's
film up outside the first-run movie theaters of Manhattan),
a career for which they had both struggled so much (and
when he said this about the two together having struggled
so much, Julio grew serious – he too grave as a dog in a

boat – frowned, and even put a protective but also in some sense conspiratorial arm around her, like comrades, two devoted valiant little soldiers who had fought together in the Hundred Years' War, shoulder to shoulder on the same front, and it's only now, over the last weeks or days, that Elena has asked herself what the front was and whether it had been the same for them both), now more than ever, therefore, was it inconceivable that he would make the trip without her, absolutely inconceivable, not only because Elena was going through an unusually difficult period, a depression unlike any she had ever previously experienced, but also because the two of them had against all odds arrived so near the top. And upon reaching this point in the discussion – a discussion often repeated with little if any variation – Elena would generally protest, because from time immemorial, ever since her youth, it has rubbed her the wrong way when women, the wives of supposedly or indisputably important men, constantly adopt the first person plural, grotesque that "we have published," "we have exhibited," "we have constructed," "they have asked us," "we have decided" on the lips of certain women – not so different from the little rabbit with long lashes and heart-shaped mouth, who has perhaps found her deepest purpose, the exact spot where she belongs in the music of the spheres, in pregnancy, and who may think her ultimate success in life consists in having gotten her husband to eat breakfast in the morning and gotten him to talk to her in that imbecilic tone in which idiots talk to children, the little rabbit who hums Schubert while combing her long golden hair before an unmagical mirror, with no little shepherd boy to admire her, the busy little mouse who sweeps the toy house with a raspberry bow (to match the house dress) on the tip of her tail and who is, in the last analysis, a doctor of law and officer of the courts? – women who don't publish, or exhibit, or build, or succeed, or for that matter ever decide anything, having lost the ability to figure things out for themselves from lack of use, although they have poured into their husband's career – whether he's an architect or a phone company employee – heaps of selflessness and, it seems to Elena, misguided effort and sacrifice, and have eliminated, erased, obliterated the first person singular and gotten used to living as if by delegation, without having a life of their own and what's worse without hoping for a more elevated life in the future, content to be able to confirm that behind every great man, or every successful man, or every happy man, we find the silent, anonymous figure of a woman, a grotesque blend – these women – of parrots who repeat, without understanding them and at times, out of an excess of zeal, distorting or misrepresenting them, the words of the master, the good and the bad, the opportune and the stupid, and of hollow cackling hens – there are few creatures, Elena thinks, stupider and more disagreeable than hens – whose feathers get ruffled and who peck without mercy anyone who dares to question the divinity of their god, all those who venture to raise objections or to criticize him, women without friends of their own – either male or female – without their own work – although sometimes they work longer hours than anyone – without their own inalienable inner life in which there are nooks and crannies – including on the conscious level – that are not shared, women who spend their lives saying yes to everything and to top it off are later often abandoned ("And those who say no?" the Wizard asks, and these are the first words he utters at today's session, always disposed to the kind, flattering suggestion, and Elena answers that they are too, and maybe with greater frequency than the former, but at least, one can hope, they're not left stark naked in the middle of the street, because it's one thing to lose your spouse and something very different to lose along with your spouse your entire life and have to start again from zero). So Elena surely would have protested when, as on other occasions and as expected, Julio had begun pontificating in a serious tone – to convince her that now more than ever she should accompany him – about the

47

inveterate struggles they had fought side by side to reach the top (and what was that "top," the woman now thinks, at what point could a reasonably sensible adult consider that he had reached the absolute peak, the highest of all possible peaks? when one of his films opened in a commercial theater in the heart of Manhattan, the heart of the world? and *then* what? for how long could one remain on the supposed peak? and Elena wonders if Julio, although he has kept on saying basically the same words and professing the same ideas, may have begun – although he hasn't confessed it to anyone much less to her – to place sensible limits on his ambition, to trim it, to lower bit by bit the height of the ceiling, because there may have been a fearful day, a shattering moment, when Julio – Julio the Marvelous, as Eduardo sometimes calls him – came to the realization that he will never be Leonardo and admitted within the realm of possibility that nothing or very little of his cinema will remain in five hundred years), so Elena would have protested, as she has innumerable times in the past, that his and his alone, not hers, only and forever his – whether or not they achieve immortality – are the movies he has conceived and directed, and if it was true that the woman had spent hours and hours discussing them, helping them along to a better birth, contributing ideas, typing the scripts, preparing mountains of sandwiches and gallons of coffee for the crew, or serving as shock absorber between the genius and insolent, suspicious producers, vain and incompetent actresses, hysterical leading men, the bottom line was she had done it because she enjoyed it, because it amused her, because she believed in Julio's filmmaking from the start, ever since that weekend in Perpignan, now swallowed up in the black hole of time, when they screened one of his first films along with those of other Spanish directors, and afterward there was a discussion in the loft of a bar, and when they were thrown out of that bar and all the bars, because at one time or another they all closed, they went on talking and debating out in the street, and again it occurs

48

to Elena, always stubborn and obstinate in her misgivings, always obsessive, that for all his insistence to the contrary the Wizard will not understand anything about anything, he just won't get it, if she doesn't manage to convey to him the living sensation – as alive as it is at these moments for her herself – of what those cinematic weekends in Perpignan were like, those getaways of the fifties and early sixties, when they would get up on Saturday before dawn and pile into a Seat 600, she, Andrea, Eduardo and two other friends, so the trip would cost less and also to begin arguing and debating from the moment they left, because in those days there was never enough time for discussion nor did the hour ever arrive to go to bed, despite having to get up early the next morning, and only very gradually, with the passing of the years, did they stop discussing the Cuban or the Chinese Revolution, the twists and turns of love and sexuality, the existence of God and of a life after death, art, the contrasting and in some sense kindred heresies of Papa Marx, Papa Freud, Papa Jean Paul, to begin talking about gossip – not about people or human attitudes, as they had in the past – or about work or the almost always trivial news that came out in the press, and then, starting very recently, about cholesterol counts, ways to give up smoking, calories, diets, affairs of money and prestige and power, and it was far more boring, not only for Elena but undoubtedly for all of them, and one fine day she realized that they no longer, or only rarely, talked their way through the night, but instead their gatherings broke up at prudent and sensible hours, because they all or almost all had to arrive bright and early the next morning at their offices, studios, ministries, now that the socialists had sprouted up like mushrooms – they didn't talk about socialists, you know, Mr. Wizard, at those cinematic weekends in Perpignan, and Elena, forever absentminded, hadn't realized there were so many – and they all had friends in the establishment, and for her this had been one of the first signs of the collective aging process – although Julio had perhaps aged less than

49

others, because he *did* still like to go around and around in impossible discussions that lasted until dawn, and he never, except on rare occasions during shooting, and even then grudgingly, resigned himself to getting up early – whereas before, in the fifties and sixties, Elena insists, there were not enough hours in the day to spend together, to hear music together, to see movies together, to debate, and they began the discussion right away in the 600 – in winter, well before daybreak – and arrived just in time to find the stores still open, to buy books and magazines – *Ruedo Ibérico* and *Playboy*, as she thought she'd already explained at an earlier session – and pharmaceutical products and cosmetics and Duralex dishes, and then two movies in the afternoon, another at night, discussions until dawn out in the street or, when it got too cold, packed into shabby hotel rooms with flowered wallpaper, cockroaches on the parquet flooring and a communal bathroom out in the hall for everyone on the floor, and on Sunday morning (even in those days many people, although not yet the majority, had stopped going to mass) one or two more movies, and into the 600 and back to Barcelona, the lungs of the soul swelled with fresh, revitalizing air, ears brimming with forbidden words, eyes brimming with forbidden images, everything forbidden, even the Duralex dishes they hid among the dirty clothes in the suitcase – they awaited one another just beyond the border, to see how the others had fared in the adventure and to return to their rightful owners the various objects they had strategically distributed in different suitcases – because there was a time, Elena recalls, as though she were a little old lady telling stories to her grandchildren before the blazing hearth fire, there was a time, my child, Elena recalls in a tone somewhere between the dreamy and the ironic, when humanity, or rather our extremely narrow enclave of academics, professionals and snobs (many of them offspring of the winning faction) fell into two groups, those who had already seen and those who had not yet seen *Viridiana, L'Avventura* or *The Virgin Spring*, and thus every

50

trip, including that brief peek into Perpignan, meant going to a different planet: the books, the movies, the newspapers, the most ordinary objects found in the department stores, all radically different, because during those years, unlike today, Spain was indeed different. And at this point Wooden Face interrupts her: "What was that again about trying to reclaim the unreclaimable through the picturesque and the nostalgic?" and "Where does Elena think her son could have picked up such off-the-wall ideas?" (which shows that at times the Supreme Sorcerer of the Tribe *does* listen to her, when he's not too bored with those ever-similar stories, repeated over and over a thousand times, or when he does not find too exciting the problem he has posed for himself on the chessboard, and he even seems capable of remembering what was said at an earlier session).

And during one of those weekends in Perpignan, which the Wizard for all he's a wizard cannot bring back to life, and here the Impassive One again interrupts her, in that smug ironic singsong that drives her crazy, even angrier now because he has interrupted her just when her discourse had entered one of those well-worn paths, like a slide or rails on which you speed along lightly and smoothly, almost flying, episodes we've told and told ourselves hundreds of times and that by dint of repetition – and perhaps this is what the Wizard hopes to avoid by interrupting her – have by now turned into literature: "Is it that I won't be able to bring those years back to life, those (he must be thinking "blessed," although he doesn't say it) weekends in Perpignan, or that I won't be able to share the image of them that you have been elaborating?" and Elena thinks that this, or something very similar, is what Eduardo sometimes implies when he refers irritably to her lost paradises, her invented paradises, those mythical paradises (as though his own weren't also mythical) which she then cannot do without and drags behind like a dead weight, but today Elena is in no mood to take into account the distrust of the Wizard, let alone that of Eduardo, so she goes on explaining, heedless and headstrong, that during one of those mythic and perhaps invented weekends in Perpignan, they had screened a short series of films by new Spanish directors, some in exile, others working in secrecy in Spain or making the most of the narrow cracks left open by the Franco censorship, and it seems to Elena that she began falling in love with Julio while watching the film, before she met him, something akin to what happens to Elizabeth in *Pride and Prejudice* (does the Wizard remember? no, of course not, the Wizard may have read Kafka, Borges, maybe even Tolstoy, but you can be sure he never read Austen), who falls in love with the hero not when she meets him at a social gathering, but rather as she peruses his house and belongings in his absence, accompanied by an old family servant, and thus she falls in love with a way of life, with a life project, rather than with a man of flesh and blood, but if she did not start falling in love with Julio during the screening of the film, it happened immediately afterward, in the smoke-filled barroom loft of endless nocturnal discussions, the floor covered with greasy paper and cigarette butts, where Elena did not ask a single one of the questions she had in mind, did not even open her mouth, yet Julio spoke all the time as though he were addressing her alone of all the people present, and the fact is that on that night Julio had not yet set limits on any of his ambitions, including love. "He looked a little like you," it suddenly occurs to Elena and she tells him, "a tall, thin, big-nosed guy, with the air of a slightly pedantic absentminded professor," and she laughs, sits up and turns around on the couch to see Wooden Face's expression, as he undaunted continues smoking his American cigarette and gazing with absorption into the infinite or at the back wall, through that body which is invisible or transparent or perhaps nonexistent, "although he was more handsome and looked more passionate and rebellious," Elena continues jokingly, and now he focuses his dispersed gaze, his gaze lost in the infinite, and asks, "Is that why you chose me as your analyst?" and Elena replies in the negative, no, that was not why, it was because she was up to her neck in a dark cesspool of anxiety from which she could not escape, and she accepted the first kind of help that was proposed to her, the first that came her way, weeks went by before she noticed the appearance of her analyst, before she really saw him.

And if she had helped him, she says, picking up the thread of her earlier discourse, it was because she enjoyed it, because she believed in his talent, in his genius even – she had never known anyone before, nor it seems to her since, who could equal him – and also because there wasn't anything in her own life so pressing or important that it could not be postponed or abandoned, and yet, despite recognizing all these things and despite knowing Julio as she knew or believed she knew him, that is, down to the most intimate hidden recesses of his mind, the fact is that Elena could not have imagined for an instant that precisely now, just when they were going to screen his latest film in New York and they invited him to attend the opening and give a series of lectures, when he was summoned from America, from the heart of the world, from that very center of the world where he had resolved to triumph, and just when the riffraff of our own country, so stale and envious and mediocre and shallow – who said that Rosario was a shallow city and Barcelona a great city? – were preparing to offer him – mere simpleminded imitation – that which on many other occasions, and some recent, they had stubbornly denied him, and moreover at a time when Elena was feeling so low, sad, tired, suddenly aged, still sunk in the depression that had brought her to this sanctuary crawling on her hands and knees, she could not have remotely imagined, then, that Julio would go without her, that he would put on her plate the possibility of leaving her behind, of abandoning her on the desert island and availing himself of favorable winds to make for the high seas, and she had said it just to say something, or for obscure reasons relegated to the unconscious and for that very reason, alas! unknown,

53

or perhaps because the emphatic, categorical "you're crazy, I can't go without you" that she was expecting, convinced that Julio would dismiss the idea without even discussing it, would have strengthened her belief in herself, have helped to dispel those dark fears, those vague and thus all the more terrible forebodings that had come unleashed within her – perhaps in warning? and if so, of what, what was the precise ill that could hurt her? – during that September of abandonment when her sons had more definitively left home and when she was about to turn fifty and which heralded the idea of death as her constant companion right up to the end. Except that, contrary to all these predictions and certainties, Julio had shrugged, kissed her on the cheek, agreed that maybe it would indeed be better for her ailments not to take a trip now, and especially not a business trip that promised to be exhausting, and he had concluded all this perfectly calmly, as though it were the most natural thing imaginable and meant nothing at all, while Elena feared that the whole world was about to cave in on them – or only on her – and dash them to bits. "That's okay, honey, do whatever you want," and of course it was true that on other occasions he or Elena had traveled separately, it was even true that on occasion he or she had traveled in the company of a third person, but this time it was different, or so it seemed to her, and for the first time, upon hearing him say "do what you want," which was just a sly and cowardly means to get his way and impose on the woman a course of action she obviously preferred not to take, it occurred to Elena that her finding things to be different, which she had believed just reflected the view of a depressed woman who could not help subjectively altering reality, could in fact correspond to the objective external reality: the crocodile who was waiting for her patiently under the bed could be real, not a hallucination, so that this time, she had discovered, it could also be a different experience for Julio, very differently lived out, and at some point in the coming days or weeks, when he returned

54

from the United States and Elena worked up the necessary courage, she would have to ask him and find out.

"It's no use pretending you're equal to men, there are things a woman will *never* be able to do," and when Elena asks him, just to be polite, what for example are some of those things, because Lord knows she could care less right now about the differences between the sexes, curled up here at one end of the bright red sofa, legs folded under her behind, enveloped in a dark blue silk robe lent her by Eduardo, a cup of steaming hot tea in one hand and a handkerchief – which Eduardo also had to lend her because never, either as a child or now, has Elena carried a handkerchief in her pocket or handbag for when she gets weepy or simply has a cold, and as a child it was terribly embarrassing to be sniffling until they left the chapel or the class ended, one of the most disagreeable memories from her childhood, and now with those times long gone, it makes her feel even more ill prepared and helpless – in the other, some lagging tears slowly trickling down her cheeks, between a sip of tea and a nibble on some exquisite English ginger cookies, and it *is* a consolation after all, the woman thinks, that even during the worst moments, perhaps like this one, when she is literally a wreck, she still responds to the aroma of a well-chosen blend of tea, to the crunchy sweetness of cookies, she still finds pleasing the soft touch of silk on her skin, a real consolation that she does not lose that voluptuousness of taste, touch, sound, that her body keeps responding promptly and obediently to agreeable external stimuli, while her mind or soul or whatever the hell it is goes on strike or goes bankrupt, and it's the body alone that stays in the thick of things and ready to help out, and the truth is nothing would appeal to her less than to be an incorporeal spirit, a spirit incapable of eating or sipping, or coming into contact with surfaces, or breathing in the fragrances of summer, and Elena is thinking about all of this, about the verses of Auden and that we must say no to Plato, and about her frustrated image as romantic heroine (who ever heard of a romantic heroine who doesn't lose her appetite or sleep? or, as much as she would have liked to identify with her in her adolescence, a Marguerite Gauthier who stuffs herself on liqueur-filled chocolates and *marrons glacés*? and all at once, abruptly, fleetingly, Elena is able to distance herself, to mock and trivialize her suffering and sadness, which does not make them any less real), and she could care less right now about anyone's opinions – and still less if the person expressing them is a man – on the limitations of woman (so just the cause of feminism, she believes, so fundamentally just, yet for a long time to come, of which she cannot envision the end, lost, so futile to have discussions with men who do not listen, or only half listen, and hear only what they want to hear), all the more so because she has not set foot on the doorstep of this house as a woman, but rather as a clumsier than usual Tom Thumb who, besides losing his way and the bread crumbs or colored pebbles, has lost his six siblings and knocks on the door of a mansion chosen at random, in hopes that it won't be that of the Savage Ogre, or as a Snow White who flees in terror from her stepmother, but whose fear does not stop her – she must have a sweet tooth like hers – from taking a taste from each of the seven dishes and then trying one after another the seven little beds, although in fact Elena has tried only one and that one not for herself alone, but shared with someone – who doesn't bear the least resemblance to any of the seven dwarves – and as far as she can recall this variant does not appear in the versions by the Brothers Grimm or Perrault, and so it's purely out of courtesy and gratitude, since Eduardo, so unbearable at other times, so sullen and stern, has today opened his door to her without reserve – at the start of this threatening weekend which she did not feel capable of facing alone – he has taken her in the way kind souls take in a poor little orphan girl or a lost mutt without a collar, and he put her in bed and made love to her gently, and then prepared for

her a bath overflowing with scented foam, and patted her
dry like a baby with a large maternal towel, and lent her
his best silk robe, and even prepared a perfect cup of tea
and got out from heaven knows where – since he does not
have a sweet tooth – these exquisite cookies, and handed
her a handkerchief at the proper moment and let her cry
in silence until at least for today she's all cried out, for all
of which Elena feels grateful and wants to be agreeable, so
she responds to his question with another question, and
asks him what for example are some of the things a woman
will never be able to do, and without altering his grave tone
of voice or losing his composure, Eduardo answers in dead
seriousness that what no woman will ever be able to do
is piss a figure eight on the wall, and now Elena laughs
until she cries again and chokes on the ginger cookies and
the dense tart flavor sticks in her throat, while she tells
Eduardo in words smothered by coughing – as he solici-
tously pounds her on the back – that it's marvelous, simply
marvelous, that it's just a question of that, just that, out of
the multiple, almost infinite and very painful limitations
she was thinking of when he asked her, and it honestly
doesn't matter, she'll swear to it, it doesn't bother her at
all or hardly at all not being able to piss on the wall a figure
eight or a figure nine or a whole flock of colored birds, as
it doesn't bother her either not participating in the virile
games at military camps, where the recruits compete, so
she's told, to see who comes closest to hitting with his stream
of urine the waste basket they've positioned in the middle
of the barracks, between the bunk beds, and unbeknownst
to him Eduardo has even given her an excellent idea how
to satisfy the Wizard, because the two of them, the Wizard
and she, have been going crazy for weeks, almost since the
start of the analysis, hunting for the Oedipus complex and
the castration complex, opening up crates and rummaging
through enigmas of lost memory, leaving everything upside
down and out of place, like a dusty old attic where you've
been looking for things without finding them and leave

57

everything a mess and in disarray, and she keeps repeating that she doesn't find a thing, despite trying with all the good faith in the world she doesn't find a thing, and Wooden Face talks about her resistances and assures her that the complexes are hidden in some obscure corner that she cannot bring herself to reveal, and it doesn't matter that she has never felt penis envy on the conscious level, since how can you prove you haven't felt it on the unconscious level, when what characterizes the unconscious is precisely that it remains concealed from us? and now, thanks to Eduardo, on Monday an exultant Elena can enter the sanctuary, the brothel-sanctuary, take off her sandals without getting into too much of a muddle, lie down on the couch and rattle off quickly, like a good little girl who has learned her lesson well: "When I was a very small girl, one day I saw some boys who were playing at pissing a figure eight on the wall and they made fun of me because I couldn't do it and I remember that I felt very distressed," and it's odd that, despite Elena's not having spoken a single word out loud, Eduardo suddenly asks her out of the blue and with no apparent relevance – in a type of nonverbal communication she often has with Eduardo and with Andrea almost always – how her peregrinations are going with the witch doctor of the pampas, with her Argentine psychiatrist, and the woman – maybe to gain time, because she really doesn't know what she can report about her adventures with the Impassive One that will sound reasonably sensible and believable, not like complete rubbish – explains once again that she is not seeing a psychiatrist (Horacio is the psychiatrist, and he treats her not as a patient but as a friend) but rather a psychoanalyst, and Eduardo says, shrugging, that they must be about the same, and Elena knows there's no point in explaining it to him, because there are scenes, characters, incidents, words that he has decided to record a certain way and are henceforth immutable, they take on permanent status although they have happened only once, because Eduardo selects at will and obeying laws unknown to Elena or himself or anyone else, and that tend to be as capricious as they are static, an often anecdotal detail or aspect of reality, and elevates it to the category of a universal truth, and so it's impossible, for example, to convince him that, although on a particular occasion you spent an entire afternoon in his company shopping for a pair of shoes, you don't feel the least fetishistic passion for footwear, or that Andrea was not a girl who always wore red stockings, like a partridge, because she only wore the stockings in question a couple of times (not even she can remember when) and that was more than twenty years ago, or that Julio is not a sucker for the writers of the Latin American boom, although he once commented that he liked very much a story by Borges and another by Cortázar, or that Elena herself does not feel a fervent veneration – of course unjustified – for the art critic she met when the two went together to an opening at a gallery, and whom it seems she greeted too warmly (which aroused in Eduardo – and continues to arouse periodically every time he remembers it – a whopping fit of jealousy, a jealousy that is also set off by any painter whose work Elena likes, although the men she may have slept with leave him cold, and competitive as the two men's relationship may be, he is not strictly speaking jealous of Julio), so it's useless to try to get Eduardo to take in, to record and process the fact that a psychiatrist is not the same as a psychoanalyst, useless to point out that they have little in common, because a psychiatrist is usually a good-natured guy who's something of a busybody, besides being extremely understanding, who pats you on the back and often suggests what you should or should not do, and predicts that everything will go better for you in the future, and assures you or implies that you are an extraordinary person, someone very special (the psychoanalyst takes every possible opportunity, even if it's only remotely relevant, to make it clear that there's nothing remarkable about you, nothing to distinguish you from other patients), that the work you're doing is magnificent, that the love of your life awaits you just around the corner, and who could imagine such rubbish that you're starting to age? (and one is tempted to point a finger accusingly at the Wizard: my psychoanalyst imagines it, and it's so hard to have someone constantly putting salt on the wound that no one should start psychoanalysis without at the same time disposing of a psychiatrist who can at least in part keep up his morale), psychiatrists generally administer and even regulate the dosage of miracle drugs – which you cling to like a talisman – drugs to make you fall in a heap into bed at night and walk around half asleep all day, life a waking dream or a dreamless sleep, drugs to curb your aggressiveness or spur it on, and even to enable you to get up in the morning – what a feat – lively and lightheaded, the psychiatrist makes you feel with every word, with every gesture, how concerned he is about your happiness, and with a little luck and savvy you can even wake him in the middle of the night to tell him on the phone about the crocodile under the bed, and it's even possible that he would give you flowers on your Saint's Day and at Christmas wish you the happiest of new years (regarding which he, for one, has no doubt), whereas a psychoanalyst – or at least those that Elena knows in person or by name – is almost always a distant, contemptuous guy, forever surrounded by a thick wall of coldness and silence, who has made a profession of the lack of cordiality and warmth – why the hell else would he choose this out of all possible professions? – a guy who wrinkles his nose as though something, which of course is not he, smelled bad in the sanctuary, and fixes on you a stare that goes right through you without seeing you, a guy who makes it plain as plain can be that you, you in particular, he doesn't give two hoots about – or at least not in any special way, and how else can one human being be interested in another? – and that your happiness or unhappiness is of absolutely no concern to him, because his job is not at all, as might presume the gullible and the profane, to look after the health and well-being of his patients, the only thing that really matters within the walls of the sanctuary is "the favorable course of the analysis" – if that course does not appear to be favorable, the fault must lie in the patient's putting up resistances, these almost always unconscious in nature, which keeps the competence of the analyst off the hook – and to ensure the favorable course of the analysis, it's basic and essential that the time of the sessions not be changed come hell or high water, that you arrive on his doorstep at the appointed hour even if you're on fire or drowning yourself, that your questions not be responded to, let alone your requests, that you not be offered comments or advice – even if you're on the point of pulling the trigger or jumping off the balcony – absolute neutrality, total asepsis, a faceless ghost, an empty clothes rack on which you can hang as you please masks and disguises, a blank form into which you can pour and confound all the characters, what's most typical of him is to let you throw yourself off the fiftieth floor without lifting a finger (could it be that analysts are screwed into their armchairs or rockers? that would explain many things), without getting a hair out of place, in a superb display of wisdom and self-control that legions of less fortunate colleagues will applaud spellbound beneath the window. Didn't Eduardo read in the newspaper a few days ago that in Madrid an eighteen-year-old girl had committed suicide upon leaving a session, most certainly because the analyst had refused to take on her problems, abandon his passivity, get his feet wet, behave like a human being? Well, the girl's parents, and even the journalist himself, were upset and querulous and even allowed themselves more or less veiled accusations, thereby giving proof of their abject ignorance and of never having read a word of Lacan, but in contrast, the most distinguished psychoanalysts the world over had declared their solidarity with the analyst from Madrid – who was also, of course, Argentine, although it seems to Elena not from Rosario – and they spoke of awarding the heroic professional, who had not flinched even before death itself from safeguarding the favorable course of the analysis – what a magnificent session they would have had the following day if only the girl hadn't died! – the medal for perfect inhumanity and the most pompous and pedantic rubbish. Psychiatrists, Elena explains to Eduardo, at least those who are not so young, have a soothing measure of pessimism and mistrust, they tend to relativize many things and seek to have us get along the best we can – with the least possible suffering, since they really *are* interested in and concerned about the happiness or unhappiness of their patients – ever onward, until the rope runs out and the movie ends, but psychoanalysts of all ages, and the younger they are the worse, like apostles of all creeds and all times, believe in absolute truths, and set their stakes much higher: none of this get along the best you can and I'll help you the best I can, but rather change a wrong way of life for another that's different, given that the game subsists on the belief that by putting on a wooden face, taking an oath of silence, laying the patient on the couch and proposing that she say the first thing that occurs to her, without filtering it through any screen whatsoever, the moment – or successive moments – will arrive when a more or less repulsive beast (almost always more, and needless to say, from it proceeded the bad smell that made the Wizard wrinkle his nose, although one didn't notice it oneself) leaps into the sanctuary, vomited up from the most turbid corner of the unconscious, whose vivisection will allow for a better organization of your life, and it turns out that to work such a miracle, the wizards of that infamous throng – or the witch doctors of the pampas, as Eduardo sometimes calls them – talk on familiar terms with God every night, and it doesn't matter if that god is called Jehovah or Buddha or Papa Freud or Papa Marx, because individuals who converse with God every night are almost always dangerous creatures, who can just as readily carry you to the bonfire intoning prayers for the salvation of your sinner's soul as undertake the vivisection of your most intimate ego on the laboratory table, and Elena is not at all convinced by the creed of José Antonio (the Wizard may not know to whom she's referring but she does not try to explain it to him): it doesn't matter if the scalpel draws blood, as long as it obeys a law of love, because it isn't determined who will administer this law, and to make matters worse, the blood is one's own, while the scalpel is repeatedly in the hands of others. And upon arriving at this point, Eduardo – Elena had by this time forgotten he was there and was talking to herself – laughingly interrupts her: "Don't you think you're exaggerating a little? And if you have so little confidence in your analyst, if what you just told me is what you think of psychoanalysis, why the devil do you keep having sessions?" and the woman is tempted to answer that she keeps having sessions because she has fallen into an absurd trap that she can't get out of, but she opts to remain silent, because it would take a long time to explain and besides she doesn't really understand it herself. So she laughs along with Eduardo, relaxed, feeling much better, emerging in part from her deepest pools of shadow, and she remembers that Eduardo told her in the little bed not shared with any dwarf, just for the two of them, "Today you are using me as your aspirin," and now she acknowledges, she admits to him and to herself, that she has indeed been exaggerating as usual, she's been ranting and raving a bit more than necessary, but these outbursts of dialectical rage agree with her and raise her spirits, and moreover it's comforting to again confirm that one can have marvelous friends, capable of turning themselves into aspirins for one's good.

"There aren't many friends like Eduardo," a yawning Elena says to herself on the second day, at almost five in the afternoon, although that doesn't matter since it's Sunday, after having slept a thousand hours and loafed around so many more in the bath and eaten on the terrace beneath a pale pre-autumnal sky, where she is now sipping a final cup of coffee (Eduardo a first scotch) and smoking a cigarette, or it might be more exact to say that she doesn't

63

have another friend like Eduardo – her relationship with Andrea may be even more intense and profound, and go further back in time, but it's a completely different kind of relationship and besides, Andrea is always wandering around lost in distant spaces, so their encounters are always brief, abrupt and inadequate – so many years of loyal mutual friendship, despite their both being so demanding and touchy and suspicious. "You are my best friend," he sometimes assures her, "and notice that I don't say my best girlfriend, but my best friend," perhaps expecting her to take offense and get into a fruitless argument about what women can be if they are not people, it's just that Elena is tired of that type of discussion, so often repeated in almost identical form that you know from the start how it will inevitably unfold, and furthermore these days she feels too sad and depressed, with that pile of apathy and discontent weighing her down and suffocating her, that bitter taste in the mouth that nothing – not even the finest ginger cookies – can remove, that urge to sleep all the time (all she has done in the days since Julio left for America, when she is not with Wooden Face or at a movie theater or taking a stroll around the office, where everything is now upside-down and in a mess – or even while she is doing one of the three – is to wait for nighttime, so she can take some pills, curl up in bed, and fall into a sleep that frees her from everything, even from dreams: the only trouble is that that "everything" awaits her promptly at the foot of the bed with the inevitable awakening), and rather than protest, she usually prefers to take Eduardo's words as compliments, although it's clear they can't just be taken as simple compliments, and she should wonder and ask him what else she can be if not a woman, or retort, "It's precisely for that reason, the fact that I'm such a person, something the majority of women apparently are not, that despite the tender and ardent whims, always literary and slightly leaden, that come over you occasionally at my side, I am the last woman in the world you could fall in love with," and it may well be the height of inconsistency, in the endless stream of inconsistencies and contradictions her life has become, that she feels if only for a few moments passed over and offended, given the fact that neither has she ever been in love with Eduardo, and since adolescence has not been able to say enough about the wonders of friendship between men and women, all leading up to the day when it annoys her to know that she is appreciated for her intelligence, her honesty, her sense of humor and not for her hair or her legs, and she feels absurdly jealous and petty, and this sets her off daydreaming about the wild crazy women, not at all people and as such very feminine, who have filled Eduardo's life for as long as she's known him and even before, maybe forever (starting with his own mother, because in the case of Eduardo it would not be too hard for the wizard of the moment – nor would it take long for the two of them, since they would not have to rummage through many closets or poke into many drawers – to bump into an Oedipus complex like a cathedral, a complex like you'd find in the first-year textbook of wizardry, Eduardo fascinated and repelled since infancy by that woman who was so beautiful and so different, for better or for worse, from the mothers of the other kids, emanating from the theatrical world – although it seems she was never a good actress – and promoted to the middle class through marriage with his father, who was much older than she, without ever being accepted into his world, always with one foot in one of the two worlds and the other dangling in the air, and maybe for that very reason contemptuous, demanding, bad-tempered, arbitrary, and above all, totally unmaternal), women whom Elena – half jokingly, half seriously – imagines donning impossible clothes and hairdos, huge red sun hats overflowing with flowers and fruit and sheer crêpe dresses beneath which they appear naked – a cocotte from the belle époque or a Venus by Cranach – or tight-fitting leather pants with knee-high boots and broad leather and metal belts – like a heroine out of the comics or science fiction – although

65

later, when she met them in real life, because Eduardo has
introduced her to almost all his lovers, they turned out to be
ordinary-looking women in nondescript clothes, but nonetheless women – and Elena knows this from what a seduced
and infuriated Eduardo has told her himself – capable of
throwing all one's luggage out the window, in a multicolored stream of ties, underpants and after-shave lotions, or
of flirting with a stranger in a restaurant from table to table,
some guy they're not the least interested in, until one finds
oneself compelled to come to blows, or of ramming the car
they're driving, just because, because something Eduardo
said irritated them, into a Rolls Royce correctly parked
by the sidewalk, also capable of attempting, just for fun,
to steal a diamond necklace from Tiffany's or a perfume
from some department store, or of taking off their blouse
and bra in a dance hall and even urinating at the edge of
the floor (that's undoubtedly where Eduardo must have
learned all that gibberish about women not being able to
piss a figure eight on the wall, although they *could* perform
no less absurd and pointless acts), thus contriving one
way or another that they all end up at the police station
in the wee hours of the morning, without Eduardo's losing even then the distant and distinguished air of a real
gentleman – what the commissioner could not dream is to
what degree he is secretly aroused and pleased – like in an
American comedy of the forties, and it's a good thing if
it's just a matter of a commotion on the premises or on a
public thoroughfare, if the bottle of after-shave or cologne
didn't hit some absentminded pedestrian, if the theft can
be put down to kleptomania, because the women of Eduardo the Bold, with the same sangfroid with which they
take off their panties at a funeral or throw canapés at the
orchestra conductor, or explain at the top of their lungs at
the Trevi Fountain, amidst tourists and pigeons, how inept
their partner is in bed and what he can't do for them and
how unsatisfied they're left because of his inexperience,
are also capable of filling Eduardo's suitcase – whether he

knows it or not – with heroin, or asking him to store a kilo of trinitrotoluene or accompany them in the armed holdup of a jewelry store, and he apparently doesn't care too much if they're young or especially beautiful, as long as they're daring, uncontrollable, unpredictable and nuts, eager to live it up or go looking for trouble, as long as they burst into Eduardo's inner world – as Andrea commented years ago – like the proverbial bull in the china shop, although Elena doesn't think that's exactly it, because it's true that the partners who have inhabited his life for months or years at a time have been overwhelming and sometimes even brutal, and it's true that beneath his multiple breastplates and shifting helmets – he never completely lets down his guard – one has an inkling of something in Eduardo's inner life as fragile and vulnerable, also as exquisite, as china, but these women have never penetrated his inner life, nor has Elena herself – although she feels closer to sniffing it out, although Eduardo himself has offered her the most signs and clues – nor anyone: Eduardo keeps his intimate life to himself and his own self-destructive ends, and he is at one and the same time the bull and the china. And if Elena suspected that some other woman had succeeded in going further than she into the inner life of Eduardo, at that point she could become terribly jealous, but as it stands what she feels is not exactly jealousy, but rather envy, a wretched envy for all the acts she'd never have the nerve to try, precisely because she's so reasonable and well behaved, such a person, the temptation to scandalize and transgress permanently contained by an incoercible shyness, an insurmountable modesty, so that makes two of them – Eduardo and she – who are bewitched and seduced by bold crazy women who perhaps have to their credit little more than bad manners and a lack of the most basic common sense, the most basic respect for others and for themselves, women who, instead of getting stupidly depressed and sleeping twenty hours a day and stuffing themselves with multicolored pills in a miserable, lackluster solitary orgy, and fighting with art gallery salesgirls or traffic cops, and dragging their nonstop sniffling to movie houses showing Walt Disney or Tarzan films, would have taken the first plane to New York and raised a spectacular ruckus, a huge row on opening night or a more private row in the hotel lobby, or better still, put on a trench coat and grabbed a gun and hunted the two of them down in the corner of some bar (if one didn't hate so much the cheap affectation of almost all French movies), women who, instead of establishing with their analyst – and why would they need analysis, when they're so coarse and primitive that they surely don't have an unconscious: barely two centimeters thick, into which nobody, not even Papa Freud, could have delved – a complex relationship of abject dependence, here and there tinged with love and interspersed with hate, would have long ago broken the ceramic jug over his head or sat on his knees and pawed him without giving it a thought ("So are those things that you would like to do?" inquires the Wizard when she tells it to him in so many words, as he raises his left eyebrow, an amused glimmer in his eye and not the least bit scared, and Elena says, "You don't get it, as usual you don't get it: it's not that I'd like to *do* those things, what I'd like a whole lot is to know that I *could* do them, which is something very different, although, come to think of it, maybe I could break something over your head one fine day . . .").

"It seems that instead of showing up at your house in search of aspirins, I came to go through a sleep cure," Elena apologizes yawning, mixing the taste of the coffee with the aroma of the cigarette, and thinking that the only thing missing was a candy or piece of chocolate to make the blend complete, and Eduardo jokes, "sleep and weep cure," and only now, when it would have been natural to bring it up much earlier, does he ask: "May I ask what's happened, what's the matter with you? Where on earth is Julio the Marvelous, Julio da Vinci, Julio Welles?" and Elena, "You must be the only person in the city who doesn't know that Julio is in New York to attend the opening of his film!" and Eduardo, making a funny face, "My Lord, so he has finally embarked on the conquest of the Americas! and has he by chance found his Malinche?" and Elena, for once not taking offense at his gibes, not feeling obliged to rush sword in hand to the defense of the misunderstood genius, "The fact is, I think he's taken his Malinche with him from Spain . . ."

"Eduardo told me a joke," Elena tells the Wizard, explaining that she has stayed in Eduardo's apartment for three days, the entire weekend, abandoning herself to sleep and tears and an erratic somnambulistic sensuality steeped in lamentation, and it seems a miracle that there hasn't appeared a single one of his crazy women, the restless feminine forms that arise like witches out of the night – and especially on Sabbath eve – maybe because Eduardo happens to be in the usual brief interlude between one affair and the next, because despite his life's being full of women and how much they mean to him, you could not strictly speaking call him a womanizer, even less, promiscuous, and he hardly ever makes love to people who don't appeal to him, he doesn't engage in frivolous affairs just because – unless, of course, he's had too much to drink – and it's rare for him to carry on two different affairs simultaneously, affairs that last for years, one or two anyway, and when they are over, usually evolve (unless the woman feels very wronged and bitter or they have hurt each other too much) into a lifelong friendship, tinged to a greater or lesser degree with nostalgic eroticism, or maybe he's in the throes of a war of absence and of silence with the woman of the present story (and this time for once Elena doesn't know the details, because Eduardo hasn't related to her his own fortunes and misfortunes, nor has she asked, too absorbed in her own distress to attend to that of others), nor has the house been invaded by black heroin addicts from a jazz group, or by that self-made crippled big shot who regards Elena – when the two meet against their will – with open hostility, but whom Eduardo

69

counts among his best friends – sometimes he even shows him before he shows her one of his paintings or sketches, which fills her with spite – so he can turn up at Eduardo's home anytime, at any hour of the day or night, as though he owned the place, and stay as long as he likes, something Eduardo would not be caught dead doing even for a prima ballerina of the Opera of Beijing, Bucharest or Prague, who is being pursued to the ends of the earth by her deceived husband – it's anyone's guess if still in love with her – along with her country's secret police, who are attempting to recover the silverware from the Town Hall, which the star has inadvertently carried off in her luggage upon making the double choice of conjugal and political freedom. No one has interrupted them, and all the while Elena has overcome the temptation to return home and wait for a phone call from New York – Julio has called her every day since he left, although the conversations between the two have been tense and forced, full of awkward silences – or from one of the boys, she has also overcome the fear that some mishap may have befallen one or another of them, the anxiety of imagining the phone ringing over and over in the empty house – when she's at home, regardless of her intentions, she is incapable of not answering the phone – but also content to know that on this one occasion (Elena can't remember another like it) Julio might have called and not found her there, for once not playing the feminine role par excellence, hovering eagerly and tremulously over the phone, consumed with anxiety, a lighted cigarette in one hand and in the other a book which she vainly attempts to read, waiting for a phone call that is late or in the worst case never materializes, with her heart in her throat each time the phone rings, and the subsequent disappointment upon finding that it's someone else calling her, not him, and this is really serious, not like that pissing figure eights on the wall: did the Wizard have any idea of the number of things that could have been accomplished – skyscrapers a thousand stories high, bridges suspended over the sea, vaccines to fight cancer, books comparable to the *Quixote* or *The Divine Comedy*, paintings that would make Rembrandt or Picasso look like child's play, the discovery of perpetual motion – with the time and energy and hopes that had been wasted and consumed – sometimes in vain – by generation upon generation of women glued to the telephone, or before the phone, spying through the curtains the arrival of the mailman, or of the stagecoach from Oklahoma? where did Wooden Face think women were when they built the pyramids, discovered America, forged the French or the October Revolution, invented psychoanalysis? Women – with the exception of those few who did not have a telephone or a mailman, and perhaps for that reason occasionally took part in history – were all glued to the phone or the window, legs folded under their backside and biting their nails, waiting for a call that did not come, or if it did, waiting for the next. "And don't you think the same thing or something very similar happens to men?" cautiously inquires the Wizard, who always takes pains not to understand anything related to the feminine condition – so Elena wonders for the thousandth time how the hell it occurred to her to go into analysis with a man – but she has no desire to discuss it again, so she continues talking about how she has spent three days, the whole weekend, with Eduardo-aspirin, Eduardo-nurse, Eduardo-my-mama-dearest – not a mother like the ones they both had, of course, but a real honest-to-goodness mother, a mother with a capital M, a mother out of an Argentine tango – an Eduardo capable of temporarily putting aside his own problems to concern himself with someone else's, and thanks to him she had resisted the temptation to return home in case Julio called or something happened to the kids – she didn't even call them from Eduardo's apartment, as she could have – and yet, as five o'clock Monday approached, the terrible five o'clock, the stroke of five on all the clocks (at least on almost all those of the old continent, it's anyone's guess what time it was in Argentina), she had felt an unbearable itch, she

71

could not resist the tug of the invisible chain, and she had run off like Cinderella, only without losing, it seems, a glass slipper or any other kind of footwear along the way, and without there being a Prince Charming inclined to follow her trail to the Stepmother's house, and "So now I'm given the role of the Stepmother?" the Impassive One protests, but Elena knows he's very pleased, because he likes nothing more than to play all the parts in the stories told by his analysands, leaping nimbly from one role to the next – the Stepmother, Prince Charming, the Fairy Godmother and even, if he gets the chance, the mouse who is turned into one of the carriage horses – the only thing he can't stand is to play the part of himself, that a tiny particle of his real self peep through some unruly crack. So Elena could not resist the tug of the invisible chain, on the stroke of five midnight pealing through all the bells of the palace, and now here she is stretched out on the couch spouting rubbish, and what was it she started to say as soon as she came in and has since forgotten? what the devil could it have been? And the Wizard, who certainly does remember, shuts up like a clam and insists that it's not important, that she keep on saying the first thing that comes to mind, and Elena protests that how can it not be important, she won't be able to talk about anything else until it comes back to her, and Wooden Face scolds her, "Why do you always have to be controlling the situation, have everything planned out? What do you think would happen if you sometime let yourself go?" and the woman shrugs and is silent, letting a light, idle hand meander along the smooth surface of the wall behind the couch until it comes upon a slight irregularity, a tiny hole in which she shields the tip of her index finger – at least it's something – she confesses that she does not know why it's so difficult for her not to be in control of situations, why unfinished thoughts or statements disturb her so much, especially now when, perhaps due to her age, for the first time there are gaps in her memory, blank spaces, and it often happens in bed, on the brink of falling asleep, of losing consciousness, when all at once, in a jolt, she realizes in bewilderment that while dozing she has lost her train of thought and she feels the vertigo of an emptiness without end, and the same thing or something very similar happens to her other times when she's talking to people, except that in those cases there always remains the doubt as to whether it's a question of a genuine memory loss or simply that she hasn't been listening to what the others were saying, as she also sometimes doesn't hear what the analyst says, and this does indeed seem strange to her, and may be due not to a lack of interest but on the contrary to how much it matters, to the excessive weight of the invisible figure – except for the tip of his shoe – of the Wizard behind her back, strange that one can miss something from inattentiveness, but also from being overly intent, and now Elena, while going over and over all of this, suddenly recalls that upon entering the office, even before taking off her sandals and lying down on the couch, she started to say, "Today Eduardo told me a joke," as though this joke were somehow representative of an erratic, blurry weekend – odd, isn't it? – and the Impassive One, perhaps to make amends for such impassivity, for so much silence and so little cooperation in the search and seizure of the lost words, the end of the tangled strand of yarn, now asks her about the joke, suggests that she tell the joke and they'll see what they find in it, and it's a very short joke, she remarks, because she doesn't generally like jokes and doesn't know how to tell them, so she can only handle very short ones like this: "Once upon a time there was a man who was so small, so very small, that he hugged a marble and declared, 'The world is mine,'" and Elena adds, without waiting for the Wizard to ask what occurs to her, that the meaning is obvious, it's obvious that in telling this joke Eduardo was referring to Julio, Julio the Marvelous, Julio the Magnificent, Julio Welles, as he often mockingly calls him, and it's one more joke in the long list of sarcastic comments, demythifying observations that he has lavished on him for almost thirty years – without their

bearing too great ill will – ever since the afternoon when
Elena had entered the studio apartment where Eduardo
was then living and informed him, on the brink of ecstasy,
of levitation, since one could say her feet no longer tread
on firm ground, that she had met at the Perpignan film
club, which on that occasion he had not attended for a
change, a marvelous man, and the two had suddenly fallen
in love with a love unequalled in the entire history of the
human race, even going back to the caves of prehistoric
times, and Eduardo had nibbled sparingly on the tip of his
pipe, turned it upside down and tapped it on the ashtray,
and put on the most malicious, glacial, sarcastic look of all
his repertoire – which was very extensive, he had at least as
many as pipes – of malicious, glacial, sarcastic looks, a look
stolen from the feline world, the look of leopards when
they draw back to ready themselves for the kill, or that of
certain psychoanalysts from Rosario when they see timidly
peek out of a corner of the sanctuary a wretched creature
vomited up from the unconscious as from a warm, moist,
protective womb, which they can immediately vivisect without anesthesia, without even having to get up from their
rocker, with the blessed and terrible scalpel – which draws
blood but which, according to the followers of José Antonio and Papa Freud, obeys a law of love – so that's how
Eduardo had looked at her, and he had explained in a
perfectly neutral voice, without inflections or shadings – as
though he were reciting for the hundredth time a lesson
that everyone already knew, but that the slowest child in
the class could not manage to comprehend – that in the
real world marvelous men did not exist – like that Julio the
Marvelous that Elena was telling him about – and that, if
she had described him the way you describe any man, with
his good points and bad like any Tom, Dick or Harry, the
story might have had the possibility of going on satisfac-
torily for some time – neither were there eternal loves in
the real world, thank God – but as she described it the
relationship was doomed to failure from the start, and

perhaps Eduardo *did* feel jealous, Elena now responds to the Wizard's question – it seems that over the last few days, at the most recent sessions he has intervened more openly, as if he has in part attenuated or revoked his oath of silence – as she has sometimes been jealous of the strange wild women whom he discovered or invented in the dark dens of midnight, bold daring women who invaded the inner life of proud, sensitive men (with poorly resolved Oedipus complexes) like bulls in a china shop, it's true that at times Elena has for no apparent reason been against Eduardo's loves (as she may also, she admits in an outburst, have been against the loves of her sons), as he has been against most of the men she has been interested in, but there was more to it than that: Eduardo, who appreciated, even to excess, so many of her qualities, real or imagined, in contrast hated her vulgar sugar-coated romanticism, bordering on bad taste and farce, typical of an adolescent, that mania to universalize and dramatize everything, to turn it all into bad literature, to overact, that apparent zeal to carry all attitudes, actions, feelings to their ultimate and extreme consequences, when she was really so reluctant to break loose, to go beyond limits, to rush into the fray and wet her ass, just as he also hated – and the two faults were so closely interwoven they could merge into one – her supposedly contemptuous good-girl airs, the bad manners of an upper-middle-class girl educated in private schools, the insolence of a spoiled child, and in such a long time, thirty or more years of friendship going back to their university days, a tried and true loyalty, they had seriously quarreled only once, on only one occasion had they let months go by – the two of them who, when they don't get together, call each other at least once a day: they report back to base – without seeing or calling one another, and it was because of a stupid incident with that self-made cripple, whom from that time on (not before, as Eduardo claimed) she came to detest, because the individual in question had pestered her the whole night at the home of some friends, taunting her with obscenities and disagreeable trash, and it's true that he and the others had drunk a lot at dinner and afterward, but this did not justify such unbridled rudeness, so Elena had donned her coldest, most distant mask, which only served to excite him more and more, until finally she'd run out of steam and patience and on an abrupt impulse had cleared out, and it seems there was something in her way of standing up, taking her coat and purse, saying goodbye to everyone, passing the cripple without even looking at him, or rather, looking right through him without seeing him, thereby denying his right to visibility and existence (yes, something very similar to what the Wizard does to her, who on a daily basis continually cold-shoulders her), something in her way of leaving the room and the house – followed by a surprised Julio, who had been totally unaware of what was going on, but in any case and whatever the circumstances, allied with her unto death, and to the general dismay – that Eduardo considered inexcusable, and it was to no avail that Elena argued on the phone later that night that it had been the other who, for no good reason and not in a joking vein, had attacked her from the start of the dinner, to no avail that she repeated to him one after another the mortifying words, the gross insinuations (except for a few that she did not repeat then out of embarrassment and does not repeat now on the couch: it may well be true that she has never stopped being a good girl, the mere promise, neither realized nor abandoned, of a mature woman), nothing could shake Eduardo's conviction that she considered herself to be of a superior breed, that the mere presence of a character like the cripple at a gathering of friends, of those she considered her equals, bothered her, made her feel unhappy and ill at ease (for a moment it seemed to Elena that it was the bitterness of Eduardo's mother, the proud, misunderstood one, the eternally passed over, that was speaking through his lips, but this idea was not enough to appease her, to make her try to cut things down to size), nothing could shake Eduardo's certainty that she had treated the cripple, from the day he introduced him to her, with the distant correctness with which you treat a lackey, until Elena lost her patience and the urge to justify herself, in some sense jealous – she admits – to see that in this contest between her and the cripple – who was in fact another obscure figure from the nocturnal depths, next of kin to the wild shameless women who, like him, dared all – for Eduardo's friendship and love, Eduardo preferred the other, and she had yelled that she did not understand on what grounds, just because he was ugly and feeble and maimed and had been born in a slum or the bed of a whore or wherever the hell it was and now passed the time pimping for the whores on Robadors Street and getting drunk at others' expense, gentlemen like Eduardo himself – or wasn't Eduardo just as much the good boy, the stuck-up spoiled gentleman as he accused her of being? – who found him picturesque and regarded him as a clown and nourished the belief that he offered entry into the world of the riffraff, and Elena did not understand why all of this was sufficient reason to forgive him what in others was never forgiven, and this setting up for him a special code of behavior seemed to her the height of aristocratic arrogance, so Eduardo and she had a serious fight and let many months go by, perhaps more than a year – because during that unfriendly interlude her first child was born and he was already crawling by the time Eduardo met him – without seeing or talking to one another. And now, it could not fail, the damned droning voice of the Great Invisible One behind her back, of that guy who is only a deliberately aseptic voice and the tip of a light brown Italian shoe swinging in the air, at one end of a rocker, and who takes every opportunity, bar none, to put salt on the wound of the dimwits who come to lie on his couch – and they well deserve it since they come and pay precisely for this – inquires whether or not Eduardo was right, not in the case of that specific incident with the cripple, but in general, is it or is it not true that Elena treats some people as if they were lackeys? and Elena shrugs and hesitates and is quiet, because it seems to her no, but she hasn't the slightest desire, at least not on this occasion, to justify herself or convince anyone, and moreover now, for a few minutes, the analyst takes the place of the cripple or of Eduardo, the three fused into the same deaf, hostile, inimical form, unquestionably masculine, so it ties in with the story of the dwarf and the marble that Eduardo had told to take a potshot at Julio, but above all to mortify her, to get a rise out of her, as she wants to with the analyst, because what Eduardo detests is not Julio in and of himself, a real Julio with his strengths and weaknesses, as Eduardo was surely capable of seeing him – and she not – from the outset, who he must recognize has a certain talent and some of whose films he has liked, although he's not so interested in cinema, nor is it even Julio's conceit – caught up in a world where everyone is envious, competitive and conceited, where Julio at least has the advantage of being more candid and frank in his vanity – what Eduardo for close to thirty years has not been able to stand, ever since that afternoon when an exultant Elena came into his studio to relate a syrupy fairy tale (that she had met Julio the Marvelous and they had fallen in love with a love without precedents and without end), is not only the relationship the couple has set up, but Elena's attitude toward that relationship: what Eduardo cannot stand is to see day in day out the proud, rebellious Elena, the spoiled little girl, the same Elena who can treat others – including him and the psychoanalyst from Rosario – like lackeys, in a state of permanent and forced ecstasy, disposed to engage, at least in part, in the dirty feminine game of worshipping her man as if he were a god and protecting him as if he were a child, willing and even glad to renounce what could have been her independent professional life to live – admit it or not, and as much as she condemns it in other women – for someone else, without managing to finish a single book of poems, a single one of her stories, and what's far worse, without its appearing to trouble her much, Elena (according to Eduardo) in a permanent state of bliss, serving at one and the same time as mother, wife, secretary, nurse, and also, at certain stages of their lives, why deny it? as impassioned lover, intervening as shock absorber, as sieve, between the genius and the outside world, freeing him from the annoyances of daily life, making sure that the boys, even when they were children, could not bother him or interrupt his work, handling all financial matters – she, Elena, who had been more disorganized and spendthrift than anyone, who had not had the least sense of the meaning of money – supervising his diet, making him swallow punctually cough syrups and pills and taking from his hand the fifth glass of whiskey – it mustn't be the second or the fourth or the seventh, but precisely the fifth, even in this regard everything precisely measured and controlled – so Elena in ecstasy, according to Eduardo, watching entranced as Julio hugs a marble, and repeating year after year, and it's been almost thirty and, still in Eduardo's view, it's starting to wear thin, repeating with unshakable faith and without the slightest fatigue, the slightest sign of having gained a sense of proportion or of the absurdity of it all, "You see, the world is all yours."

Every morning – Eduardo told her, half jokingly and as though making fun of himself, because he always makes this kind of confession in a comic vein, while they both know he's more in earnest than he seems – he opens the mailbox (when he goes out for a cup of coffee, or a first drink, because Eduardo often drinks from the time he gets up and it's a wonder he can continue working all day, as she knows he does) hoping to find a letter from the Museum of Modern Art in New York – so for him too real success, success with a capital S, passes through the land of the Yankees on the other side of the sea, Eduardo too dreams of conquering the Americas – or from the Albertina in Vienna, expressing an interest in buying a complete series of his drawings – it might be the one they together entitled *Crazy Women in Hat* – or in organizing an exhibition of his most recent work, or a letter from a woman he has never met but who is destined to become the great love of his life, because he too believes in the possibility of a great love, although upon saying these last words the sarcastic expression on his face becomes more pronounced, and for him too, Elena thinks, there are only two important realities – love and painting – and only after – despite having signed hundreds of protest letters and manifestoes, having donated paintings to be sold at auction, having taken part in sit-ins and demonstrations, and being one of the very few people Elena knows who would have been willing to carry the protest to the end and risk his neck – and only after, in second place, comes the concern over what is happening in the world – in Beijing, in Nicaragua, in the Middle East – so his interest centers on a hypothetical letter that is surely never going to arrive (this waiting perhaps not so different from the wait by the telephone, so the Wizard might have been right that something very similar happens to men as to women) and only after comes the purchase of the newspaper, which is still more than Elena herself does, who doesn't even read the papers although she finds them every morning on her desk, the parts the secretary thought might interest her marked in red, so she doesn't learn that there was another coup in Central America or that the Israelis occupied such-and-such regions of Lebanon until someone around her comments on it. And this bothers the Wizard: although he does not unseal his lips to make the slightest observation, the woman has learned by dint of scrutinizing him week after week to distinguish those small signs – a lift of the eyebrows, a wrinkling of the nose, a certain way of running his hand through his beard or rubbing his eyes beneath his glasses – of rebuke and displeasure, although she has not learned to detect with equal skill – yet there *must* be some, there have to be, Elena repeats to herself, terrified by the mere possibility that they might not exist – the flashes of solidarity, the currents of warmth and friendliness, only, at times, a hearty, uncontainable roar of laughter, or a gleam that like a will-o'-the-wisp, an elusive yellow-coated feline, darts across the depths of his foggy eyes; always more obvious, more tangible, easier to detect the negative than the positive, and Elena thinks that the overwhelming need she has dragged along with her like a heavy, tiring load ever since infancy, the need that her thoughts, her feelings, her acts, her words be approved by someone on the outside (that childish need to be endorsed by others, that mama would tell her "What you did is very nice, you're a very good girl," a need that some years ago, although not so many, detached itself from the figure of the mother to shift to that of Julio, and then – in a world that has witnessed the death of God, the death of Marx, the death of Papa Freud, and one feels so alone – to that of nobody), as of three or four weeks ago has settled on the person of the psychoanalyst, and it would be very comfortable, an excellent solution, to leave things as they are within the sanctuary, for him to allow her to leave things as they are, whom could it offend or harm that the Wizard – who has played so many roles – assume the role of God in the life of a woman who feels empty, perhaps a failure, and is inevitably starting to age? But Elena knows it is not possible, that the last thing Wooden Face will allow is that the relationship that has been established between the two of them – so asymmetrical, of course – stabilize, reach a point of equilibrium, and become immobilized there (the Impassive One could come to be identified with God, why not? but it will always be a changing, transitory identification), and this point may well illustrate the striking difference between what the two of them propose, what they expect from psychoanalysis, because for the Wizard they are now at a stage in a process that will lead her not to depend on anyone and to what is called maturity, since the Wizard is in the last analysis a man of faith, who has surely stopped believing in God, or perhaps never believed in Him, and may even have acquired a certain skepticism – although he continues reading the newspaper conscientiously every morning – a certain detachment with regard to politics and the possibility of improving the lot of the human race in this world of cretins and lunatics, but who has the faith of true believers – the faith of fanatics, which amounts to the same thing – and works out of the conviction – it must be marvelous for him, or for anyone, thinks in wonderment Elena the skeptic, Elena the disbeliever – of being on the side of the truth, that taken as a whole the psychoanalytic system works and that analysts have at their disposal an effective tool – the *most* effective, not just one of the most effective – to help others, to come to the aid of their fellow man – not on the global level, not humanity en masse or in large groups, but from individual to individual, individuals who may in turn influence the rest and even alter the social reality – and carefully draw him out of his private and particular pools of darkness, and it is this seamless monolithic belief that frightens Elena, because she divines something hard and inhuman in the back room of all dogmas (including psychoanalysis), something that can make one – her, for example – end up, for the greater good of one's sinning and immortal soul or to reclaim the most valuable portions of oneself from the unconscious, burning at the stake, and Elena doesn't care if the blaze is set by the Inquisition or the followers of Papa Freud or a child who's innocently playing with fire (or with a firearm, it occurs to her, and it's undoubtedly true that on occasion her analyst has seemed to her like a child, playing and threatening her with a revolver that by chance has fallen into his hands), and the fact is that the Wizard is advocating a cure that will eradicate the illness forever, whereas all she seeks, all she asked for the day she groped into his office blindly and on all fours, like a zombie, is a recourse that will allow her to drag herself along as best she can toward death – which is probably not so many years off, and maybe she would be looking for more radical, definitive solutions if she were about to turn twenty instead of fifty – so a bandage, a patch, a support, a crutch, and at this point Wooden Face makes a fuss, or pretends to, in one of his coquettish outbursts, "So in short that's what I am for you?" derisively, "merely a crutch?" and Elena turns over on the couch and looks him straight in the face, "What more do you want to be? Do you think a crutch is a trivial thing? Isn't it important to help a cripple remain upright or even walk?" and she knows, although he has instantly regained his vacant air and doesn't say a word, that what the Wizard wants is not to play the role of a crutch – although he'll accept it as one more in a long series of disguises – but rather to induce her to walk on her own, and for that supreme end he is willing to carry her, if necessary, to the torture chamber or the stake, the witch, the backslider, friend of the Devil, who has signed an abominable blood covenant with the unconscious, and keeps hidden there, behind seven walls, seven bolted doors, seven unbridgeable moats, an Oedipus and a castration complex whose existence she stubbornly denies, and even runs to consult a psychiatrist who can administer some accursed multicolored pills that will help her keep up her resistance and defiance, and even seeks, oh sacrilegious monster, to tear the high priest down from his seat of honor before the altar, to place him in the ranks of ordinary mortals pure and simple, and once deprived – owing to his loss of magical powers – of that which the Christians call a state of grace, to set up with him on that basis a relationship of friend to friend, or enemy to enemy, it doesn't matter, the important thing is that it be a relationship between equals, not that asymmetrical relationship postulated by psychoanalysis. "I acknowledge that the relationship between the analyst and each of his patients is asymmetrical," he had said in an indifferent voice, while he scrupulously cracked each knuckle in turn, so Elena would see that he did not differentiate even among them, no favoritism for the little finger or the thumb, but cracked each one when its time came, and at that point Elena could not gauge what that asymmetry meant and was far from suspecting – and by the time she did suspect it was too late – that in this game whose most elementary rules she ignored you could stake your soul or your hide, and also at one of those initial sessions, at the end of a stifling August, the Wizard had commented as though in passing and without giving it the least importance – only later did Elena discover that analysts, or at least hers, almost never said things just in passing or did things just because, but on the contrary everything was timed (like the length of the sessions), weighed, and precisely meted out – that patients were wrong who complained about the asepsis surrounding the figure of the analyst and psychoanalysis itself, because does the patient protest against the surgeon's wearing a white robe and rubber gloves and a mask (read: beard, interlaced hands, super-thick glasses, Elena deduced) that partly cover (hide) his face? It was just a question of basic hygienic measures, designed to ensure the safety of the patient and the success of the operation, and of course the Impassive One had said this to reassure her, to calm her fears, to nip her suspicions in the bud, only it had had the opposite effect, because for once that free association that he proposed to her in the sessions and that almost never worked had functioned, and for a few seconds Elena had associated the idea of surgery with mutilation, defense-lessness in another's hands, possible death, and the figure of the surgeon implied a monstrous indifference toward the pain of those whom he coldly, dispassionately cut open in the operating theater, and that was when the motto of José Antonio or of another Falangist leader, she wasn't sure which, came to mind for the first time, a motto she must have heard in high school or in the workshops of the Social Service, which she had not paid particular attention to and had never thought of again until now: "It doesn't matter if the scalpel draws blood; all that matters is that it obey a law of love," and the grave thing was that the person who de-cided what law the scalpel obeyed or did not obey was the ex-act same one who had it in his hands, and in the specific case of psychoanalysis it was easy enough to determine whose

hands those were – you better believe it was an asymmetrical relationship! – so at times the Wizard inspired in Elena a
fear very similar to that she might have felt before a monk of
the Inquisition chanting bad Latin at the foot of the bonfire
for the salvation of her soul, or before a fanatic of any
ideology or kind – in the end they all turned out about the
same – who had a firing squad under his command, or (an
idea she had had on other occasions) a serious, innocent
child who was playing with a revolver that might or might
not be loaded, and when these things occurred to her,
besides lamenting that she was going through analysis with
a man instead of a woman, and with a foreigner who had
not experienced Franco's Spain and thus could understand
next to nothing about what had happened since, she also
lamented that such a young wizard, many years younger
than she, had fallen to her lot, thus one not yet beaten down
enough by reality to be obliged to relativize his own beliefs,
and on a few occasions Elena had communicated these
doubts to the Wizard, and the Stranger had responded
with an ironic smile – it's unlikely he felt even remotely
offended – and shrugged in a gesture that seemed to say
(although to date he had never verbalized it and it could
have been just another product of Elena's imagination): "If
it is as you say, why don't you quit the analysis? Why don't
you change analysts and select a Catalan woman who is over
fifty years old, among the many competent ones whom I
myself could recommend? Or why not rush into the arms
of one of your psychiatrist friends who are so warm and
understanding, and stop playing a double game? The door
is open, isn't it, for you to clear out whenever you like?"
But the truth was no, pure crooked rhetoric, the door was
not open, in fact there wasn't even a door in the sanctuary,
and even if there were it would be of no use, given that
something or someone, maybe the Angel of Death himself,
kept her from leaving, as in Sartre's hell, kept her from
clearing out and looking for some other wizard (there must
be scores, of all nationalities, races and kinds), who would

85

be content to play the role of God with his patients and to allow the beatific and impassioned sessions to go on until death – it was bad luck enough to have landed on the doorstep of such a pigheaded and pedantic guy – or a wizard who not even the looniest of loonies could enthrone on an altar; something or someone stopped her from taking refuge – since the Wizard's suggestion was basically reasonable and would have been another solution – in the paternal arms of Horacio, the friendliest of psychiatrists, for he *did* indeed know life and its setbacks and had seen hundreds of neurotics and psychopaths of every ilk and would probably be disposed to be kind, without time limits, to permit a comforting lifelong relationship of sensible, moderate dependency – none of this being his lordship's dog – and to continue giving her tender pats on the back, wholesome advice, pleasing incantational words regarding the future, and it was for this very reason, for having shown himself to be so humane, so close, that it was impossible to assign him the role of God, and his approval and praise could not be elevated to the level of universal acceptance, so Elena was spending her life waiting to hear words from the lips of the Wizard which, spoken by him, would have an infinite worth and power, while the same words spoken by Horacio did not have remotely as much worth or power, so Horacio would have accepted all of this, as he now accepted an infinitely less gratifying situation (not only did he accept it but in a sense promoted it, since it was Horacio who – at the most painful moment, the worst crisis in the analysis, when she had turned to him as a patient for the first time, the only moment, it seemed to her, when she might have been capable of abandoning the temple of the false gods and of leaving very crestfallen the high priest of that established and infamous cult – had persuaded her to continue, contrary to all reason and all logic, because while he did not believe that psychoanalysis constituted a universal panacea, he had told her, in Elena's particular case it could prove useful, and that attitude of Horacio's had infuriated her, since she would have a thousand times preferred, or so she thought, that he had taken her side and helped her break off with Wooden Face – this was her only chance: beyond this point it would no longer be possible), a situation in which she was miserably dependent on a stranger who certainly did not know what the hell to do with this headstrong, unruly woman, absurd in her suspicions, excessive in her demands, always off the wall, and then she would show up at Horacio's office – almost always appearing out of the blue and calling him in a state of extreme distress – all done in, dragging herself on feet that were suddenly invertebrate, the bones having dissolved, so he could put her together again, raise her spirits, set her back on her feet – tottering but upright – ready to instantly return to that game of masochists or crackpots that she had invented along with Papa Freud for her own self-torture and that seemed to be a never-ending affair.

So Eduardo opens his mailbox every morning hoping to receive a proposal from the Museum of Modern Art, an offer from the Albertina, or a letter from an unknown woman, whom hopefully he had not known during other periods of his life and then abruptly forgotten and above all is not now breathing her last in the squalid bed of some sinister hospital, an unknown woman he can meet soon after at the airport or the train station, with whom he can perhaps arrange to have a date at a bar, one of those bars near his home that are his inevitable haven every night, after finishing the workday, which Elena knows to be arduous and long – it surprises her, who is so abstemious and well organized, that he can work that way with so much drinking and staying up to all hours – to have a drink before dinner – at midday he threw together whatever he had at home or simply didn't eat – chatting with the bartender, the waiters, other regular customers, so the gathering initiated casually and spontaneously at the bar usually continues afterward at some nearby restaurant and goes on until close to dawn at one of their homes or at another night spot that doesn't close, or at least doesn't close for them, and this informal circle is roughly equivalent to a club, and Elena thinks that this is the only kind of social life Eduardo can stand, with friends who appear to have as little in common with each other as with him, and who may just as well include in their ranks a lame self-made big shot as a retired colonel who collects garters or matchboxes, a bullfighting critic, who over the last thirty years has only missed the bullfights he offered to the Virgin for the success of his mother's cataract operation and who, when someone asks him to name his favorite bullfighter, says Manolete, and if they insist that he name another who's still living says Manolete, Manolete and forever Manolete, and if no one asks him, sticks in the joke whether or not it's relevant, an eminent chiropodist who for many years has been writing a great cosmic poem and considers himself to be the only epic poet of the twentieth century, the nurse of a cardiologist (Eduardo met this one in the morning while having a first cup of coffee – or a first beer to clear his head from the previous night's hangover – when she came in to get some coffee for her boss, and only through her relationship with Eduardo – which didn't go very far, because while he assured Elena that the girl had a perfect body, the rare perfection of an object that has been polished and finished down to the last detail, like a Dupont cigarette lighter or a painting by Vermeer, she was neither a kleptomaniac nor a nymphomaniac nor even a hysteric, and she even treated him with tenderness and affection, when nothing in the world terrified Eduardo as much as tenderness, which covered his delicate modesty with embarrassment and shame – did she come to swell the ranks of the early-morning brigade, in which she continued to serve long after her affair with Eduardo had ended, although not their friendship), some aging rich kids, some of whom have been friends since their adolescent days with the Jesuits or at La Salle, others since college, in certain cases the relationship lost for a long time and then revived, after a chance meeting on the street, in a restaurant, at a funeral, or at one of those bars where from then on they showed up regularly, almost all straddling two worlds, the respectable upper-middle-class and the stronghold of lost sheep and oddballs, so they spent their mornings in the factory or the customs house or the doctor's or lawyer's office or at the board of directors, and even ate the midday meal at home, surrounded by the wife and kids, thus not for a moment cutting the umbilical cord with the world to which they belonged, and it was only later, in the course of the afternoon, that they began coming apart, so by nightfall they had reached such a degree of suffocation and boredom that they would have died of sheer ennui if they could not have taken refuge at the counter of some bar and had a few drinks with friends who were not presentable at other hours, who bore no resemblance to those they frequented at the tennis club or the opera or on the golf course, with women who also had little in common with those they had left at home, some separated from their husbands and determined to take their chances on the adventure of nightlife in the city, most dedicated to a select and exclusive form of prostitution reserved for a select clientele, and this type of woman Eduardo took up to his flat only on rare occasions and always after drinking too much, not given to erotic adventures that did not include a heap of complex buried emotions and a back room well stocked with literature and ghosts (it was anyone's guess what would become of Eduardo and his sexuality if he ever went through psychoanalysis), thus as little inclined toward prostitutes as toward decent women, and to all these people, these inhabitants of the city nightlife, he offered an unhesitating and total loyalty and would not accept in their regard – although at times he allowed himself sharply witty descriptions or caustic remarks – any criticism, or at least any criticism from Elena, prepared, it seemed, to swim with them across any channel or join them in placing a bomb in police headquarters

(Elena had been quite uneasy during the affair with that little good girl turned revolutionary, who dauntlessly gave him for safekeeping a kilo of heroin or trinitrotoluene or a cache of jewels they had stolen, by her account, in the armed holdup of a jewelry store, and Eduardo swallowed it all hook, line and sinker, although she seemed to Elena affected and absurd and rather dimwitted the night she invited her with Eduardo and other friends over for dinner, and the girl spent the dessert and coffee hour sitting on the floor, her back against the sofa, stubbornly etching over and over, with long, sharp, for Elena's taste too red nails, the A for anarchy on the carpet, without deigning to open her mouth – not even to eat, because she confined herself to reluctantly picking at her food – or paying the least attention to what they were talking about, very much in the role of the tough little resistance fighter who has by chance fallen – and it's essential to keep one's distance and make clear the distinctions – into a stronghold of the most abominable bourgeoisie, in short a vulgar, showy sim-pleton), friends Eduardo almost inevitably discussed when they went out to lunch together; recently Elena preferred lunch invitations, because he had not started drinking or, purely because of the hour, had drunk only a little, and thus it was more likely they could talk about so many things they were both interested in (art, love, death, what was happening in Nicaragua or the Middle East), and by the same token it was less likely they would get embroiled in nasty senseless diatribes against almost everything or in dis-cussions of principles carried to the absurd, or that awkward situations would arise with the waiters or those dining at the next table, situations which Elena the timid, Elena the fainthearted, Elena the prude could not abide – although recently she too has provoked them, and then they embar-rassed her even more – and Eduardo regarded this as one more sign of her not so much bourgeois mentality, because the authentic bourgeoisie, like the aristocracy, could bring themselves to do almost anything – it's a shame, the woman thought or told him, she wasn't the Duchess of Alba or belong to the Baader-Meinhoff gang, so Eduardo would not be wasting his precious time having lunch with her – as petit bourgeois, traces of an affected, formal upbringing which she had never overcome, designed to make her into a lady, so it was better to avoid all these difficulties and rough spots, and get together whenever possible during the daylight hours when the sun was shining, before the coffins of the living dead came open and the werewolves started sprouting teeth and fur all over, just as it was also preferable, Elena thought, to always end up at the same restaurant or restaurants, partly out of her inclination for repetition and ritual – she liked doing the same things in the same places with the same people – and partly to mini-mize the chance of brushes with the maître d' and the other waiters. So on days when they lunched together Eduardo told her about those nocturnal friends, so different from one another and allied, it seemed, only by being in one way or another – some by personal and free choice, if this type of decision could in fact be made freely (which Elena was starting to doubt), others, the majority, because that was their roll of the dice, because try as they might they had not managed to fit into the world they originally belonged to or had wanted to join – outsiders and in some sense losers, excluded from the privileges and comfort and security enjoyed within the fold, but also free of the shackles and restraints, or at least of some of them, entailed in inserting oneself without too much friction into the common herd, and it suddenly seemed strange to Elena that among such a colorful, heterogeneous fauna there was not, apart from Eduardo himself, a single artist – no painter, no sculptor, at most an unemployed Latin American architect and a commercial artist – although there *were* two or three jour-nalists and novice writers and mediocre actors and even a movie director (it was clear that for Eduardo, and maybe one could find in this a certain veiled hostility toward Julio, film did not remotely fall into the category of art and perhaps not even of licit entertainment, and the last time Elena had dragged him to see a movie, *The Twilight of the Gods*, stubbornly insisting that the things she liked her friends must of necessity also like, he had cleared out of the theater snorting before the halfway point and she had to go looking for him later in all the neighborhood bars, until she found him, ill tempered and morose, in the darkest corner of the most sordid bar, masochistically downing a beer, when everyone knew that of all possible drinks beer was the one he detested, and only drank during morning hangovers). So on some days, while eating at one of the two or three usual restaurants, Eduardo told her at great length and with real enthusiasm and passion about those other friends, inhabitants of his nights, whom Elena did not know or knew only very superficially, and proposed that they get together some day – for lunch or dinner, it didn't matter – not all those who happened to be drinking at the bar, of course, but only the closest friends – who at times numbered four, and at others magically decreased to three, without curious Elena's ever inquiring about the cause of such mysterious disappearances and reappearances – the most beloved (the four being male, by the way, and thus, one assumed, qualified to piss a figure eight on the wall), and Elena said yes, whenever he liked and arranged a date, although she did not express great enthusiasm or feel very confident about it, given the bad outcome of her attempt to be friendly with the cripple and how badly Eduardo had taken it, and it's possible he too had doubts, as much as the idea tempted him and he brought it up time and again, because the much talked about encounter kept getting put off from day to day, from week to week, from month to month, and seemed destined never to come to pass.

And it seemed to her, Elena is telling the Wizard, that Eduardo responded with the same ingenuousness – because Eduardo was profoundly ingenuous, for all that those who knew him only superficially mistakenly labeled him a cynic – the same limitless and unconditional devotion, the same mythification, to his friends, his few real friends – she the only female among them, since Eduardo developed a very different kind of relationship with his ex-lovers – as he also placed in his hopes for the future, his professional aspirations – and they were more than aspirations – the future successes reaped by his paintings, the selective exhibitions he would celebrate in New York or Rome or Berlin, the exceptional girl he would meet any day now, at the counter of a bar, at a dentist's office or just around the corner, although what remained obscure was exactly what that woman would be like and in what would consist her exceptional nature. "Do you envy him?" the Wizard asks yawning, no doubt tired of hearing Elena, who before was not free-associating as he asked, saying the first thing that came to mind, but was at least talking about herself (as she had at the first sessions when she really spouted off), now spending entire sessions holding forth on all subjects human and divine, while not on a bet departing from a general and impersonal "one" that does not implicate her at all, or prying into and scrutinizing the words, attitudes, problems of others (like at the moment those of Eduardo), acting as though she were the psycho-analyst and were using him as her supervisor, when she doesn't go still further and begin pondering and fantasizing about Wooden Face himself, thus entirely reversing roles, until the Stranger finally loses his cool and patience and protests with more or less annoyance, depending on the day, "I'm not the one who's being analyzed" (and on one occasion, on an impulse of truthfulness and precision that did not go well there, that was out of place within those four walls, in the sphere of the brothel-sanctuary, where he was not accountable to her or his other patients for anything, or almost anything, so the guy must have regret-ted his words even before they were out of his mouth, "or in any case, I'm not being analyzed by you"), and it was amazing, even to Elena it seemed amazing that in the course of those two long months of sessions she had tried

93

or proposed the most diverse and seemingly preposterous activities – ranging from setting up a musical café where they would serve roast beef and sing, or even dance, tangos (she'd even come up with a name: it would be called "Transfer") to coauthoring a book about her analysis, wasn't this an endeavor of fundamental scientific interest? a kind of secret and parallel double diary that the other would read only upon completing the process and starting the search for a suitable publisher, an idea the Stranger had refused even to consider – almost anything except being analyzed (despite the fact that at one of the very first interviews she had expressed her desire, which at that point was perfectly sincere, to do just that), as she had also struggled blindly, passionately, as though her life or her honor depended on it, to establish with the Impassive One some kind of real bond (in the sphere of the imaginary or the symbolic there was no conflict and everything was permitted, anything could come into play within the narrow confines of orthodox wizardry – and perhaps, more than permissible, it was imperative in this colorful game of mirrors reflecting masks and phantoms – and Elena could without difficulty imagine her analyst, not only as the mouse-footman of Cinderella, but even as her own mama, that coldhearted mama who had not loved or pampered her much as a child, or as the little old learned doctor who sat her on his lap when she was very small and asked her for a kiss and scratched her face with his pointed goatee, or as her lover or washing machine or typewriter, with all of whom she had especially unhappy and conflictual relationships since she had never learned and never would learn how to handle them properly: everything was allowed in psychoanalysis as long as one used the "as if" rather than the "is"), and at times, when this strange way of behaving cropped up during the sessions, Elena suggested in a half-conciliatory, half-sarcastic tone – since they both knew it was not to be taken too seriously – that it must be due to her multiple and complex resistances, enormous resistances, motivated by the secret urge to preserve untouched in the unconscious that Oedipus and castration complex that must perforce exist in some vile corner of her being, in the deepest, dirtiest cell of the labyrinth, and which she would give birth to some day by mouth in an abominable delivery, Lucifer himself emerging from her bowels – with no need of a bonfire, which was nonetheless a consolation and a relief to confirm – before the wise and valiant invocations of the Exorcist, who was much more convinced of the existence of the Devil than were those who were supposedly possessed – the torture rack, another thing to be thankful for, replaced by what Elena called punishment sessions – and then the hairy rat, terrifying and grotesque, would go scurrying around the office, along the bookcases, under the rocking chair and the couch, over the desk, as Elena and the Wizard, united at last in a common cause, chased it while defending themselves by beating it off with their shoes (it would be a pretty sight to annihilate Satan by breaking between his horns a ceramic jug from La Bisbal . . .), in hopes that her vomited runt would not in turn – such things had been seen – devour its mother. And yet, what could it be? Elena has often asked herself, and inquired more than once of the Supreme Sorcerer of the Tribe and the Pampas, what can it be – asks Elena the skeptic, Elena the Cartesian, Elena the sacrilegious, inclined to believe in forest gnomes, in water nymphs, in Tinkerbell, but by no means in the Devil – this presumably atrocious truth that the unconscious jealously guards and hides from view, a creature so dangerous and harmful that we would rather get sick than bring it to light, and which induces us to organize our entire being around it, erecting mountains of silence, emitting deceptive screens of smoke and shadow, opening deep pits without bottom or end? what can be revealed, or can I discover about myself, at this stage of history and my own story, so close to fifty years old, half a century of life, in a world that has witnessed the death of God, the death of Marx, the death of Freud, and we all feel very lonely but also in some sense liberated, a world where even housewives at the beauty parlor and the supermarket announce without batting an eye that their son has a whopping Oedipus complex – without batting an eye and usually brimming over with satisfaction – and books, movies, even television overflow with tales of incest that no longer frighten little old spinsters, or the indescribable old ladies of the villages, and no one – at least no one in the world in which Elena moves, because maybe in Rosario these matters function differently – considers his own or others' homosexuality or bisexuality cause for tragedy, and we assume without prudery things that the ever so puritanical Papa Freud surely never practiced (at least not with his own wife) and classified as perversions by hearsay (that beautiful round word, dense and mellow, that fills our mouths and speaks to us through its very sounds of elaborate and exquisite pleasures, what would love be reduced to, Mr. Wizard, if we did away with perversions?), and Elena does not find in herself, except, of course, in that story of pissing a figure eight on the wall, the smallest sign, the slightest trace ("on the conscious level, only on the conscious level," Papa Freud might have pointed out, and Wooden Face occasionally notes, making Elena spout toads and snakes, not roses or pearls or diamonds, because of course it's on the conscious level, if the unconscious is by definition the unknown!) of that blessed castration complex?

"Do you envy him?" the Wizard asked, and Elena – it often happens to her on the couch – was caught off guard for a few seconds and without words, and in this case it was not that the question took her by surprise or that she had never thought about it, but rather that she had turned it over for a long time without arriving at a definite answer, although the truth was that rather than compare herself with Eduardo – the two so different in character, with such disparate goals, that there were hardly any elements on which

96

to base a comparison or sustain envy – she has compared him with Julio – both highly ambitious, although their ambition takes radically different forms, and moreover both very close to Elena through a long period of their lives that has yet to draw to a close, so she has had plenty of time and occasion to study them – Julio the great victor, the born leader, the spoiled child (first by his mama, this one definitely out of an Argentine tango, an overprotective mama who also propelled him to the greatest heights, followed by a long series of friends, admirers, coworkers, lovers, and heading the list, his own rightful spouse), Julio white knight of the anti-Franco movement and of democracy, Julio conqueror of the West Indies, on the color cover of Spanish magazines, then European, and finally North American (at least two she knows of for sure . . .), Julio who has managed, through a combination of seductiveness, charm, sheer force of personality, and also undoubtedly through his talent, to always inhabit the center of the world (and it may be a restricted, fragmentary world, but she does not believe that even in joking it can be compared to a marble), always surrounded by a crowd of admirers – always also by another crowd of enemies, because in people's attitude toward Julio there is no middle ground: it is either implacable hatred or boundless love – indulging his ego and feeding his inflated narcissism, happy to figure among the faithful and to have been allowed on board his ship, even as the lowest-grade cabin boy, to set out on the conquest of the known world and the unknown, Julio who now, upon his return, will be able to shoot whatever film he pleases, with the script he selects himself and technicians and actors of his choice, without budget problems and at last – and it's taken many years and much sweat to achieve this – without having to tear his hair out and expend some of his power of conviction, his seductive arts, in the struggle to scrape together the necessary coppers, sometimes from several different sources, other times from a vacillating and bewildered and almost always cowardly producer whom you have

97

to convince all over again every morning, because Elena is sure that upon his return, and despite the increased rancor and ruses of the envious, everything will be handed to him on a silver platter, so Julio da Vinci, Julio the Marvelous, Julio the Magnificent, Julio Welles, although upon arriving at this point she isn't sure if Eduardo is referring to the fact that Julio had wanted to be Welles, which would indicate a very high and laudable degree of ambition, or to the fact that he believed he had already attained it, which would indicate a very high degree not only of the naïveté that sometimes characterizes him, but of sheer stupidity, and in any case Elena's curiosity went beyond this to wonder if at some moment in the past, and if so when, Julio had come to the realization that he would never be Welles – or at least he would not be Leonardo – during a moment or series of moments she could not pinpoint in time and which they had never talked about, because Julio never brought the matter up and she did not have the nerve to ask, but if there had existed such a moment, if the genius had begun to place reasonable limits on his ambitions and dreams ("And what would that have consisted of?" the Stranger asks, "what would it have changed in practice?" and Elena, without hesitation, "In not making only the movies he wants to make, no matter what, the movies that no one else in the world can make, do you understand? In giving in to the temptation to please others, to be applauded by others, and thus arriving at a compromise, a comfortable arrangement"), in that case Julio might have felt some obscure stabs of envy toward Eduardo, although the latter led an infinitely more difficult and precarious existence, and lived in the final analysis alone (Julio was incapable of walking alone to the corner bar, since they had met he had not once sat alone in a restaurant), without a long-term partner, or children or any kind of family, and without friends other than Elena herself, the five or six women he had really loved during certain periods of his life and the tie with whom he had never afterward broken off, and the night birds who frequented the same bars at the same hours, although above all he had not managed to achieve, despite his hard work, what is generally regarded as success nor did it seem likely that he would achieve it in the future, because the critics had dealt little and badly with his work, for whatever reason, and on the occasions when they had attended to it, it was to write inanities that irritated rather than gratified him, since even those who thought highly of him, Elena feels, did not have a precise idea of what Eduardo was seeking and intending to do in his painting, and moreover those few who, rightly or wrongly, determined who's who in the art world, were almost never those who really mattered (and at the head of the list, the most powerful of all, was the guy she had met one day with Eduardo at an exhibition, and whom she had greeted, he said, with extravagant to the point of ridiculous affection), and it was true that Eduardo held periodic exhibitions, in fact almost every year in the same gallery, and his paintings even sold pretty well (it was a mystery to Elena who bought them, since she never again saw them afterward), but it never got beyond this, and it was hard to believe the number of people connected with the art world who, when Elena mentioned his name, did not even know to whom she was referring, and only after knitting their brow for a few moments in fruitless effort recalled having seen one of his canvases on some occasion or having read his name somewhere, so it seemed to Elena to be an extreme case of invisibility, and perhaps the great-est difficulty in dealing with Eduardo, including on the level of an intimate friendship, or maybe above all on that level, consisted in knowing how to ignore or camouflage or sublimate his failure, a failure that was there, harsh and plain for all to see, like an amputated limb or a burn in the middle of the face, does the Wizard understand what she means? an amputation or a burn that makes you not know if it's better to turn away and not look, or look the person straight in the face and pretend not to notice, or look at it and strike the most ridiculous of all possible or impossible

99

poses of naturalness (it would all be much easier, of course, with a humanity who had been psychoanalyzed en masse, where one could roam the world happy as a lark without a nose or without legs or with a retarded child at one's side, and where Elena herself could go on greedily sucking the lobster legs despite having a monster or a dwarf sitting at the next table), so the relationship staggered under that excess load, one always walking a tightrope and on the brink of slipping or stumbling, and became fragile and complex and brittle, and of course, something very similar occurred with other friends or acquaintances whose work was not recognized, or was recognized but not highly enough, that is – and now Elena explains to the Impassive One what she means by "enough" – without any reservations or limits, given that in other professions relative values sufficed, so a dentist could feel satisfied if his office was full to the brim, and an engineer if he had built enough bridges and highways and drilled enough tunnels, and a linguistics professor if they published his cum laude doctoral dissertation and he got a professorship at the university, and a textile manufacturer if his fabrics sold well (and the be-all and end-all would be to be received by the king in the Moncloa Palace, along with a hundred other textile manufacturers, and for the event to be televised), and a shoemaker if his shoes sold well (in this case the be-all and end-all would be to export them to Nigeria or the North Pole), and even a psychoanalyst like the Wizard if patients or snobs lined up to go into analysis with him and he occasionally gave a talk at a conference in Stockholm or published a short article in a specialized Buenos Aires journal (did he?), but none of this meant a thing or had any weight whatsoever in the world of art, where one was always dealing with absolute values – to be or not to be, one could not halfway be – so everything was a matter of life or death, existing or not existing, and thus it was understandable that artists set their sights higher than seemed sensible or than one might expect, so a friend or critic could not tell Julio, for example, in an outburst of friendliness and goodwill – it did not always have to be a question of twisted motives – that he was one of the best Spanish filmmakers of his generation, because Elena knew that he was measuring himself against the best directors of all countries and all times, from Méliès up to the latest release at the most recent festival, nor could one of those female fans of Andrea who sprouted up like mushrooms and identified with the characters she portrayed on stage or screen and came up with any possible pretext to see her and to be heard – not to listen, which mattered to them a lot less – win her favor by assuring her that she was the best living Spanish actress, because Andrea might feign a smile and even babble some kind words of thanks, but she would forever cross the simpleton off the list of people she could, and then only at a distance and at very long intervals, asso- ciate with; so it's almost impossible to dole out compliments on the level the artist secretly (and sometimes, as in the case of Julio, openly) desires. ("And couldn't one overdo it, go too far in one's praise?" the Stranger asks, for once really curious, "Couldn't the admiration be so excessive that the artist felt uncomfortable or foolish?" and Elena answers no, that no praise is ever enough, that one could blush to the ears at the dithyrambs, the panegyrics declaimed by others, but the guy in question was listening entranced, without the least sense of proportion or of ridicule.) And if this was true for everyone, or at least for the vast majority of people she had known and dealt with throughout her life, which came to a sizable number, it was especially true for those who, without ever wavering and giving up and devoting themselves to some other kind of work, stayed the course and never arrived (and she was using the word "arrive" as it is generally used in these cases, because it's obvious that when it comes to arriving, that is, really arriving, no one ever arrives anywhere, except upon their death), as though, as the failure grew and deepened, became more and more irreparable, their ambition, instead of diminish- ing proportionally, increased, so ever greater the gulf, the gaping void between reality and desire, because in their case self-esteem fed not on flattery but on humiliation, and vanity was borne of wounded dignity or pride, and Elena could no longer find new excuses not to attend movie openings, to flee as soon as the film ended and the lights were going up, not to enter theater dressing rooms, to view the unavoidable exhibitions taking advantage of the minutes when the painter or sculptor put in an appearance to have a cup of coffee and do one's duty by leaving a message, a polite little note, with the doorman, because she could no longer resort to the "very interesting" and she was terrible at lying – even those banal half-truths imposed by life in society – and she did not have the nerve, as Julio did, to remain silent or tell the truth, or what seemed to her to be the truth, without beating about the bush. It was hard enough for her to remain loyal and steadfast, or at least neutral, by his side, to refrain from acquiescing or trying to smooth things over – as she had during their first years of life together, always with terrible results – when he came out with monstrosities – the fact that they were glaring truths, widely held beliefs, did not make them any less monstrous – and an uncomfortable silence fell on the room and you could have cut the air with a knife, because the bitter envy and spite grew thick and dense around them, around the two of them, "Any day now they'll grab you by the throat or stab us in the back," Elena would joke uneasily, "Heaven help us if we take a false step and fall on our faces, because they'll trample on us for sure!" and he, "If they don't want to hear the truth, why the hell do they ask my opinion?" and "It's the best thing anyone can do for them, or do you think you're doing them a favor with that tangled web of flattery and lies?" and again, with a smile, "And let's hope you don't slip up, honey, because no matter what I say and even if I shut my trap, they'll still trample on us."

Although Eduardo is a case apart, not only because the three have been such good friends and buddies for such a long time, but also because Julio, while not sharing his opinions on art or on almost anything, the two having such different, almost contrary approaches to life (unlike Eduardo, Julio in no way fits the image of the damned creator or the lone wolf), and above all, not managing to comprehend (the truth was he hadn't tried very hard) what he was striving for in his paintings, respected him (to say that he envied him, Elena now decides, would have been a bit excessive), not for what the other might have achieved, which seemed to Julio and might in fact have been very little, but for the magnitude of the wager he had been able to make and then sustain, everything he has and is placed on a single number of a single round of a crazy game of roulette, more dangerous in a sense than Russian roulette, since what was at stake here was perhaps more precious than life itself, while others, the vast majority, and maybe on some occasions Julio himself, and this might give him cause for envy, spread their money around on different numbers, on multiple rounds at multiple tables, or did not bet on just a few numbers but played by color (and you? what are you betting on, what's your game – the Wizard should now ask – playing a chess match without a king?), so the successes and failures balanced each other out, and with a little luck and smarts the final result could be positive, or at least not catastrophic. But the Wizard, instead of putting salt on the tenderest part of the wound and asking about her own wagers and games, about her inexcusable fear of playing, confines himself to asking, "And do you like Eduardo's paintings or not, is he or is he not a good painter?" and she answers hesitantly that she's not sure, she thinks he is but in any case her opinions aren't worth much in the field of the visual arts, because her strength is words, not images – she even approaches film as a novice, focused primarily on the unfolding of the story, on what happens, rather than on how it's presented – and she would venture to offer an opinion with some confidence – and even this is foolhardy, given that critics and the public constantly make mistakes – about a novel or even a book of

103

poetry, a theatrical performance, but not about a painting or sculpture, and what's more, in this field which is not hers, and although it gets on Eduardo's nerves, she feels a tenacious, childish weakness for outdated warm sensual forms, an art designed for children, an exquisite boudoir art, and not, of course, for the stark and difficult compositions of Eduardo and many others, who are not in the least trying to please (Elena is sure that when Eduardo is painting, he does not for a second consider whether or not people will like the painting, or what he could add or take out or change to make it a little more pleasing), as dry and difficult and spare as a mathematical equation (could the Wizard appreciate the beauty of a mathematical equation? of course yes, so Eduardo's paintings might fascinate him, not her), in an investigative work that has moved forever in the same direction – there has undoubtedly been evolution but no sudden breaks – because whether he has progressed a little or a lot or hardly at all, he has not deviated by a millimeter from what his objective was when she first met him. Something very similar, it suddenly occurs to her, because she had never before noticed the similarity, to what goes on with Jorge, stubbornly obsessed with an idée fixe, a single idea (once at a gathering some friend of theirs, of the parents, had commented that he had abandoned the field of biology or astronomy or electronics, she couldn't remember which, because so much was being discovered in those areas, so much new research was coming out, that he had felt incapable of learning it all and keeping up to date, and Jorge had burst out laughing with a certain vanity and insolence, in this a little like his father, and had rejoined that the problem of the scientific researcher, like, he supposed, that of the creator in any field of knowledge or the arts, was precisely the opposite: both the scientist and the artist should work wearing earplugs, with balls of wax in their ears, should heed nothing, see nothing, remain ignorant of everything going on around them and of how it was received, mindful only of a single idea, which almost always sprang from a magical intuition, a sudden, unexpected revelation like a bolt of lightning or a priceless gift from the gods, which often occurred at a very early stage of life but would then take one's entire life to realize or prove), because there were some people, a great many, who drifted their way through life, bending whichever way the wind blew them, and there were others, also many, who did set goals and lay out a course of action, but later got tired, distracted, frightened along the way, and ended up walking in zigzags, but there was also a third group of people, infinitely more scarce, bewitched, obsessive, half-crazy characters (and Elena is not so sure she likes including Jorge in their ranks), who set themselves a single fixed goal, from which nothing or no one could ever distract them, among other reasons because they have lost sight of all other realities that fill the world, and this was perhaps what Julio (who alas, with his many all too human weaknesses *had* amused himself along the way, a Little Red Riding Hood here and there led astray by the wolf, but who would nonetheless arrive safe and sound at grandmother's house) could admire – to say envy, Elena insists, would be going too far – or she herself (who had remained to play on the doorstep of her house or had climbed onto others' wagons to follow the pilgrims' parade) in Eduardo, that absolute dedication, that total sacrifice on the altar of a single passion, painting, as an end in itself, not as a means to gain wealth, fame, women, praise, even a small piece of immortality, so Eduardo up to his neck in the riskiest game of all, which could lead him only to the finds of genius or to insignificance.

"Meine liebe Elena," the Argentine whispers in her ear, their two heads almost touching on the pillow, "meine kleine liebe Elena," he croons, in an accent that is not from Rosario, like the Wizard's, nor from Buenos Aires, but from some obscure humdrum town of the interior, "meine liebe kleine Elena, who weeps at dawn like a little girl and won't tell me what's the matter," and she can't bring herself to protest – as the man takes her by the shoulders, sits her up in bed, leans her against his chest and starts kissing her tear-stained cheeks – that she feels ridiculous at this stage of life and of the night – because the dawn has not fully arrived, but there's a hint of it in the grayish tone the darkness is taking on on the other side of the windows – being mollycoddled in German, but she does protest that for better or for worse – perhaps more for better than for worse – next to nothing remains in her of the little girl, not even her tears, and furthermore it isn't true that she cries particularly at dawn, because she cries at all hours (at least over the last few months, since last August when she fled terrified from the toy house of the little cartoon character – who to top it off is pregnant – and a son who had all at once turned into an idiot, or so it seemed to her, and suddenly without warning she felt engulfed in a dark well, the exact depth of which she still could not fathom and where she lacked air to breathe), because in earlier times, including her childhood, she had cried very little, as though she had spent half her life amassing tears in order to spill them later all at once without rhyme or reason: so she has cried almost every day since August, at any hour and in the most diverse circumstances, although especially at the end of Tarzan movies or when Bambi calls for his mama or they all tease Dumbo on account of his ears and also, of course, at times during punishment sessions (and now she has to explain that she is in analysis with a guy from Rosario, who everyone says is very intelligent and wise but has turned out to be a pighead, who refuses to treat her in a sensible or at least agreeable manner – to appreciate her, like her, support her, understand her – stubbornly insisting on that nonsense about the Oedipus complex, castration complex, narcissism and the resistances), although it *is* possible that today there are more real, immediate reasons for tears, and Elena starts telling this almost unknown Argentine, whom she and Julio had been introduced to long before at the home of some friends, and whom she had not seen again until running into him today – really yesterday, since it is now quickly growing light on the other side of the panes – in mid-afternoon, after a very difficult punishment session, in the lobby of a double-feature movie theater where they were showing back to back *Letter from an Unknown Woman* and *Casablanca,* and Lord knows why she had passed up such a magnificent and almost once-in-a-lifetime occasion to cry, and had let herself be talked into – the truth was it hadn't been hard to talk her into it – going for a cup of coffee and then another, and then by car to the breakwater – it had been such a long time since anyone in this supposedly seaside city had invited her to go look at the sea! – and they had remained there a long time, inside the parked car, observing the night falling little by little and the lights coming on on the boats, reflected in water that slowly grew more dark and viscous, in a harbor image that fascinated her and that she would have thought you'd have to go to Marseilles or Hamburg to find, when you had it so close, and then they went to a Chinese restaurant for a very late dinner and to hear tangos at a small café, where Arturo had greeted everyone, and she had withdrawn – alone and yet accompanied, something very different from loneliness – agreeably sheltered in a corner, amidst the cigarette smoke and the too shrill music, while Arturo talked to a guy who had sat down at their table about the black heroin addicts of New York, who in his view represented the most sublime condition attainable by the human race, the maximal degree of potency, of freedom, of raw self-affirmation, the maximum not only of physical but also of moral power, and he's even tempted to write a theatrical work with only two actors, the head of a concentration camp and a black prisoner – the latter a heroin addict and jazz musician, of course – who would confront one another in such a way that little by little the roles would be reversed, and the black prisoner would end up triumphing over a German Nazi who had been reduced

107

to a dummy, and Elena felt too sluggish to enter the conversation and suggest that maybe it was not a question of balls or moral strength in situations where the power, or simply the arms, are on the other side, and instead of saying this she had begun telling an Arturo who wasn't listening, or was only half listening, "You know, I have a painter friend who opens his mailbox every morning hoping to find a love letter from an unknown woman or a proposal from the Albertina, and I have a husband who it seemed would devour the world but has ended up perhaps, I can't say for sure, hugging a marble," and Arturo had put an arm around her, had embraced her while with the other hand placing a joint between her lips, had signaled furtively to the waiter to bring more drinks for the three of them, and it seems he must have been listening to her, even if it was only half listening (it's possible, it had occurred to Elena, that that sound interlocutor that guys like Arturo talk about, that interlocutor in search of whom they roam the far reaches of the earth, is an interlocutor who not only does not understand or respond, but does not even listen), because he had forgotten about his friend for a few minutes and inquired with a smile, "And what role do *you* play in these little stories? what do you hope to find in your mailbox in the morning?" and it was odd that this or something very similar was what the Great Witch Doctor of the Pampas might have pointed out, and maybe it was a vile custom of the Argentines, a people who had indeed been psychoanalyzed en masse, had spent years and years stretched out on the couch, to later move on to occupying a rocker behind it or going through life spouting analytical rubbish (which doesn't stop them from continuing to be analyzed, or from starting in with a new analysis, because a new conflict has arisen, material that had not been dealt with in the previous analysis, or because, they confess in dismay, they were analyzed by a Kleinian, and in view of the magnitude of the outrage they believe, and they express it in these very words, that they deserve a second chance), and if Elena gets irritated during the sessions, this carrying psychoanalysis over into daily life – this going around substituting for analysts in a frivolous parlor game – literally drives her crazy, and it costs her dear to imagine Papa Freud raising his index finger instead of his little finger while drinking his tea, or admonishing his friends in a box at the Vienna Opera, although maybe this was justifiable in his case, given that he had invented such a splendid plaything out of almost nothing and felt exuberant like a child with new shoes, so he could do with it – and in fact did – whatever he liked. So Arturo had said to her something very similar to what the Wizard might have said, although the latter would not have embraced her or smiled at her with affection – although yes with the same irony, the same comic spark in the depths of his eyes – and Elena had felt coming on one of those disproportionate attacks of rage that make her see red and send a shiver through her spine – fits of anger that, along with the parallel fits of weeping, must be a symptom of an illness recently contracted and until now ignored, which could well be lack of love or old age – so she had withdrawn rather brusquely from Arturo's arms, rejected the damned joint – which always leaves a bad taste in her mouth and doesn't lift her spirits – raised one of her own cigarettes to her lips and waited defiantly for him to offer a light – sorcerers' apprentices have no choice but to light her cigarette, and if Arturo, thought an Elena driven to distraction, dares make the most remote and veiled suggestion that asking for a light is a hidden demand for love, I'll pounce on him and tear his eyes out with my nails – and she had assured him firmly that she did not even have a mailbox to open, since she receives almost all her correspondence at the office and the secretary leaves it opened and sorted on her desk, and those letters that are marked "personal" on the envelope are invariably from some more or less dangerous shark who recounts his life story in hendeca-syllables or, if the letter is addressed to Julio, threatens him

109

with the eternal fires of Hell for some presumably infernal, unholy and Voltairian scene in his latest movie.

And afterward, when the café closed, they had gone to Elena's house and gone to bed together, without its appealing very much to either of them – Elena suspects, although she could well be mistaken – just because they had lacked the imagination or courage to come up with a different ending for the evening, and maybe that obligatory, trite ending mortified her a little, and she even felt a remote, very remote hostility toward the guy, but she wasn't sure that she would not have felt offended – without cause, but definitely offended – if Arturo had behaved otherwise, and on the other hand she *did* know with absolute certainty that she had no desire whatsoever that he accompany her home and leave her with a kiss on the doorstep, no desire to enter the empty building alone, empty since she had left it so many hours before (to make things worse the cleaning woman was sick), with the objects in exactly the same places – it was almost enough to make you stop believing in witches and elves, who should have hidden things and changed everything around – the half-drunk Coke by the phone, the open book lying face down on the arm of the sofa, the bath towels on the floor, the half-opened patio doors, the light left on in the kitchen, so without objecting she had let Arturo come in and quickly take over the place and the situation, put on music, serve them both drinks, start kissing her on the sofa, and then carry her to the bedroom and undress her and put her in bed – much like what had happened last time with Eduardo: could she have stopped being a woman who puts herself to bed, to turn into a big rubber or china doll that you take the play clothes off of and tuck into bed? – and start caressing her, while not for a moment – as he turned her over, manipulated her, parted her rag legs, flexed them, put the perfectly jointed arms in one position or another, touched her all over, licked her, sucked her, led her hand with his, spurred her on, pounded her, penetrated her – not for a single moment stopping talking – and now you get like this, sweetie, and I do this to you and this and you feel this and that and you see how luscious it is – only silent during those moments when his mouth was too busy with other things, and even in those cases the description of what was going to happen preceded the event or was delayed until after, as though the only way to experience pleasure was through the word, so it did not seem to Elena-robot, Elena-china-doll that they were really making love, it bore almost no resemblance to a real-life scene, but on the contrary seemed like a broadcast of an episode from a radio serial, where the listener could only grasp what was happening from what he heard, or as though they were inventing stimuli to excite a blind voyeur or some depraved person who was listening on the other side of the wall or under the bed, and when the man remained motionless on top of her, silent at last and panting (exhausted from the double effort, Elena thought, because that had been like playing a tennis match while singing *La Traviata*), she could not keep from laughing, and she hugged him hard, swung him to and fro as if he were a sailor and she the boat, got him down off his mount and rumpled his hair and kissed him on the nose, and assured him, to justify the laugh, that she felt cozy and nice here by his side, and it wasn't exactly a lie, but then, a little later, the woman had noticed with surprise that tears were filling her eyes and rolling slowly, softly, saltily down her cheeks, and it was then that Arturo had talked about little girls, romantic adolescents who weep at dawn and do not, cannot, will not explain what's the matter, or maybe they don't even know themselves, and Elena had begun telling him that over the last two or three months she has cried at all hours and without knowing why, although perhaps today there were in fact more obvious and concrete reasons for tears, because that very morning – that is, yesterday morning – she had found on her desk some material concerning the premiere of Julio's movie in New York, the list of more or less famous people who had attended the opening, of those invited to dine with the consul, statements made by various people to the press, the reviews and criticism published before and after the opening, the interviews (in which Julio appeared magically transformed into a hero of the resistance, the champion, or almost, of the anti-Franco movement, who now, upon the dictator's death, has finally found the space he needs to show the full extent of his talent; he was depicted like this, with these or very similar words, in two or three of the interviews, and of course the reporters were to blame, at least in part, always inclined to twist the facts to make the story more sensational, but even so, did Arturo have any idea of the number of people who were going to reveal their hidden talent upon Franco's death, a talent stifled by repression and censorship, and then came to nothing or less than nothing? although it seems to her that this was definitely not the case for Julio, who *did* have genuine talent, and had shown it before, went on showing it now, and would hopefully continue to show it until his dying day, but in that case why did he climb on the bandwagon, why did he, at the wrong time and for the sake of cheap publicity, sign on to such a farce and such a lot of hot air? so quite unlike Hernán Cortés upon his conquest of the Indies, more like a Cid with silver armor and shining sword), so there were the interviews, and the text of the words Julio had pronounced on different occasions, especially what he said on stage as the screening ended amidst applause, and the worst of it was not, although it was bad enough, the fact that in various photographs – including the color covers of two specialized magazines – he appeared with that little chick at his side or very near him, a thin girl, dressed in casual clothes even at the formal dinners, face without makeup, at least not that could be detected in the photos, long straight hair – so very different from the woman you would expect and that Arturo must be imagining at the moment, very different from the spectacular, sophisticated women who appeared at film festivals accompanying important men, much closer to a university or fine arts student, much more

112

like the girl she herself had been years ago – but even at that, the worst of it was not the fact that Julio had become infatuated – or fallen seriously in love, impossible to know until his return – with a schoolgirl half his age, or the fact that he had been unable to resist the temptation – after all, why should he? – of showing himself off with her in public (if Elena had not been feeling depressed and strange, she would not even have felt jealous), the serious thing, the worst part of all, was something so humiliating, so ridiculous, so petty, that it didn't square with the image Elena had of herself and tried to sell to others, and she was actually embarrassed to tell it to a guy she had just met that afternoon, although she knew she could not possibly confess it to a friend, not even to Eduardo: the serious thing was that neither in his speech on stage nor in any of the interviews, in none of his statements to the press, did Julio make the slightest allusion to her, Julio offered his success to half the world and gave thanks to the other half, because there they all were, down to the last nincompoop, whether or not they deserved it, since in these matters Julio was a generous guy – it would not do for us, for Arturo to confuse egoism with egocentrism: Julio could give almost anything to others, what he could not do was imagine for a single moment that he occupied any place other than the exact center of the universe – so there they all were, everyone, Julio had offered his success to the producer and then to everyone who had assisted in one way or another with the filming, and then to the public of all countries and all times – which was already pushing the limit of arrogance and losing all sense of proportion: maybe he did in fact believe he was Julio Welles – but not to Elena, so that she, in her role of creative muse of the great genius – the idea and the script could almost be called the brain child of the two of them – had been silently eliminated, and also in her other roles, less poetic of course, of collaborator, secretary, budget director, tamer of cameramen and actors, she had likewise been erased, since her name did not appear anywhere in the endless list of credits that headed the film, and so it turned out that that Julio who could not exist alone and needed someone with him to buy himself a jacket or make a turn at the first corner, upon arriving at the top, higher perhaps than they had ever imagined, did not find enough room there for two.

So Elena had arrived at the psychoanalytic session that afternoon – already yesterday afternoon, for now it was completely light on the other side of the panes – in a state the likes of which she had not been in for a long time, prostrate on all fours, and since reading the papers and seeing the photos early in the morning all she could think about was how she was going to tell it to Wooden Face, she'd been counting the minutes until five in the afternoon, and she had not lain down on the couch as she almost always did now, but had sat on the edge of the seat, looking the Wizard straight in the face, and in one breath she had poured out the tale of her bitterness and rage, had explained to him the monstrous injustice of which she had been the victim, but the Impassive One had not batted an eye, again looked her way without apparently seeing her, and then calmly lit a cigarette, again today without offering her one, so Elena felt obliged to take her own pack out of her purse, and then the Impassive One had not offered her a light – who knows whether due to a lack of good manners or the mysterious rules of analysis – and when Elena asked him for the lighter, because she had left hers on the counter of the bar where she had just had a cup of coffee, he gave it to her so stiffly, so disagreeably that it seemed to her, or at least it was recorded this way in her memory, that he had thrown it at her, although it was possible that he had handed it to her, and then she had gone on ranting and raving, and he in silence, not a word, not an expression of sympathy or support, not the remotest help, again with his foggy gaze and distracted air, until Elena had exhausted her double reserve of indignation and words, and then she did what she had vowed never to repeat, even if her

114

life depended on it, she implored him, "Say something please, don't sit there silent in your rocker and me talking into the void like an imbecile," and it's true that she was pleading, yet not submissively but with anger, from the tone of voice it seemed almost like an order, and then she had realized too late that she was making a kind of demand that was not destined to thrive within those four walls, so the Stranger had sustained another long pause, thoughtful and bemused, a pause he perhaps used – assuming he was not thinking about other things and had even forgotten she was there – to ponder and decide on his next move, as though it were a question of a round of poker or a chess game (if I ever go into analysis again, a desperate Elena promised herself, all the while fully aware of the absurdity of the situation, without this alleviating her distress, not only will it be with an older woman from my own country, but I'll make sure she does not even play Parcheesi), and at last the Impassive One had unsealed his lips, when Elena was no longer expecting it so, as on so many other occasions, his voice made her jump, he had boldly unsealed his lips and suggested, "And doesn't it occur to you that there may be a good deal of jealousy, or in any case, of wounded narcissism and pride in that painful and violent reaction of yours?" and then, without changing his tone of voice (why should he change it?), "And how does your current reaction tally with those theories of yours about women who use the first person plural and aspire to live through their husbands?" and at that point Elena had lost all control and manners and shame and had started screaming, and she couldn't remember now, as she's telling it to Arturo, what exactly she had screamed, and then the Wizard, when he could get a word in edgewise because she inevitably had to stop in order to breathe, had asked in his most innocent, distant voice, "So what was it that in your opinion I was supposed to say to you?" and hearing these words Elena stopped screaming at him, all she could do was drop it or kill him, so she had lain down on the couch – and today, of course, this was not a gesture of submission – resolved not to open her mouth again, he in punishing silence and she on a silence strike, until she had gotten up, a few minutes before her time was up, and had cleared out without really saying goodbye, without giving him time to come up and shake her hand, assuming he was planning to do it today, and so there she was in the theater lobby before six in the afternoon, feeling much more desperate and furious than at any other time that day, and the curious thing, the strange thing was that now, as she's telling the story to Arturo, the business of the New York movie premiere and the thin little long-haired girl who resembled the girl she had once been, and the fact that at the moment of triumph she had been excluded or forgotten, seemed to her trivial, the prank of a spoiled egocentric child who at a given moment had wanted to have the whole stage to himself, while in contrast the memory of her argument with Wooden Face drove her crazy, it was strange to confirm that all of her anger and resentment had shifted object, had left the figure of Julio to settle on that of the Wizard, as though it were the latter and not the former who had degraded and wronged her. Elena was, in short, detesting Wooden Face for something he had not done and had little to do with, and she – she now assures Arturo with a certain ridiculous air of disdain – was honest and lucid enough to acknowledge and accept it.

Perhaps, Elena thinks in the chilly redoubt, which seems less like a theater than a parish auditorium where they might have held Christmas plays or festivals to celebrate the end of the school year (assuming they put on Christmas plays and end-of-school-year festivals in this lower-class part of town), or not even that, a warehouse or garage where they've made only minimal preparations, little more than erect a stage and put out some rows of folding chairs, almost all empty, which makes the cold feel even more intense, although it's scarcely mid-October and there's a mild breeze blowing in the street, and she does not know how to wrap herself better in the vicuña shawl lent her by Arturo – and maybe the time is approaching, the woman thinks, now that I'm turning fifty and am in analysis, to carry in my purse matchboxes, handkerchiefs for crying, and a jacket on the shoulders or on the arm, don't I embody for Julio and even for the kids the practical side of life? – that, according to Andean mythology, should provide not just adequate but a searing warmth, although it barely covers her shoulders, her neck and a small bit of cheek, perhaps, Elena thinks, the time has come when without further formalities or delay we can begin turning into contemptible old women, and perhaps you, always more resolute, always ahead of me or taking the lead, have already taken the first steps, she silently tells that completely new and unknown Andrea, dressed any which way, with badly distributed makeup staining her cheeks (maybe she too cries involuntarily and at the most inopportune moments, as for example before going on stage), much thinner and more haggard than in any other period of her life, although she has never been fat, this Andrea who moves around the stage like an automaton, and it's not just her, they're all moving like zombies or sleepwalkers, it's not walking so much as drifting along in the direction of a port they will never reach, and each one recites his lines whenever he feels like it and not on your life addressing the other characters (they'd be divine in Ibsen, even in Chekhov, Elena whispers to Arturo, nostalgic and possessed, each absorbed in his own incommunicable sorrow or madness, in a moist twilight atmosphere, nordic and corrosive, but none of this makes sense in Arthur Miller, who the hell had the bad sense to choose this work?), so that nothing goes with anything else, it's all utter nonsense, and the audience, the scant thirty spectators who are cringing numb and bewildered in the folding chairs – what moreover could have dragged them to that wretched, godforsaken place, if not the obscure desire she too had felt to see Andrea again after such a long time, and Arturo's eagerness to meet her in person? – constantly fear that something terrible or extremely grotesque may happen, that one of the actors will forget the size of the stage and plunge into the void of the pit or have a sudden fit of real madness or go dumb and catatonic in the middle of one of the dialogues, it seems impossible that in that collective high they manage to remain standing and even jabber some lines, which die out before reaching the first row of the audience (now Arturo puts his mouth near her ear, and in a fatherly way advises the naïve little girl whom he has decided to train for life, the sheltered little old lady whom he has resolved to return to her youth, "If you're ever caught by the police and you've been shooting up or inhaling drugs, be sure not to lick your lips, so they don't see your mouth is dry," and Elena laughing, "Don't worry, big boy, if the police ever pick me up it will be for murder, for doing in my analyst by breaking something squarely over his head, for strangling a traffic cop or the salesgirl of an art gallery, for riddling with bullets a famous filmmaker who just happens to be my husband, not for a matter of drugs, and I'm afraid it won't make much difference whether or not I have a dry mouth," although it *is* true that the sleepwalking actors seem to be dying of thirst and are laboring to get the words out as though their mouths were full of shortbread, and maybe it is indeed happening as the two women half jokingly predicted long before, when they were no longer young and the university years lay far behind them, but old age was still too distant to have acquired consistency or a face – more like a ghost that deep down you don't believe in than something that could really happen to you – and they had still not begun the terrifying countdown, not calculating years lived but probable remaining years of life, and above all what can be fit into them (in the case of Eduardo, how many paintings he still has time to paint, which are not all he has in mind, how many women he still has time to meet and love, to meet and hate, to invent and destroy, not by a long shot all those he has dreamed of, as Eduardo often objectively and pessimistically tallies up – if you can describe as pessimistic an attitude that implies still having such high hopes of life – calculations he makes in regard to himself and to others, although others don't show the least interest or enthusiasm and even try to avoid it when they can, and now there is no longer any doubt that they have passed not only the midpoint of life, but the two-thirds mark, maybe more, thus much shorter the future that awaits them than the past they have left behind, and at one of the last sessions with the Wizard Elena recalled that many years before, in a pizzeria in Siena, she had heard some kids at the next table commenting on how unthinkable and horrible was the certainty of dying, and one of them had wondered how old people, for example, those over forty – and at that point the kid was lucky that Elena's homicidal impulses had not yet risen to the surface – could handle it, having death so tangible and close, in order to keep going, to keep on existing without being overwhelmed with anguish and terror, and after much calculating and haggling with Eduardo, because Elena is more optimistic regarding the amount of time left the two of them, they agreed that they can have real and satisfactory lives up to the end of the century: and celebrate the new millennium on Fifth Avenue, Elena proposes, "and down barbiturates or hemlock in the last glass of champagne," Eduardo concludes), the acceptance of the unavoidable fact that time impels us mercilessly and against our will toward the abyss, placing ever tighter limits on our existence, and maybe Andrea has again taken the lead this time, as so many others – the first to stop attending mass on Sundays, to stop wearing a girdle and even a bra, to join the anti-Franco activists at the university, to sleep with a guy, to leave her parents' home, and always going a bit farther than an admiring and envious Elena could, the latter held back by her shakiness and fears, her never-ending vacillations and doubts – and is taking the first steps, even before crossing the strict threshold of old age, toward turning into a contemptible old woman (Eduardo the aesthete, so concerned with avoiding the deterioration of his own image – at times Elena thinks that the business of opening his mailbox every morning is merely an aesthetic pose: he likes to picture himself as a guy who every morning awaits a love letter or a letter from the Albertina – doesn't even want to hear about elderly gentlemen who have lost their dignity, and thus advocates barbiturates, the last glass of champagne in New York, in Rome, in London, wherever she chooses), Andrea perhaps driven – sucked down to the depths of the swamp, hurled off the highest cliff, wafted to the clouds by a cyclone, because it's been ages since Elena has seen or heard from her, and she hasn't a clue what could have impelled her to this raving performance given by a group of drug addicts, which seems more like a drama therapy session at a mental hospital than a normal performance – by one of those absolute loves that have always been the single, sufficient, driving force in her life, because from the very beginning, from the first day of school when they showed up at the same Latin class (a fat little priest was pontificating untold rubbish – Elena didn't seem to have luck with her Latin teachers, which is per-haps why she never managed to learn the language – and Andrea, sitting in the seat behind, handed her a series of mock verses in a burlesque or invented Latin, and for a few days they hardly talked to each other at all, amusing themselves with the game of passing slips of paper back and forth in class), she recalls Andrea's being madly in love with someone, and this dates back to long before the university years, Andrea has often pointed out upon discussing it, practically forever, as far back as she can remember, because at the age of four she was passionately devoted to one of her single aunts who lived with her family, and every night left drawings, small religious pictures, candies and colored prints beneath her pillow, and at seven she was crazy about a frail young priest who was preparing them for the first communion, and this set off an ardent mystical phase, with chickpeas in her shoes, lunches without dessert, snacks without chocolate, communion on the first Friday of every month (although she never managed to assemble those nine consecutive Fridays that would have guaranteed her entry into Paradise; maybe the Virgin foresaw what would happen later and decided against getting involved with such a sinner . . .) and fervent longings to convert the heathens (starting with her own parents and moving on to the little girl who lived next door to their summer house, who was foreign and Protestant, thus a double sinner), and at fourteen she fell head over heels for the language and literature teacher (she read from cover to cover many of the India-paper volumes of Aguilar, including the *Episodios Nacionales*, and she could rattle off everyone's works, at least the works of all those who were included in the book they were using in class), so Eduardo and Elena remember her perpetually in love, not only in her childhood, as she has informed them, nor in her youth – besides, who hasn't loved that way in their youth? – but in every phase of her later life, as an adult – Elena doesn't know if it's still true today – loving as one usually does at the age of seventeen (if anyone asked her or if the subject came up, she made it clear that she could not conceive of any other way to love, and upon saying this she looked Elena straight in the face, an ironic, scornful smile on her lips, as if to say – or at least that's how Elena took it – that the occasional affairs the other may have had over the course of her life, never serious or passionate enough to endanger her relationship with Julio, and even the latter relationship, which they both speak of with a beatific expression, eyes raised to the heavens, have little in common with the crazy, passionate love of seventeen years, and although Elena sometimes protested, deep down she always suspected that her friend might be right, and it might be true that for that kind of love, as for so many other endeavors, she had always lacked the guts and spirit), and the very brief parentheses between one love and the next, in the infrequent cases in which the old love has run its course before the dawning of the one that is to succeed it, have been parentheses of shadows and silence, the woman drawing in on herself, sleeping within her silk cocoon, hibernating, because for her not loving is synonymous with not existing, and thus it's quite possible that it's a recent foolish love, a passion of the last months, almost two years which Andrea has spent out of the country and about which Elena has heard almost no news, that has plunged her to the depths, wafted her to the heights of a contemptible old age, allowing her to shed at the start of the path, the final path, the few conventions she was still dragging along with her, to rid herself of the persistent fears, to violate the last threatening taboos that until now had kept her from giving up being a lady to become something else and that have finally lost their sacred character, so to give up safeguarding – and maybe it's in this respect that Elena knows that, try as she might, she cannot follow in her footsteps, nor can Eduardo – even in part her own image, in a more definitive transgression than the others and one that does not allow for a turning back, maybe Andrea has crossed the dividing line, almost imperceptible but conclusive, and has taken her place in her own right among the mythical black heroin addict musicians of Harlem, among the no less mythical Eduardian women of the night (and upon arriving, at the sessions, at this recurrent conflictual point in her discourse – although she thinks she has never perceived it as clearly as she does now, in the freezing, half-empty barn of a theater – that hole she falls into and remains stuck in more and more often, like a musical motif that slips in, looms up, retreats and returns throughout the entire symphony and in the final strains invades and overwhelms it, the Wizard generally asks about her own envies and bedazzlements, and he doesn't even have to ask, because Elena has been asking herself the same question, and she admits, without anyone's having to suggest or ask, that maybe she *does* envy after a fashion the black heroin addicts, those blacks she has seen advance through the streets of New York, powerful and magnificent, unspeakably beautiful and in their eyes one of the most disdainful looks in the world, with a pair of sleek and unsettling Dobermans on the end of a leash, so it seems the street and the city are theirs by rights or they may at any moment rush to conquer them – which does not of course imply they could reverse the power relations in a concentration camp, badly nourished, without Dobermans, and with the dogs and arms in the hands of the guards – Elena admits that from time to time she feels bitterly envious of Eduardo's women, prostitutes, women of the night, real women – and at this point she talks very fast so he won't have time to ask her what being a real woman consists of and why she assumes she is not one – who take what they want without shame and demand whatever takes their fancy and can raise a terrible ruckus without the floor moving an inch under their feet or getting a hair out of place, yet in both the case of the blacks and the women – and much the same could be said with regard to Andrea or even Eduardo – Elena does not envy them for their greater beauty, their greater talent, for all that they presumably have achieved, for success, love, moments of bliss, which may or may not be greater than hers, but rather for their daring, their overwhelming passion for risk that leads them to stake so much holding so few cards, for being able to soar to the greatest heights without first checking – as Elena undoubtedly would, who only seems to take calculated risks – the state of the parachute or the functioning of the motor.

"You know, it's been very hard spending these three days, the whole weekend, without you," Arturo suddenly mutters, taking Elena by surprise, and it's a good thing they're in almost complete darkness, she thinks, inside the car and parked at the jetty, as on the day they met and many other evenings, facing the dense shining sea, shining like an enormous reptile, a whole brood of reptiles coiling and uncoiling their rings, like a melted down or liquid metal, of quite a different consistency from the sea she bathes in every summer ("Have you noticed?" once asked Andrea, who shares with Elena her boundless love of the sea, "have you noticed that the water's touch is different every day, the way it brushes against our bodies is different, some days like fine needles of ice, others the tepid softness of cotton, others pure silk or velvet?"), and it must be very dirty and covered with a film of oil or tar, but seen like this, from the jetty at nightfall, it looks beautiful, a mercurial sea beneath a moon that ascends like a huge lantern, a red silk paper lantern lit up with a candle from within, or the silver moon they lower from the wings in the theater so Harlequin can sob his heart out, more a theatrical prop than a real moon, and it's a good thing they're here in the car in the twilight darkness, because Elena started and felt the blood rush to her face, blushing like the adolescent Arturo claims to have discovered in her, since only an ever so young Elena can restore to him in turn, like a reflecting mirror, that youth which is gone never to return, the two in blue jeans smoking joints and skipping along the Ramblas hand in hand, laughing like idiots over any little thing, from kiosk to kiosk, because every night at two or three in the morning it suddenly occurs to Arturo that it's a matter of life or death to get a copy of a particular paper from Madrid, and that it's a sure thing to find it at such and such a newsstand on the Ramblas, and although they still haven't found it there any night, it's certainly a good excuse to descend the Ramblas hand in hand spouting nonsense down to the sea, and even to strike up a friendship with the kiosk vendors, who on the third or fourth night obligingly offer to reserve a copy for them the next day, to which Arturo flatly says no, because it would not be the same, Elena imagines, it would not be as thrilling as this desperate nocturnal chase, night after night coming to nothing, night after night started up again with renewed vigor, nor would it be the same if she brought him the copy she receives every morning in duplicate – one at home and the other at the production company – and hardly looks at, and in this nocturnal *via crucis* not only have they made friends with all the newspaper sellers, but also with tobacconists, waiters, prostitutes, lottery vendors, Latin American vendors of the craziest and sometimes most fascinating things (like those marvelous birds that soar high above in beautiful circle and filigree patterns, and never work when a dazzled Elena takes them home), guys who earn a few cents sketching the Mona Lisa on the pavement or playing the flute and drum, and they always, always, always bump into some friend of Arturo's, one of those friends of whom there must be thousands because you run into them everywhere without fail, and it's almost impossible to go out with Arturo without finishing the evening in a group, and it seems he has friends stationed in every corner of this city that is not his, or perhaps in every city on both continents ("friend of all the world," Elena laughingly called him on a couple of occasions, torn between envy for this ease in getting along with others, even those who are not really of his world, this irresistible geniality and charm, and the suspicion that being a friend of everyone is the closest thing to having none at all, and declaring oneself a citizen of the world to feeling like a stranger all over), and they always end up listening, sometimes with Arturo at the keyboard, to Brazilian music or jazz until dawn, along with young kids half or a third their age, and Elena can't figure out why he has chosen her and not one of those twenty-year-old girls to take along on this voyage back through the slippery tunnel of time – who ever saw a Gretchen who's approaching a half century old, and where will they find a Mephistopheles interested in buying their souls? – and what Arturo needs is a young girl like the one Julio took with him to America, or the cardiologist's nurse Eduardo fell madly in love with for a few days, as perfect in form as a Dupont lighter and only eighteen years old, almost schoolgirls, inexperienced eyes through which one can vicariously rediscover the world (because she is not jealous of the nights of lovemaking, nor even that Julio's girl has shared in the honors and glory of the supposed genius: what makes her wild with envy is the pleasure of showing New York to a person one loves who has never been there before), a warm young body from which to suck vampirelike the juices of life, someone who still believes, as she breaks the colored ribbons, impatiently tears off the tissue paper used for gifts, that she may find the moon inside ("And you?" asks the Wizard, when she tells him of such things, "are you still hoping that someone will present you with the moon one fine day?" in the same tone in which Arturo asked, "What do you expect to find in your mailbox every morning?" and Elena protests to the Wizard, "You don't understand, my case is far worse, because I *was* given the moon, wrapped in tissue paper with gold ribbons, I truly had it, and that's why, since I lost it, I am forever sick with nostalgia," and then in a whisper beneath her breath, as though someone else were speaking through her lips and saying something she did not want to say, or at least did not want anyone to hear, "or I didn't know what to do with it: it can be a nuisance, you know, finding yourself day after day with the moon on your hands," and she looks furtively around her, afraid of what may come of her blasphemy, a disgusting creepy-crawly or a hairy rat scurrying loose between the legs of the couch, but nothing in the sanctuary seems to have moved, it doesn't even smell of sulfur, and as always the Impassive One goes on rocking, hands interlaced before his mouth and a distant expression: it's difficult to know if he has been listening to her at all). Some afternoons, then, since the day they met in the movie theater and shared that radiophonic sex act constructed mainly of words, he has waited for her at the end of her analytic session, but most often he shows up at her home at the most ungodly hours of the day or night, indeed sometimes the intercom has woken her just at daybreak, "Something happened that I want to tell you about, can I come up?" without having called ahead, hardly ever making plans beforehand from

126

one day to the next, Elena much freer than usual during this parenthesis set off by Julio's trip to America and her own nervous depression, because she still spends some time at the office every morning – except on unusually bad days when she lacks the will to get out of bed, and turning off the alarm clock wraps herself up in the sheets as in a warm nest and goes back to sleep, her face turned to the wall – but after that she sees almost no one throughout the day, and even her contact with Eduardo has been limited these days to reporting back to base (she lets him know by phone that she has met an Argentine musician, who besides music does many other things, rather intrusive and bossy, as highly strung as a piano, but intelligent, stimulating, fun, who is striving moreover to patch up her life, hers and everyone else's, he too determined, like the Wizard, like Eduardo himself, to make her give up her lost and illusory paradises and to return her to the age of eighteen, and Eduardo listens very attentively, even slipping in some agreeable comment – in any case, you never knew with him at what point amiability coincided with sarcasm – but then a little later he suddenly calls back and, without even bothering to say who it is, rattles off everything he thinks of Argentines in general and Argentine musicians in particular, and warns her to dispense with these inauspicious relationships she has gotten into recently that will lead to no good, keeping in mind moreover that Elena, and this the Argentines do not know – she certainly hasn't explained it to the Sorcerer of the Pampas, with whom she should first and foremost break off – was at the age of eighteen an impossible baby: "I like you more the way you are now, idiot!" and he hangs up without leaving her time to re-act or respond, even to clarify if she should in the first place feel offended or flattered), so when Arturo calls on the intercom she always tells him to come up, lets him in, fixes him a first drink, asks if he wants something to eat, brings him an ashtray, while he's putting the record player on full blast (something as fateful and unavoidable

127

as trying to get a newspaper at two in the morning on the Ramblas, or ending up – despite her declaring herself a fan of American cafeterias, with enormous glasses of fruit juice and combination platters and hamburgers – at some awful dive, the floor littered with cigarette butts and sawdust and prawn shells, and a television set up in a corner), and then he prepares more drinks for himself and rummages around the kitchen and talks nonstop about everything under the sun – Elena no longer has to read the headlines or wait for the TV news to find out what's happening in the world – and then about what's happened to him, which is always a lot and spectacular, during the few hours since they last saw each other, and none of this stops him from at the same time putting a slack, sluggish, hostile Elena through a third-degree interrogation, and as much as his suggestions and interpretations often remind her of those formulated with much greater caution by the Wizard, at that point the similarities and coincidences end, because Arturo, besides being nosy, is a real busybody, determined to repair by hook or by crook the lives of everyone and his uncle (even Pablo's and Jorge's, whom he's never met), thus a far cry from impassive, from Wooden or Poker Face.

And it's true, thinks Elena at the jetty facing the sea, relieved that the darkness prevents his seeing that she has blushed to the roots of her hair, that the two have spent many hours together since their chance meeting that afternoon, which seems lost in a remote past, but was really only ten or twelve days ago, and it helps her and she enjoys this invasive, discordant presence in a house that would otherwise seem terribly empty and where she would have trouble sleeping alone, so she likes finding the kitchen turned upside down, the record player – now there's music around the clock – or the television on or both, or a half-finished letter in the typewriter, and she likes having a friendly shoulder to cry on at the movies, although Arturo doesn't take her to see *Bambi* or the old Bogart or Tarzan films, and he teases her affectionately when she cries buckets at a movie chosen by him, "Meine liebe Elena, who can't manage to free herself from her lost paradises, meine kleine Elena, who cries like a little girl when Diane Keaton and Warren Beatty make love to the sounds of the International," and he puts his arm around her or takes one of her hands in his, touched, it seems, by the woman's boundless sentimentality, because to him the idea of running along Nevsky Avenue locked in a tight embrace and screwing, like lions or gods, to the strains of the International seems like a cheap sham, unacceptable at least during the decade of the eighties – like Latin American protest songs that no one listens to anymore, at least not in public, or that foolishness that a man and a woman shoulder to shoulder in the street can be part of something greater than themselves – and the movie almost irritated him, whereas of course Elena, who weeps even at Mickey Mouse cartoons, struck it rich that night and cried her eyes out without modesty or reserve, practically sobbing, soaking handkerchiefs – the two brought by Arturo – and she didn't even care if someone surprised her with red, slightly swollen eyes when the lights went up – nor did it occur to her to put on the sunglasses she had acquired for such occasions and still carried around in her purse – what difference does it make if there are people she knows in the audience, at this late date who cares, what does it matter if they think she's crying because she has suddenly aged or because Julio has a lover half their age, when the truth is she isn't even sure herself why she's crying, at the stage of life she's now entering of contemptible old woman, or what exactly are the lost or fictitious paradises – which Eduardo at times, and the Wizard many times, have spoken to her about – from which she has been – like Keaton and Beatty and all those who once dwelled within them – expelled, a friendly shoulder on which also to weep over more concrete and personal sorrows, and afterward she enjoys spinning out the night in dives and low-class cafés, hearing music, discussing art, politics, psychoanalysis, meeting people who have little or nothing to do with her, who will never come by her office at the production company and whom she will not meet at the homes of any of her friends – we have spent too long, she discovers, always frequenting the same people, only our own kind, whether we're in Paris, London, Rome or New York, always the same types, talking about similar questions from interchangeable points of view, with the one exception, naturally, of Eduardo, who absolutely cannot stand those people and has to stretch his principles to accept and even like me, being as I am so tied to them – in search of the locale that closes its doors the latest or that will agree to close them with their crowd inside, because by now it's too cold to continue the discussion walking along the Ramblas or sitting on a bench on the avenue or at some sidewalk café, and then, with the approach of dawn, breakfasting on fritters and hot chocolate at the dairy that opens earliest, and then going to bed ever so late and sleeping until practically noon. Or some mornings – before the fritters and hot chocolate – she likes to go up to the top of the Tibidabo, everything still closed and not the slightest trace of human beings, so they can leap like scamps over chained fences, go out on the lookout point, the gray, misty city at their feet, and then Arturo hugs her hard, hard, euphoric and content, picks her up in the air, covers her face with kisses, "It's your city, will you give it to me?" and Elena laughing, slightly dizzy and bewildered, as she wonders if men need the words of women to possess the earth, amused to find that on this occasion it's not a matter of a marble serving as the world, but only this mediocre, endearing city, which she *does* feel to be hers, and which is emerging now in different shades of pink and ochre, "It's yours," she says, "what the hell are you waiting for? Take it already, it's all, all for you!"

Or she likes to drive along the jetty as they did today, and park the car with the hood pointing directly at the spot where very soon the sun will appear on the horizon of the sea, on the cassette player jazz of the most black, heroin-addicted, savagely individualistic, potent blacks of Harlem or the Bronx. And it's certainly true, Elena admits to herself, that despite their friendship's being so young, so recent, despite all they do not know about one another, they have already developed strong ties of trust, great tenderness, and yet she was startled by the words Arturo had spoken in the dark – did he need darkness to work up the courage to say them, as Elena needed darkness to hear them without apparent confusion? – "You know, it's been very hard spending these three days, especially these three nights, without you," and they make her feel not only surprised and embarrassed, but also remotely guilty, because it seems to her that this puts their relationship on a different footing, not like the kind made by alley cats who meet by chance on the rooftops and miaow in unison to the moon, or the kind between two ships that intermingle their sirens' laments while crossing paths on the high seas, because if it is hard for him to spend three nights without her, it means they have to some degree developed a relationship of dependency, and this implies an inescapable bent toward continuity, when it is very clear to Elena that they are living out an adventure without a probable future, and she does not have the slightest intention to open the window to cats prowling around the rooftops, or to rush forth or allow passage on board a pleasure yacht or a sailing ship.

"Is psychoanalysis also for you a calculated risk?" the Wizard asks right off the bat, the minute she takes off her shoes and lies down quickly on the couch, eager to tell him about, to lament the three ill-fated days she spent in Rome last weekend with Jorge, about her clumsy weakness in turning to her son in search of a kind of solace and support that he was not at this time able to give her (so why, then, had he encouraged her to make the trip? why hadn't he at least warned her, so she could make an informed decision as to whether or not to go, that she would find in the tiny apartment another man and a woman, why hadn't he told her that he was living out with one of the two or both, she couldn't be sure which, a crazy, highly intense love affair that left room in their lives for nothing else, nothing beyond themselves? so that for Elena it had been like landing out of the blue in an unadulterated psychodrama, something out of an English or American author of the sixties, the three characters constantly spitting up monstrosities and illuminations, and everyone on edge, her younger son also reduced to a state of profound oligophrenia, even the flies forgotten, her son, she concluded in astonishment, for the first time in love, with one of those all-encompassing loves – Andrea's kind – that turn the world upside down and obliterate everything that doesn't involve the beloved, and Elena couldn't tell for sure if it was a question of the man, who she was told taught at the university, a blond fellow with a moustache, not very tall or good-looking, or the girl, a pretty but common redhead, plump, certainly not so young, with a tight sweater that set in relief two enormous breasts and pretty legs sticking out of her leather skirt, and looking at these two, Elena missed not only the gorgeous, spectacular, undoubtedly mute women – as far as she could recall she had never heard them speak – who would discreetly vanish at a glance from Jorge whenever his mother came on the scene, shutting themselves in their room or temporarily moving to a friend's house, but even the know-it-all, very pregnant little rabbit), in search of a solace and support, then, that Jorge could not now offer her, or that he perhaps had never been able to provide, because this is not the role of one's children, much as Jorge has been on so many occasions and in so many ways the best child imaginable, just as likewise the role of the psycho-analyst apparently does not include offering his patients understanding and affection – it's taken her a long time, a very long time to realize that Poker Face is not sitting there in his rocking chair four times a week, at five o'clock sharp in the afternoon, to "understand" her, and if at times he inevitably does understand her this is entirely useless and he will make every effort not to show it, as he will take great pains not to set up with her a relationship that is remotely human – whence it follows that Elena has spent months or years or her entire life turning to the wrong addressee and seeking what she desperately needs in the most unsuitable places, although this is undoubtedly a very widespread, generalized affliction, and people must feel very lonely and yearn to have someone listen to them, since they all seem to be rushing through life in hot pursuit of what Arturo calls a sound interlocutor, a soundness that she is discovering does not consist in particular intelligence or exceptional moral gifts, but just some remote capacity for patient listening, feigned interest, supportive words, and she is not at all sure that it's more absurd to seek this sound interlocutor, to try to hunt him down, on the couch than, for example, in the dark caverns where one spins out the night with the aid of drink and jazz, or with the occasional bedfellow, the trouble is that even there she has not found him, and it seems to her the worst possible timing that just today, when she's been weaving together her little speech the whole way over and has obediently thrown herself down on the couch intending to fire it off in one volley, the first words already quivering on her lips, the Great Silent One should for once take the lead and ask her point-blank the irrelevant question of whether or not psychoanalysis is for her a calculated risk, apparently picking up a thread that had been left hanging at some earlier session, that Elena does not recall, and the fact is that he is asking just for the sake of asking, since at this point he must of necessity know, no matter how little he's been listening to her, that the answer is no, that for once in her life Elena did not check the motor or take along a parachute, that for her analysis was not a risk of any kind, controlled or uncontrolled, but rather she threw herself headlong into it in total ignorance of the danger – unthinkable in someone who was born and lived near the Pampas, woolen scarf around the neck and jug of maté in hand, but understandable and even unavoidable on this side of the ocean or the sea, despite having read Freud at the university and visited his home in Vienna and even been seduced by Freud-Clift on the silver screen – total or almost total ignorance of what could be unleashed and take shape and be decided within these four white walls: an office desk surprisingly plain and empty, occasionally holding just a couple of books or a blue folder, an ugly gray-green couch, one of whose cushions came undone days ago at one end, obscenely displaying its plastic guts (a far cry from the sumptuous couch covered with Oriental rugs that Papa Freud used in his consulting room, whose cushions, in the unlikely event that they had come undone at the seam, would have shed a cloud of the softest white feathers: of course, going through analysis with Papa Freud would have been an entirely different experience, Elena stresses insolently, and then is surprised to find that as soon as she says it she suddenly, although she doesn't express this out loud, has doubts: not even that can be taken for granted in this game of absurdities), a Kennedy-style rocker, where you can lull your ego and stir up wild fantasies of power, a window facing an inner courtyard, so the desperate patient who threw himself out would only succeed in breaking a leg, a dull, pallid print in which intermingle flowers without perfume and birds with no song (it wasn't there at the first sessions and suddenly appeared one Monday, set in a simple sheet of glass held in place with metal clips, which leads her to believe that the Impassive One spends his weekends bric-a-brac hunting like any Tom, Dick or Harry, although it doesn't occur to him, or to his wife, who must be an impossible Buenos Aires woman, the kind who never stop talking and make a big impression and claim to know everything there is to know about almost everything, from how to boil spaghetti to the artistic-political-sexual education of their three-year-nine-month-old child or the solution to the Middle East conflict, to repair the torn cushion), some bookcases where the books grow and multiply and pile up in wild excess, under the protection of a Wizard who tenderly, passionately loves them, at the risk of hurling into the void a fine, authentic folk art ceramic jug (whose lamentable end by defenestration, and not the numerous little trifles invented by Papa Freud or Uncle Lacan, would signal – and this she's sure the Wizard is not aware of – the termination of the analysis), and that slight but oppressive presence, which seems to permeate everything while taking up almost no space at all, only, when she's stretched out like today on the couch, the tip of a light brown shoe swinging to and fro, sometimes annoyed and impatient, the sound of a lighter or matches, or the orderly ceremonial cracking of knuckles, ten brittle brotherly sounds, without missing one, so at the end Elena feels like applauding, all of this so unreal that at times, when the Other has brandished the deadly weapon of one of his relentless and devastating silences (no one who has not experienced them, in analysis or some similar experience, although Elena can't imagine any similar experience the world over, is capable of understanding the degree to which a silence can be deadly and devastating), the woman finds herself obliged to ask, "Hey! Is someone there?" and she tries to say it jokingly, of course, but they both know that they are – no, just Elena is – hovering on a tightrope over the abyss, and any moment she may break out in a wild fit of rage, because she cannot stand, she cannot or will not get used to the notion of stupidly talking into the void, of talking without someone listening, whether he be a sound or unsound interlocutor, and then, if Elena controls herself and doesn't press him too hard, the Impassive One may deign to give some token sign of his presence, that he is still there and hasn't even gone to sleep, and yet it occurs to Elena that if she went a step further and asked a second question, this one for real, the answer to which she thinks she may partly know but which sometimes seems like a matter of life or death to confirm, "But you, who are sitting there and at times listen to me, who are you?" she would get no reply at all (unless the Impassive One had one of those rare and always unexpected attacks of frankness that moved him to unusual concessions, like the time he felt impelled to specify that perhaps he too was being analyzed, although not by her, or that he did not plan to paint the office and thus efface the tiny hole in the wall that was a desolate Elena's final refuge – "Any day now you'll paint the office and then I won't even have this," Elena had lamented, and he had simply said "no," so she was left wondering, and not daring to ask, if he had answered without hearing what she had previously said, if he was just indicating the innocent intention not to paint, or if he was taking on the woman's desolation and wished to comfort her in her extreme distress), or unless he decided, and this was another possibility that had occurred on similar occasions because he still retains something of the university professor or small-town schoolteacher, to be didactic and instruct her, in which case he would surely say something like this: "Nobody, for you and within these walls I am nobody" (and it would be difficult for an Elena suddenly demoted to the rank of Cyclops to explain to her people – and who the devil can she count as her people for this business? – that it's Nobody who hurts her, Nobody who rejects her, Nobody who has blinded her with frustration and rage, in this unequal yet ruthless contest in which he always comes out unscathed whereas she of necessity emerges scarred and defeated, although she has to admit that rather than a war between two people this is a private war that she is waging all alone against herself, and surely you do not find such a fierce struggle in the course of every analysis, and it's clear that it is not the Wizard's intent, despite being a bossy, dogmatic type who will not tolerate resistance or accept failure, to hurt her so much: it's Elena who by means of the other attacks herself, like a moth that, having at its disposal the whole expanse of night sky, plunges into the flame or against the light bulb, or a bird that clumsily and blindly knocks against the bars of its cage, not realizing that the doors are wide open or that the cage perhaps exists only in its imagination, or a poor lunatic who in the middle of a field smashes his head against a wall, not seeing that he has free passage everywhere except precisely at that wall, and it would be unfair to judge the flame, the cage or the wall responsible for the harm done, although neither is the moth, the bird or the madman capable of behaving otherwise, no matter how much you argue and reason with them, but for what reason, a reason that escapes her under-standing and that the Wizard, if he does know, slyly does not let on, has Elena established that kind of relationship in this aseptic laboratory where everything is handled with forceps and almost nothing intervenes from the outside world? or could it be, and this seems most likely, that this is the type of attachment – conflictual, competitive, exces-sive, demanding – that she has engaged in throughout her entire life without being remotely aware of it, or at least without admitting it to herself, but that in this total vacuum she can no longer attribute to unlucky circumstance or to the awkward or unkind behavior of others? strange too how in a place where nothing real ever happens, the slightest accidents swell to the magnitude of tragedy). "In this room I am nobody," the Supreme Sorcerer of the Tribe would thus declare, "at most an empty clothes rack on which you can hang as you please the masks and disguises of all of your phantoms," and it is precisely in order to make this feasible, to be able to adopt all roles and take the place of the diverse, sometimes opposing characters of the farce, from Little Red Riding Hood to the Boston Strangler, that the Wizard must forego a personal face, should as much as possible erase his own characteristic and strongly individual traits, because if he behaved otherwise the game would perhaps lose much of its mystery and magic, the Impassive One deprived of his secret powers, and it would be impossible to go on with the analysis, and then Elena-Polyphemus could escape from the sanctuary-brothel and retreat to some dark corner to lick her wounds and try to understand what has happened to her, and yet, the woman believes in the deepest recess of the most remote chamber of her inner

life – not including her unconscious, which is in its essence
unknowable – the door to which she has never opened to
anyone, not even in love, and which she herself enters on
tiptoe and holding her breath, and yet, as much as she has
often laid on the Impassive One disillusionment or grief or
anger provoked by others, and though at other times, more
for fun than for other reasons, she has pretended to foist
on him the mask of the little old doctor who sat her on his
knee when she was little and scratched her with his kisses
with the prickly barbs of his goatee, or the bookseller on
the corner whom she fell madly in love with at the age of
ten and to whom she wrote dozens of sonnets in a square
notebook, or the treacherous Stepmother of Snow White,
or her own highly treacherous yet seductive mother, or
even the Lord God Almighty, and yet, in spite of this, the
Stranger *does* have his own unmistakable face behind the
wooden mask, a face that appears at times, never when a
melodramatic Elena has outdone herself in trying to drag
out of him some kind of sympathy or warmth, never when
she has attempted to force and compel and tear him away
from that damned rocking chair and corner him against
the wall, but yes, for example, when she says something
inadvertently, usually without getting the joke until afterward, that strikes him as extremely shocking or funny and
makes him roar with laughter, and then for a few instants
he is not the supreme-sorcerer-of-the-most-fucked-up-tribe,
but only a young-man-who-is-laughing, or when something
in her tale, never something deliberate, moves him and
sets his eyes alight with deep twinkles, and always, almost
always – if Elena hasn't ranted and raved and flung signed
checks from the couch to the sanctuary desk, and slammed
doors, and doesn't still have on her lips the bittersweet
taste of her latest impertinence – when he shows her out
at the office door, especially if the session has been very
hard, as though the compassion and understanding that
he has denied her, that he has denied himself, that Papa
Freud has forbidden them both throughout fifty minutes

by the clock, allowed or demanded at the final moment this minimal compensation which is nonetheless enough and momentous in import, in order that the fragile and complex mechanism not break down, because it is invariably a hurried, distracted guy who lets her in upon her arrival and greets her with such an aseptic, hasty handshake that even before withdrawing his hand they're already moving one behind the other down the corridor, but it is without doubt – of this Elena has not a grain of doubt – a real human being who warmly shakes her hand at the moment of leave-taking, as he gazes at her with different eyes, eyes that sparkle with something much like affection, or at least with warmth and friendliness, and then it is Elena who puts on her mask of indifference, who gestures impassively and dons for the occasion a poker face, since she certainly would not want the Wizard to notice her excessive reactions to that handshake by the door at the moment of taking leave, and although she would give a lot, an awful lot, to know if this represents on his part a natural, spontaneous gesture endlessly repeated, or if on the contrary it's a calculated decision made in her absence for the good of the analysis, as the diligent professor makes a note in the margin of his treatise on how to treat unruly, suffering patients who have gone astray, or even worse, discusses it with his peers at a case review session, she will not venture to ask anyone, not even Arturo, though of everyone she knows Arturo is the most sound interlocutor on this subject, the one who could best understand such extreme lunacy and nonsense.

Does Arturo understand – Elena asks him in the dawn, the two lying on the living room floor, she stretched out on the carpet with her head on his lap, so the man is behind her, in a position similar to the one she adopts on obedient days in the sanctuary, although here it's easier to suddenly turn around and look the other in the face – why a supposedly adult woman, who until now had not given stunning proof of profound oligophrenia, would feel mortally humiliated and offended because her analyst refused to give her a light – a cautious, wary Elena has almost stopped smoking over the course of the sessions, less to avoid her rage when Wooden Face doesn't offer her cigarettes or a light than to avoid her own feeling of shame for flying into a rage over such stupidities – and, after referring her back to some earlier session with a slight lift of the eyebrows and an icy look (a session when he must have explained to her, didactic and patient, that behind the request for a light lurked a demand for love, and that it could not be accidental – hardly anything is accidental – that she had spent half her life, besides not carrying a jacket on her arm in case she felt cold or a pocket handkerchief for occasional sniffles or tears, leaving lighters in friends' homes or on the counter of bars), had confined himself to handing her brusquely a box of matches? can Arturo believe – Elena insists, after lazily stretching her arm to lower for the thousandth time the volume of the record player, which he'll automatically turn up again a moment later without even being aware of it, and to switch off the table lamp so they're left in semidarkness, as she likes it, as the dawn rises on the other side of the panes – that the woman in question feels as though she is going to die, literally die, if in the course of a session, in the middle of her discourse or even of a sentence, the guy gets up from his rocker and leaves the room to answer the phone, leaving her, so to speak, with the words in her mouth, which seems to her the height of disrespect toward the patient who is at that moment being analyzed, in this case her, but that she also feels terribly mortified if the phone keeps ringing and the Wizard doesn't move from his rocker, because that clearly shows his contempt for all the loonies who are in analysis with him and who sometimes call him with extreme urgency during his working hours, which is not her case this time, but which well could be on some other occasion, Elena quickly identifying with the wretched person who's calling? can Arturo explain – and without looking at him the woman removes the cigarette or joint from his lips, takes two short puffs and restores it to its place, and huddles a bit more closely between his knees – the fact that she feels a strong urge to kill him when by chance, one time in a hundred, scarcely two or three times during her months of analysis, Elena's mind wanders to the point of losing her sense of time and it's Wooden Face who announces the end of the session, or even worse, that on those days when she has decided beforehand to be docile and cooperative and has promised herself not to even glance at her watch, or better still to take it off and, as is fitting, let him monitor the time, when the occasion arrives she cannot carry it out? or that a woman who has never been particularly jealous and who even now, in this difficult phase, is taking with relative calm and good humor the fact that her husband has gone off to conquer the West Indies with a schoolgirl on his arm, leaving her behind, sees red and does not even manage to respond to her greeting when she passes on the stairs or out on the street an anachronistic girl, wearing a hippie-style flowery full skirt with long dark hair covering her shoulders, who is going to replace her on the couch, still warm from her own body, and lean her head on the torn cushion, and it's even possible that she too, distracted or distressed, runs the palm of her hand over the surface of the wall until she places the tip of her index finger in the tiny hole, almost invisible to the eye but so comforting to the touch? can Arturo believe that when she by chance discovered that the most vain and odious actress who had worked with Julio – or the one who from that moment on seemed to her the most vain and odious, who knows – was in analysis with the same wizard, she threw a terrible tantrum, feeling vilely cheated and betrayed, and even considered breaking off her own analysis, as though the gray-green couch, which isn't even covered with Oriental rugs, had been transformed into a bed in the round where lustful, cretinous women made love trysts and promiscuously blended odors and words? "And doesn't it occur to you," Arturo breaks in for the first time, "that there may also be men in analysis with the Wizard?" and Elena astonished, of course it doesn't occur to her! some rubbish! and what the hell does that have to do with it? and she immediately picks up the thread of her recently violated monologue, had she told him that once she had dreamed, and she doesn't think it's a difficult dream to interpret, but one that's within the grasp of the most simpleminded sorcerers' apprentices and even of her, that the ominous telephone was ringing over and over, and Wooden Face got up and left the room more wooden faced than ever, and then she tried to hear what he was saying but she couldn't make it out, and suddenly she began discovering in the corners of the couch – which has hardly any crevices in real life but did in the dream – under the pillows, peeping out of the hole in the torn cushion, black lace bras, red garters with embossed painted hearts, stockings with intricate and bold designs, brief moist multicolored panties, the complete arsenal of intimate apparel for a young ladies' boarding school or a brothel? was Arturo aware – who was meanwhile muttering, without her listening, that maybe the dream was not in fact so obvious or simple to interpret – had she already told him that one day she came upon an astrology manual, and Elena had read everything related to Aquarius, although perhaps paying more attention to the negative aspects – and for starters it was curious that the first sign she looked up was the Wizard's and not her own, or Julio's or Eduardo's or the kids' – and she had arrived later at the sanctuary-brothel like a monster, literally enraged, as though whatever bad things the manual said – and to top it off Elena had never been interested in astrology and did not even believe in it – were characteristics of the Wizard and she had suffered their consequences in real life, assuming you could brand as real anything that took place within those four white walls, and perhaps for the first time the indifferent expression on the Impassive One's inscrutable face had changed to a new expression of uncertainty and bewilderment, because clever though he was, it still took him a few seconds, quite a few, to comprehend what was happening and what in hell that crazy broad was accusing him of today, even before taking off her shoes and deciding whether or not to lie down on the couch or in any case giving him time to take refuge between the arms of his rocker? does Arturo understand – Elena goes on with her rhetorical questions, to which she does not expect or maybe even allow an answer, the man who's all words for once reduced to silence – why out of all the people in her world, a great many of whom appreciate and respect her and some of whom truly love her, all that really counts is the Stranger's approval, the Stranger's praise, the Stranger's show of affection – so scant the approval and praise, let alone the affection – as though through the Wizard's acceptance she would gain universal acceptance and endorsement of everything she is and does by all the gods, so the Wizard, like the Virgin Mary – and this is a new disguise she hadn't applied to him until now – sole mediator of all grace? does any of this nonsense, this pile of rubbish – and now Elena sits up abruptly, sits cross-legged before the man, lights a cigarette, picks up a glass in which only some half-melted ice cubes remain, which she jiggles together – does any of this game of the thousand-and-one absurdities make sense to Arturo, who was also born in a town near the Pampas and later lived in Buenos Aires itself (and naturally has a vicuña scarf and a silver sipper for maté and may even possibly know how to handle bolas), and has been analyzed by Kleinians, Freudians, Lacanians, by orthodox analysts and heretics, by women and men, by analysts of every type and persuasion, besides experimenting with drugs and psychodrama, and therefore must of necessity know the tricks and secret codes of all varieties and sects of wizards? and now Arturo, with a serious look and not even the hint of a smile, as if nothing Elena has said can be taken as a joke, answers yes, he does believe it, he does know, he does understand, of course he understands, things like those she has described, and even more unusual

143

and far more terrible things generally occur in the course
of psychoanalysis – there's no reason to consider herself
such an exception – and that passion that seems to the
woman unaccountable, that isn't exactly love but at times
proves to be more urgent and devastating than love, that
passion that impels her to declare herself her lordship's
dog, when throughout her life it seems that Elena has
never been anyone's dog, nor is she inclined to be one
now, is none other than the form taken by her resistance to
being analyzed, so it's not a question – Arturo continues,
while Elena pours a stream of whiskey over the melted ice,
drinks, and is quiet – of needing to see that rare passion,
which in the last analysis is not so rare, reciprocated, or
of needing the affection and approval of the Wizard in
order to survive – hasn't Elena herself told him that over
the years she has had the love and approval of so many,
and isn't it true that none of this has apparently helped
her overcome her anxieties, her melancholy and fears,
or avoid sinking into depression? so how will it help that
the analyst behave like the others, that he repeat with
her a tiresome story that is doomed to failure from the
start? – nor is it a question of principles, as Elena sometimes
pretends, that she cannot as a matter of principle accept
such a son-of-a-bitch asymmetrical relationship, help that's
offered so coldly, from so far away, so high above, not at
our side and shoulder to shoulder, almost apologizing for
offering it, which in Elena's view is the only acceptable
way in which a human being dare offer aid to another,
nor is it a question – as the woman proclaims upon reaching the height of grandiloquence – that her individual attitude, in the context of her own analysis, responds to a
moral debt to all humanity, that is, to universally do away
with – and Arturo keeps talking in dead seriousness without even breaking into a half smile – that dreadful, underhanded, the more dreadful for being underhanded, form
of subjugation (since I'm incapable, Elena now thinks, of
doing away with my own personal misery and dependence):

to once and for all reject the false or perhaps true gods, Papa Freud, with or without rugs on the couch, just as destructive as Jehovah himself, to unceremoniously tear the high priests down from their rocker altars, their pulpits, their pedestals, to raze Valhalla, from the flames of which a new superior race of men will be born, a race of supermen who are not analyzable, who refuse to go on vomiting up or aborting obscene little pieces of their unconscious, giving birth to intimate abominable monsters who no longer find shelter in the labyrinths but are carved up mercilessly by wizards on the vivisecting table without anesthesia, using a scalpel that one must accept obeys a law of love, rather it's a question – Arturo continues, and Elena thinks: so he *has* been listening to me, yes, sometimes he hears what I say and records it so well that he can repeat it days later using my exact words – it's just a question of the volatile, chameleonlike forms taken by Elena's resistance to being analyzed, because she already knows enough about analysis – from what she has read, from what she's heard from others, from what she recalls from the university years, from what she has experienced in her own life – to understand that, while the process cannot take place without establishing a transference relationship between the analyst and the analysand, that same transference relationship, if carried to the extreme, if it bursts its banks, can likewise make all psychoanalysis impossible.

I won't listen, thinks a frightened Elena, I won't hear a word more about all of this, this heap of savage events that really took place and that we cannot therefore, neither I nor anyone, in the least attenuate or change, because they belong to the past and those who played – and endured – the leading roles have almost all died and the past is irreversible (despite the Wizard's vigorous denial one day, which left Elena surprised and incredulous, and his obstinacy on this point was understandable only if one bore in mind his tendency to shift everything to the plane of the symbolic and the imaginary and to beget phantoms – an entire universe of ghosts illuminated by Papa Freud – and the Impassive One has often reproached the woman for being so literal, so coarsely realistic, for assigning words a single definitive meaning, when living as she does in a world of artists and creators you would expect just the opposite, or are the elements that appear in Julio's films, that compose Eduardo's paintings, that figure in her own stories and poems perchance literal and univocal? and Elena admits of course not, they're bursting with complexities and ambivalence and lend themselves to multiple interpretations, because this is one of the characteristics of all art, but in life, as against fiction, there always comes the time when one bangs one's head into reality, which is death, and there the multiple interpretations are exhausted, or at least become useless in the face of a game that has already ended, and it's the knowledge that she and all of us must arrive at that point that greatly concerns Elena, and almost all human beings, no matter how ignorant they are or appear to be, and compared to this the fact of handling more or less skillfully the death drive is irrelevant, so the one who really hit the mark was not the Viennese professor, but another Jew who lived almost two thousand years earlier, magnificent Christ's promise, don't you think? – and here Wooden Face frowns, always touchy about favorable references Elena may slip in to psychiatrists, feminism or religion, as though it made him jealous to consider sharing with such rivals the souls of his patients and being obliged to make his own magic triumph over theirs – the most glorious promise made to mankind throughout all history: "He who believes in me shall not perish," and the Wizard, "So why don't you believe in him, if you find his teaching so appealing and so convincing?" and Elena, now shedding her mocking, emphatic tone, "Because I like it a great deal, but I find it totally unconvincing, because I cannot believe, I simply cannot, because something inside me screams loud and clear that that unlikely story of a god who turns into a man and lives among men and dies on the cross for the love of men, and whose body men have eaten for centuries past in the Eucharist, and who has a personal relationship with every one of us, cannot be true," and lowering her voice more and regaining her ironic tone, "just as something inside me also screams it cannot be true that in the deepest, dankest hole of our interminable halls of shadow, in the most profound part of what you call the unconscious, are lurking absurdities like the Oedipus and castration complexes"), thus the past is irreversible, no matter what the Wizard says, and the death of those we have loved, of those we have hated, of all those we have known or simply heard about, brings to a final close the little story, situates them irrevocably outside us, forever beyond our reach, and there's nothing more that can be said, nothing for better or for worse we can still do for them, and revenge is as pointless – for those who died, although not perhaps for oneself – as piling heaps of flowers on coffins, erecting monuments, composing symphonies or poems in their memory, or giving their name to some street in their native city, and for all these reasons Elena is loathe to hear more details of such horror and useless wasteful death, since she knows the details are the worst part, what makes the account really unbearable, because they make the collective story individual and concrete and hence more human, and the woman thinks that not only she, but everyone, has his own highly personal horror museum, images we've been collecting throughout our lives, almost always in spite of ourselves and since infancy, and that only death – and it's one of its few advantages: that dissolving, that erasing of everything within it – can reduce to nothingness, and meanwhile they remain there, stored away and very much alive, not even relegated to the unconscious – Frau Depression, bursting at the seams with narcissism and the castration complex and other pretty little trifles, must have deemed them not worth the time and trouble – ready to appear before us transparent, complete, at the most unexpected moments of our waking hours – sometimes when we're extremely busy, surrounded by people – or in the middle of the night in dreams, which is what must have happened to Arturo, because Elena heard him cry out in his sleep, and she had to shake him gently by the shoulders, take his hand, call him over and over by name, to finally awaken him, and now he sits up in bed, eyes open and heart lost in distant realms, in places she knows nothing of, and only after a few seconds does he sigh deeply, "Thank God it was you" (Elena doesn't have the nerve to ask who else could have approached him in the night, whether a woman of flesh and blood or Mrs. Dry Bones herself), and he clings to her the way her children used to hang around her neck, her waist, during nights full of nightmares and ghosts, shaking uncontrollably from head to foot, his face, which he keeps stubbornly hidden in the woman's shoulder, moist with tears, and Elena takes him firmly in her arms, rocks him back and forth in a soothing, rhythmic motion – as with her kids in nights of bad dreams – caresses with her fingertips his cheeks, his hair, his forehead, around his eyes, murmurs sweet silly words – also similar to those used with children – asks him time and again, "What's wrong? Tell me what's the matter; what were you dreaming?" and it seems to her they've gone through a thousand eternities there, the two of them holding each other at the edge of the bed, he in silence, she playing mama – in a role, she thinks, feeling for a few seconds ridiculous, that has been assigned to women from the very beginning of recorded time – until at last Arturo withdraws from her arms, stops her with a gesture, "No, don't turn on the light," leans back against the pillows, lights a cigarette and starts to relate – in a surprisingly calm, controlled voice, as though none of it had anything to do with him, as though he were repeating foolish tales told by an idiot thousands of years ago – not the content of tonight's dream, but other worse nightmares that occurred only yesterday in a reality that is still not over (the same voice, recalls a frightened Elena, as that

148

of the woman on the television screen, she had missed the beginning of the program and did not even know if she was Israeli or Palestinian, and the woman, motionless in the foreground, was telling how the soldiers had invaded the town and put all the inhabitants to death in a brutal slaughter, including her entire family, while she watched the scene from some hiding place where they could not find her, but it was Elena who applied the terms "brutal" and "slaughter" to the event, the woman had used much calmer, more neutral language, as though she were describing the weather or broadcasting a chess game, not for a moment had she altered the monotonous singsong of her voice, she had made no gesture, she had not shed a single tear, and Elena had calmed down incredulously thinking it could not be true, it was not a news report, later it would turn out to have been an error or some hideous television joke, the woman could not be telling something so appalling in that way, but in the end it turned out that it *was* all true, that in less than half an hour and before her very eyes they had killed everyone in the world she knew and loved, including her children, and Elena had discovered that by far the most terrible thing was that neutral voice, a voice one can only attain, she thought, upon reaching the end point of horror and suffering, when the worst has happened and whatever may happen in the future no longer matters, and no crying or sobbing can afford comfort or relief, and the compassion and solidarity of friends or strangers can no longer help, whether of a few or the entire world, and not even suicide offers a soothing or seductive way out, a mere futility that may or may not occur, what's the difference, since one is already and forever worse than dead), and now Elena feels weak and frightened and thinks she won't listen to any more, because she already knows more than enough about what happened in Argentina, as she learned everything – everything you can know without having been there – about the Nazi concentration camps from a dreadful, unforgettable weekend in Perpignan, and enlarging her own personal horror museum is not to anyone's benefit, it won't change an iota of what belongs to the past, and what's worse, neither will it help to prevent such atrocities from recurring in the future, so Elena would like to tune out, leave, close her eyes and not listen any more, recite to herself a poem or the multiplication table to block out Arturo's voice, as she closes her eyes and covers her ears at the movies during horror films or violent news reports, except that it doesn't work, it's okay in a movie theater but here she cannot do it, nor does she dare interrupt Arturo to say "stop now, don't tell me any more," because she suddenly feels ashamed of being so timid and fearful, the good little girl who never grew up, fruit of an unnatural marriage between Francoism and French existentialism, the legacy of which she will never get over, because therein lies the source of those lost or illusory paradises where everyone agrees she got stuck and which she would have to leave behind, and so here she is entering old age – and maybe not even a contemptible old age – without hardly ever, except by chance, having walked the paths of adulthood ("We humans do not mature: we rot," Eduardo is wont to declare, always charitable toward himself and the human condition), bound to and bowled over by a miniscule world made of cheap ambitions, small-time dreams, petty rivalries, of dwarves who embrace a marble and think they possess the world, of poor idiots who look in the mirror and never find – they would die if they found it and that's why psychoanalysis can be lethal, assuming that from Papa Freud on down someone sometime has really been psychoanalyzed – an image that even remotely resembles their own, or the image that others have of them, of women who go into ecstasies, or pretend to, before the man hugging the marble, or before the illusory landscape glimpsed by their man on the other side of the mirror, women who praise, support, propel, glorify – although later they always, always retaliate or send the bill – who treat their men – whether the latter fancy themselves to be

Leonardo, Napoleon, Marcelo Mastroianni or the top star of the Bolshoi – as though they were at once children and geniuses – and the eternal feminine must consist of this, a mask with two faces: the rapidly interchangeable roles of mama and Beatrice – who grant them possession of the world and all it contains, just for the asking, and Elena herself, obsessed with her stupid miniscule wounds, taking refuge in an unhealthy dark hole, the better to lick them at her leisure – it's anyone's guess whether to heal or contaminate them – throwing herself headlong onto the couch, greedily hoarding pills of all shapes and colors, because in short she cannot bear – it's something so simple – starting to grow old, because Julio has gone off to America with a little girl by the hand and has left her behind, because he has not publicly acknowledged all he owes her, or the great deal that Elena – who had never looked at it this way before – believes he owes her, because he has not pronounced her name in speeches or interviews, because in short he has not proclaimed loud and clear on the streets of Manhattan that she is his Beatrice and his mama, Martha and Mary wondrously combined in one person (which has undoubtedly been the dream of all males of the human race for as long as they've been scurrying around the planet Earth), because Elena even feels stupidly jealous of her sons' women – whether they're pregnant little stuffed animals or front-page pinup girls – and after having always maintained that a mother's relationship with her children is by definition asymmetrical, since there's almost nothing they're obliged to give or that one can rightfully demand of them, suddenly she is asking them for something they cannot and should not have to give, and really what she cannot bear is no longer being the center of this insignificant miniworld that she – in the same way men do with other kinds of miniworld – took for the whole show, and maybe the decision to live entirely or partly for others is not so disinterested or noble, if one expects in return to be enthroned at the center of their universe, and Elena is no longer certain – as of the last days or weeks, although she hasn't discussed it with anyone nor has it come up directly in analysis – of being so different from most of the women she knows, and she is starting to ask herself the real reason why her work in the production company, raising her children, the multiple roles she has played in Julio's life, have completely monopolized her time and attention without leaving room for what she wanted above all to try to achieve, why all her literary projects have remained unfinished, the stories and poems by her own choice unpublished, and the woman has been turning all these things over in her mind, maybe in part to shut out the voice of Arturo whom she does not dare interrupt, since he is undoubtedly lightening his personal horror museum, which is far more dreadful than Elena's, by telling her about it and sharing it with her, and this is something she feels she cannot deny him, so she lets him go on to the end, until the man's voice gives out like water welling up from a fountain, at last just a fine trickle and then gone, and the man is still, lies back on the pillow, remains motionless with his eyes closed, and the anguish and fear have been thickening around them, closing in on them viscous and foul like a damp, polluted atmosphere, and Elena feels a lump in her throat and a weight on her heart, a sorrow that seems without limit or end, and she slips softly onto Arturo, pressing his body against hers, eager to cut through so much anxiety, to protect and warm him, to somehow pull him out of his immobility and silence, to break the evil spell, and she takes his head in her hands, she again moves her fingertips lightly over his temples, around his eyes and mouth, as if she were redrawing his face, she kisses him on the eyelids, stubbornly closed and still wet, she kisses his lips, still trembling, she licks with the tip of her tongue the salty aftertaste of his tears, and Arturo asks in surprise but without protesting, "What are you doing?" and the woman feels, like the flapping of a bird's wings, the first brief flutter of his sex beneath her thighs, and it gives her keen pleasure to feel it still so small and uncertain, so unaggressive and scarcely playful, and only now, when he asks "What are you doing?" and she feels the first thrust of his sex on her womb, does she think, "I am loving you, it will last only some minutes or some hours, but at this precise moment I am loving you," and then she realizes what is happening, she observes with astonishment – like a dark, obscure sound rising from the deepest caverns of the most impenetrable labyrinths of the complete unknown of her own body, an imperceptible, hardly detectable shiver, but which unerringly announces the rising, uncontainable approach of the waterspout or the hurricane – the unquestionable presence of desire, a desire she has felt so seldom for years and the whereabouts and paths of which are unknown to her, a desire she does not have the powers or witchcraft to invoke – so she cannot show others the way, reveal its whereabouts, teach them the magic spells, she has no thread that will allow Theseus to reach the Minotaur – and which appears suddenly just because, almost always without warning, always for her a miracle, leaving her afterward with the fear or suspicion that this may have been its last visit, the fear that it may never again return, a desire that has been vanishing from her relationship with Julio, without either of them knowing how to avoid it, a desire she has never felt with aspirin, best friend, mama dearest Eduardo – and why is that, the woman would like to know, why? what ingredient is too much or what is lacking? – a desire routinely absent from her casual affairs, much as she imbues them with passionate romanticism – perhaps the body, always more lucid and powerful, refuses to take part in the clumsy farce – a desire until today absent in her relationship with Arturo, who could not arouse it with his avalanche of words, which only reminds Elena of a love scene broadcast on the radio, nor the complicated positions and caresses, which always seem so ridiculous and false, which tire and inhibit and bore her, nor the sophisticated blends of herbs and to-baccos, which she has smoked with the best of intentions, nor the very fine line of white powder going from inside the empty pen up her nose, while Arturo asks eagerly, "And now, tell me what you're feeling! Are you feeling better?" and she has often lied "yes," partly not to disappoint him, but even more to put an end once and for all to these attempts that she knows are doomed to failure from the start, to stop him from making bothersome interpretations – she has to put up with more than enough of those from her wizard-analyst and from Eduardo, and Elena hates parodies of psychoanalysis at the hands of amateurs even more than her sessions on the couch – from getting lost in endless suppositions, making farfetched connections, and then plunging in again with new blends of herbs, powders and tobaccos, the more sophisticated the more desperate he gets, which Elena is sure will give her only growing nausea and a splitting headache.

Perhaps that sudden irruption of pleasure and desire, she is telling the Wizard the following afternoon, without giving him time to lead the session in more likely directions, since the woman feels she has come today with new elements to analyze and try to explain or resolve, and maybe it *would* have been more logical to start with Julio's return, now imminent, tomorrow afternoon by direct flight from New York, a return at once so feared and so desired, in any case so discussed, about which in recent days she has amassed a heap of predictions and conjectures, not only regarding his frame of mind upon his return, what he may have planned for the two of them – or perhaps for three – maybe even including a future in which Elena has no place or in which she will play an entirely different role, but also regarding how she is going to react – during these days of waiting she has been unable to determine, apart from what Julio may have planned or decided, what she really wants, what she's still feeling or has been carrying around for years, without even realizing that her feelings have changed for this man with whom she has shared

154

two-thirds of her life, so she is as curious and anxious to see what may come from her as what may come from him – and the Wizard was surely expecting to hear from her lips today something related to Julio's return, that reunion of the two, neither of whom may well be the same, but Elena, without even taking off her shoes, a sign of extreme urgency, and without lying down on the couch, but sitting up very straight and staring him in the face – as always when she's going to talk about something serious, something that poses a threat to her well-being, that is really important to her, the couch reserved for the ingenious exercise of free association – has begun telling him about the previous night's unforeseen awakening of desire and pleasure (even now she feels surprised that at this stage it's still possible, that it has been granted her once again by the generally stingy but occasionally benevolent and generous gods, when she thought she had lost forever – without this constituting a tragedy – the drive and the will and the in-clination), which would carry her easily, naturally, almost inevitably – from a certain point on it was as though they were lifted and cradled and tossed about by a wave that was foreign to them, or at least that's how the woman had experienced it, as though the two were asleep and dream-ing the same dream that they could not control and in no way sought to elude, whatever was happening beyond the domain of their conscious will, their bodies fused in the same warmth, the same gasp, the same prolonged moan that seemed without end – to the very peak of pleasure, for once crowned without effort (and she assures Wooden Face, so he is not left in the slightest doubt and does not start imagining rubbish, that there is no reason to get all worked up and dramatize things, since orgasm – while it's extremely enjoyable, and despite all that Papa Freud, Uncle Lacan, and even Reich, the friend of the family, have expati-ated on it – does not constitute the center of her existence), where she thought she would never again set foot, and perhaps, although she isn't sure, it was because she had felt the pressing need – on the unconscious level, she for once concedes, since she only thought of this afterward when she tried to understand what had happened – to pit against so much suffering and inexplicable cruelty and senseless death – not only in Argentina, but everywhere and always, from time immemorial – as the only minimally valid or at least acceptable response, the most simple, round affirmation of life – perhaps, it now occurs to her, something similar to making love in a cemetery, can the Wizard understand this? – at least the most basic that the woman knows (can the Impassive One believe that for a few seconds while they were making love – or while love was making them – she wanted to conceive, to produce a child in seconds and deliver him there among the tombs?), perhaps without its mattering too much what actual man was lying with her, so Arturo himself may not have played a major role in that macabre dance of death full of phantoms ("Would that have made a big difference? Would it have somehow changed the situation?" inquires curiously the Great Witch Doctor of the Tribe, and Elena, after a pause, still hesitant, "I don't know, I think so, not as regards the pleasure itself, but because finding it with a particular man and not with others must mean something, as if the body, always wiser and surer than the mind, has given its own response – but what do you think?" and Poker Face shrugs, smiles enigmatically, raises an eyebrow and is silent), although maybe this was not the reason – at least not the single decisive reason – and maybe the fullness of her pleasure was due to the formidable power of tears – masculine tears, of course, since women's tears, by dint of being squandered and even exploited, soon lose their effectiveness and become almost worthless, and maybe that's why we tell boys from the time they are little not to cry, that men do not cry, so they zealously collect and store up their tears and they come to contain a magical power, so that, when one of those men who by definition do not cry, very much in spite of himself sheds a few small tears, we women fear that, if we don't instantly put a stop to that dreadful weeping, the sky will fall on our heads, the force of gravity will cease and we'll all be hurled up to the stratosphere, the fountains will spout blood and apocalyptic bugles will sound, and maybe, it now occurs to Elena, that hackneyed castration complex, that blessed and ever so feminine penis envy that appears in all the essays but which the two of them, she and the Wizard, have tried to track down in vain, without ever finding it, might consist just as much in the lack of some magical, powerful tears as in the mortifying inability to piss a figure eight on the wall – so it's quite likely that masculine tears – whether Arturo's or any other man's she cannot for the moment tell – may have aroused Elena's compassion beyond measure (that *Ungeduld des Herzens* that Zweig talked about) and the compassion brought tenderness in its wake and the tenderness almost inevitably culminated in desire, and perhaps – the woman goes on amused, at the risk of the Impassive One's at any moment accusing her of declaiming a monologue from a couch transformed into a stage, at any rate, a stage is better than a vivisecting table, isn't it? or even crossing her off as a maniac, an odious word he had sprung on her the day she arrived at the sanctuary for the first time minimally upright and lively, not crawling along the wall like some filthy maggot, and that has that slightly aseptic, pedantic smell of words taken from a manual of psychiatry or psychoanalysis – perhaps this is her personal road to orgasm – surely it's not for nothing that the best Spanish novelist since the generation of '98 says that we each come as we can – and in her case, when men ask her what she wants them to do, what are her erogenous zones, the positions she likes best, she should disabuse them about the possibilities offered by the Kama Sutra and other similar tracts, explain that despite a long coexistence she knows almost nothing about her own body, and tell them all the same, "Start crying," although perhaps the Wizard – who has been silent for quite a while – believes that what was different the night before, and propelled her so easily toward desire and pleasure, might also have been (it's another open possibility) the fact that for once she was leading the game, for once she was not the one being besieged, summoned, pursued, that she did not feel forced or obliged to do anything, on the contrary she had to overcome the passivity, if not the resistance, of the other, that "What are you doing?" uttered by an Arturo who at that moment was thinking about anything in the world but making love, that timid helpless sex between his legs, and now at last the Wizard opens his mouth, his expression indifferent as usual, but in the very depths of his eyes behind the glasses, almost imperceptible to someone who does not know him, there's that amber gleam of the hunter on the watch who has just sniffed the still remote presence of the prey, the same expression that must light up his face when he glimpses a checkmate, or just got the fifth card in the royal flush, "And doesn't it occur to you," says Wizard-Cardsharp, the Great Solitary Hunter of the Pampas, "don't you think that that ability to experience pleasure, that recovery, which you yourself admit to be unexpected, of the orgasm – which I realize does not con- stitute the center of your life, but which you acknowledge to be pleasurable – may indicate that you are over or almost over the worst of your depression?" and Elena laughs, "So in short, I owe the unexpected orgasm to you?" and then she hesitates, and ends up admitting that she *does* seem to have emerged from the darkest part of the well, although at times she still feels very deep distress – the Impassive One should not judge her state of mind by the good humor she sometimes, like today, displays on the couch – although she still goes through moments of almost unbearable anxiety, although she still cries at the wrong times and for trivial reasons that don't serve as a valid excuse for tears, although she still does not venture to spend an entire night alone at home, and Julio's return tomorrow fills her with apprehen- sion and fear, and she can't remember the last weekend in Rome with Jorge without feeling a flash of grief and despair, and now for the first time, as she brings it up in the sanctuary, since the Monday she got back and planned to tell him about it the Wizard had refused to listen or simply hadn't realized that Elena had something to communicate to him, just as she formulates the first hesitant words, "You know, I spent last weekend in Rome, and it was Jorge who insisted that I go because he thought I sounded bad on the phone, but upon my arrival I found without prior warning that the apartment had been invaded by a strange guy, much older than he, who they said is a professor at the university, and by a well-endowed redhead, as a result of which Jorge paid almost no attention to me and we could not even talk on a one-to-one basis," just as she explains with the failed hint of a smile, "I guess I had an acute attack of maternal jealousy and that's why I felt so bad," she realizes for the first time – despite her having told the story several times earlier to Arturo – that perhaps that was not exactly what had happened, and she begins to formulate in words something she is still not consciously aware of, the words once again dragging the thoughts behind, "It could also be that Jorge, although he knew from our most recent phone conversations that I was depressed and anxious, couldn't stand seeing me reduced to this state: weak, needy, frightened, bitter," and then, after a pause and in another voice, the couch voice although she remains sitting up because she can't bring herself to lie down on the couch now, much as she'd actually prefer to, "I imagine he couldn't stand seeing me for the first time as an old woman," so it probably was not true, or not exclusively, that her son was so absorbed and consumed by a romance à trois that it left him no time or space or ears for her, on the contrary it might be that he had interposed the other two, consciously or not, deliberately or not, as a kind of shield to protect him from a solitary face-to-face confrontation with his mother, something he lacked the heart and nerve for – doesn't the Wizard think it could have been that? – it's often terrible for children to see their parents age, to witness the deterioration of a once so mythical image, and even more so when the relationship has been as intense, passionate even, as that which prevailed for years and years between her and Jorge, and suddenly Elena recalls that on a certain occasion long ago, when Pablo and Jorge were still children, a motorbike had run her down before their home, and they had carried her into the apartment – they were still living in an apartment building in the Ensanche, not in a house as they are now – her clothes dirty and in disarray, with a thin line of blood running down her face, unable to stand by herself for a few minutes or to string together more than two or three words, and while Julio and Andrea made her comfortable on the sofa, carefully placed a pillow beneath her head, dabbed her forehead with a towel soaked in eau de cologne, talked about calling a doctor (obviously not necessary), asked her twenty times a minute if she was feeling a little better now, while a Pablo with eyes wide as saucers took her hand and stubbornly refused to let go, Jorge, sitting at the other end of the living room, had taken refuge behind the pages of a comic book, had focused all his attention on a jigsaw puzzle, his toy train, so absorbed in all this that he had not for a second glanced up, had not once looked at her – or maybe he had and she hadn't noticed? – had not until much later addressed a single word to her, so Elena had begun to be much more concerned about what the child might be feeling than about her own fright, which was already starting to pass, or about Pablo's obvious and spontaneous distress, doesn't the Wizard think that something very similar might have occurred last weekend in Rome, something which, if at some future time he decides to lie down on a couch, Jorge himself will have to try to explain to the diffuse ear of the wizard of the moment (or rather the wizardess, because it was just as unthinkable that her son, notwithstanding the three-way affair with the university professor and the well-endowed redhead, would go through analysis with a man as that Elena, despite playing with the idea on occasion, could be in analysis with a woman)?

160

We're all here, everyone's come, Elena mechanically reviews the troops, a glass of very cold champagne in her hands and a wan smile dancing on her lips, because it almost makes her laugh to think that tomorrow she'll have to tell all this to the Wizard, to explain to him what has happened and what is going to happen from here on, and how Julio's return, so longed for and feared, in any case so talked about, analyzed and debated, that meeting of the two that would of necessity represent a milestone in the woman's life and perhaps also in Julio's, that reunion she has been preparing for, strengthening herself for day by day, session after session (she has even inaugurated some new pills that Arturo gave her for the event, these really miraculous, no matter what happens leaving you in a state of total serenity, of an exquisite violet color, although they taste like hell and almost inflict a wound if they stick to your palate or get caught in your throat, and she has even memorized the multiple speeches she might have to make at the airport or later on, depending on the turn of events), that blessed meeting about which they have all – Arturo, Eduardo, Horacio, even the Wizard, but above all she herself – erected among themselves an enormous mound of more or less nonsensical and delirious fantasies – depending on the day, the changing color of the sky or of the pills – in a broad spectrum of possibilities ranging from the dramatic to the burlesque, so that blessed meeting has led to this, a social gathering very quickly organized and which, despite being on the spur of the moment, has brought them all, or almost all, together at the house (the Wizard already knows, because Elena has explained it to him on other occasions, that that "everyone," all Barcelona, boils down to about a hundred notables, who all look very much alike, and are on the other hand extremely similar to, or at least equivalent to and interchangeable with, those one might meet in London, Paris, Rome, New York, maybe even – although they'd be more delirious and crazy and fantastic – Buenos Aires, although it's a bit difficult to imagine the Impassive

One at one of these soirées), an entire world closed and turned in on itself, absorbed in contemplating its own navel – convinced it's the only one possible, that it occupies the exact center of the city and hence of the universe, set on disclaiming the other worlds with which it coexists, with the same obstinacy and candor with which the others disclaim it in turn – has congregated in full-dress gala, in plenary session, to welcome home and congratulate the hero who sailed the high seas in search of fame and fortune and now returns victorious, despite there not figuring among the spoils of war a chest full of objects of gold and silver (as for plaques and medals, they have granted him a few) nor an unsettling mestiza with firm skin and dark bewitching eyes (and what the devil has become of the demure little schoolgirl? did they leave her sleeping on the first beach of some remote island peopled by fauns and bacchantes? did they check her in on another plane, like one more piece of luggage? did they have her get off the plane with the other passengers, the two pretending – how embarrassing – not to know each other?), and now Eduardo, since on this occasion not even Eduardo has failed to make the date, although it seems he's already had a few too many, his dim blurry gaze wandering indiscriminately over the bodies of all the women at the party, whether they appeal to him or not, in fact it's quite likely that upon reaching a certain level of intoxication and sour grapes – impossible to gauge for sure if he's already arrived at that point or has a little way to go yet – all women attract or repel him equally, so Eduardo peering into the dark chasm of the low-cut gowns, trying to put his hand under skirts, abruptly and rudely, with model insolence and brutishness worthy of higher causes, breaking into conversations of which he has not heard the beginning and whose outcome does not interest him, an Eduardo in short – Elena thinks as she sees him making his way over to her – who is more depressed and thus more contentious than usual, because this impulse that draws him toward low necklines and under skirts has little to do with sexual arousal or even sensuality (Eduardo-aspirin, Eduardo-my-mama-pampers-me-very-much seems far away, as though in another dimension), and he comes up to her, takes her coldly and crudely by the waist, gives her a noisy, grotesque kiss on the mouth – his tastes harsh and bitter – and whispers in her ear, as if he had been reading her thoughts and were prolonging and responding to them, "My congratulations, what magnificent drawing power!" and it bothers Elena a little, who has been thinking the same thing with similar detachment and sarcasm, to have someone else say it, "In any case," she protests, "the drawing power must be his, not mine," and now Eduardo, in his most sinister guise of enfant terrible, "And where, may I ask, is the little girl he took with him to the Indies?" and Elena is about to tell him to go ask Julio, what does she know about it, but she opts to shrug her shoulders and murmur, "I don't know, it seems he didn't bring her here," and Eduardo corrosive, as if he wanted, heaven knows why, to burst out crying or to hit her, transformed by the alcohol into an arrogant, aggressive soap opera character, "But *you did*, right? You did bring your Argentine tango dancer, incomparable joint maker, night owl, friend of all the world?" and as the woman peers at him in silence, uncomfortable and slightly angry, "I'll be damned if you too can't take pride in your drawing power! So you've gathered the three of us together here, the only one missing, and I'm not even sure of that, is your psychiatrist," and Elena remains silent and in a sense concedes the point, and she thinks that whether or not it was she who drew them, here the three of them are (not the Wizard, of course, and by the way, it's as useless to explain to Eduardo yet again, when he's tight as a vat, that it's not a psychiatrist but a psychoanalyst, as it is to clarify that the Argentine musician is not especially interested in tangos but rather in black heroin addicts from New York, and Brazilian music and rock): so Eduardo, without the slightest doubt headed for a colossal, apocalyptic meltdown, a couple more drinks and he won't be able to stand up, but as long as his legs support him, and even after, vomiting up with each poisoned word evil vapors borne of bitterness, envy and resentment that are brimming over, without his being able to stop it, because it's so hard to struggle hour after hour with the fateful suspicion – ever more well-founded and credible with the passing of the years – that one may well not be a genius, and that maybe it's not just one's obtuse, discredited contemporaries, who can't see what's right before their noses, who deny one all glory, but also, and this is far worse, posterity, so much struggle and effort with nothing to remain on earth after one's death, and Eduardo may be seeking an impossible compensation (art sublimated as sexuality and not the other way around, as Papa Freud pretends) in the form of sordid, banal relations with dull, more or less crazy and bad-mannered girls, who he alone – with the indispensable aid of some drinks and the complicity of an Elena who at times joins in his fantasizing and at others simply lies through her teeth – can exalt and metamorphose into fascinating women of the night, it's very hard in these circumstances to keep up one's morale, against all odds, at least high enough to open the mailbox every morning with strained and artificial – not genuine – excitement, and now here too we have – Eduardo spied him out and even identified him, without having previously met him and in spite of the liquor – the Argentine music man (Elena is incapable – out of self-respect, if not for more altruistic reasons – of abandoning anyone on a remote island, even one that's overflowing with fauns and bacchantes, or of checking him in like luggage on another plane, or of pretending not to know him on the stairs or at the arrival gate), citizen of the world and of nowhere, full of remarkable gifts for numerous professions without ever on your life settling on one, bursting with a talent that he only displays among his own, at café bars, friend of all without really having a single close friend, perpetual exile – from all countries, all ideologies, all revolutions – and first and foremost from himself, with the hope, always up to now kept alive or after brief parentheses recovered, of someday reaching safe harbor – a new wandering Dutchman – and casting anchor forever in its tranquil waters, redeemed and rescued from all evil spells by the love of a native girl – again the recurrent myth of the Malinche – capable of throwing herself for his sake, innocent and lovesick, a supreme prayer of passion on her lips, from the height of the rocky cliffs, and in this way to follow him unto death and even beyond death itself, since love – what room is there for doubt, when it's been repeated by poets through the ages, going all the way back to the Scriptures? – is more powerful than death, doesn't Gretchen commit the most abominable crimes for the love of Faust? when in truth the limits to Elena's daring are set by the port on one end and the Tibidabo on the other (her boldest deed: to include Arturo at a party like this and introduce him to some of the guests), Arturo determined to prove to her and above all to himself that the two are still young, perpetual adolescents by the grace of the benign gods from whom they don't have too clear an idea how they've won the favor and who have decided to erase in them all traces of the passage of time, bent on proving to Elena, and above all to himself, that the two together are emerging – assuredly holding hands and without being able to determine precisely who goes first, who should take care not even once to look back – from the mournful subterranean realms of depression and death (many years earlier in Fidel's Cuba, an old witch had prophesied from reading the remains of a sacrificed animal that upon turning fifty he would meet an extraordinary woman and together with her would start a new life), resolved to gamble on a future that must not exist anywhere, Elena thinks, and now here, tonight, concocting for his own exclusive consumption unusual blends, daring cocktails never before tried, in which he ably mixes – he'd leave any psychiatrist in the dark – alcohol, various herbs and powders, and a whole arsenal of drugs that he must have gotten by softsoaping a well-intentioned pharmacist or with the prescription of some doctor friend, and that he hoards in a bag that he keeps with him always and doesn't part with for a second, even to go to the bathroom – very similar, Elena imagines, to the carpetbag carried by Mary Poppins, inexhaustible and full of ever-changing surprises designed to fill the need or fancy of every occasion – convinced that being strange and stoned is the way to be truly charming and scintillating before all these people he doesn't know and whom he would like to impress favorably and win over, when what really occurs is just the opposite, and this guy who is intelligent and entertaining, a superb conversationalist, after so much alcohol and muck ends up diminished and gray, his eyes clouded over and a silly half-ass smile stuck on his lips, and now, how strange, after seeking him out with her gaze in every corner of the overrun house (they've even opened the patio doors and some people have gone out into the garden, despite the cold damp of the autumn night), she finally discovers him in the kitchen by the refrigerator, clumsily taking some ice cubes from a tray, and a woman with him is holding the container into which they're falling one by one and the woman – Elena doesn't know when she arrived, or how it's possible that she didn't see her until now, or whom she came with, and she doesn't rule out the possibility that she descended from a star, using Mary Poppins' magic umbrella (which Arturo may well have taken from his bag and lent her) as aircraft engine and parachute – is Andrea, and at the exact same moment Eduardo has also discovered her, and he rushes over to Elena, grabs her by the hand, pulls her toward the kitchen, and there the four of them are by the icebox, and the two women come together, literally fall into each other's arms in a dense, interminable embrace, as if the two were alone in the universe, sole earthly survivors of a nuclear disaster, or astronauts with their engine damaged beyond repair – and moreover neither of the two knows a thing about mechanics – who have turned up on an unknown planet without signs of life, or on an island located beyond the seven seas where there are no bacchantes or fauns who can keep them company and carry them off to splendid, divine, crazy orgies, and Elena feels tears coming to her eyes and she realizes that the other is also crying, and when they finally separate they have damp, slightly red eyes and shaky, rather embarrassed smiles on their lips, and Eduardo takes them by the arm, one on his right and the other on his left, "So now we're really all here: the sheep has returned to the fold whom we had given up for lost forever!" and he's using that tone of voice between sarcastic and sentimental that he uses when he's had far too much to drink, because it's obvious that the wine makes him sad, although it's not so clear that he's enjoying the sadness, and Andrea, smiling through her tears, letting them keep running down her cheeks without bothering to wipe them off, "My Lord, how old and fat and ugly we all look!" and since no one ventures to contradict her, "How terrible it is to arrive from other worlds and see oneself reflected all at once in this mirror!" and Eduardo declares that raw, naked reality, without the intervention of the arts and liquor to dress it up, is intolerable for humanity, and that certain very high levels of lucidity – and isn't this akin to what Elena says about psychoanalysis? so it was an ill-advised idea on Freud's part to invent a process that can bring us closer to the truth, when what we all need is somehow or other to adulterate it – can bring death in its wake, and Arturo hands Andrea – whom he has just met, because the night when they saw her onstage in that catastrophic performance put on by drug addicts Elena preferred not to go backstage to greet her, but with whom he has immediately hit it off – a large glass full to the brim with whiskey, with a single ice cube slipping all alone along its surface, and then he serves himself another like it, and puts his arm around her and leads her to the living room sofa where a convenient space has just opened up, and now Elena is telling Eduardo, "Serve me something to drink too," because it seems to her impolite, unseemly even, not to show solidarity with the guests – something like walking around dressed and with one's gloves on at a nudist camp – to remain sober amidst the contagious and general intoxication, it's anyone's guess why everyone's drinking so much today, much more than usual, maybe Eduardo's right that reality is unbearable without enticements and palliatives and consolations, never unarmed – as the Wizard certainly pretends or hopes – and although almost everyone has come, all Barcelona (at least all Barcelona that is rapidly heading toward its fifties) and the party can be considered a success, it's not at all clear that the majority of the guests are really enjoying themselves – could it be that some are feeling, as Andrea put it, ugly and fat and old? – much as they all come over to her, a smile and a kiss poised on their lips, as she wades laboriously from one end of the living room to the other, much as they congratulate her for an evening that has been, continues to be, marvelous, and for how marvelous she also looks, much more attractive and youthful than twenty years ago, and the most naïve, how does it feel to be married to a genius, someone who has reached the height of success in his field, the very top? and the surprising thing, Elena thinks – although deep down it doesn't surprise her too much – is that the genius, Julio Welles, Julio da Vinci, Julio the Marvelous, the happy mortal, one among hundreds of thousands who has made it to the top, got off the plane with a sullen expression and a twisted demeanor, and then strolled aimlessly among their friends – those who went to meet him at the airport and those who have gathered here – with a funereal air, not even a smile, as though nothing that had taken place was even remotely marvelous or what's more had anything to do with him, and as though he were brooding over very deep sorrows, painful secret wounds, and then he went out to the garden and sat down in the darkest corner, and Elena follows him there, after courageously wading through the cloying river of praise, kisses, smiles, and she sits down beside him on the stone bench, and this is the first time she has had a chance to exchange more than two or three words with Julio alone, and she asks him, "What's wrong, may I ask, what the hell's the matter? Did something go badly? Aren't you satisfied?" and Julio looks at her scandalized, as though Elena has just given signs of profound oligophrenia, a condition infrequent in her, or as if the woman wanted to inflict on him a new wound, this one much harder to bear because it comes from someone so close to him who should know and treat him better, of course he's not satisfied, does he by any chance have cause to be? and Elena (silencing the thought that the adventure with the traveling schoolgirl might have ended badly, or that Julio might be annoyed – who knows what others have maliciously told him or he has imagined – by the presence of Arturo in the house), "But wasn't this, precisely this, what you, or the two of us, had always dreamed of? To have one of your movies on Broadway, at the very heart of New York and of the world?" so had he forgotten that distant day, almost thirty years earlier, the first time the two had traveled together to America, when he had stopped in the middle of Times Square, amidst all the hubbub, all the lights, he'd lifted her in the air, started spinning around with her in his arms until the woman felt slightly dazed and dizzy, he'd kissed her on the mouth and decreed once and for all that this and only this was victory, real victory: to see one's film up in neon lights on one of the movie houses on the Square? but Julio shakes his head sadly, with the most doleful of his wide repertoire of expressive looks, and begins telling her about his trip, and she's the only person he can tell it to, Elena thinks, because she alone possesses the keys not only to understand what he means but to know instantly how to react, the suitable phrase, silence, caress, and naïve little girls with timid schoolgirl smiles cannot fill this kind of role, so all these days he must have had to swallow the words (impossible to explain it to her on the phone, besides which Elena didn't give him the chance), so now at last he begins telling her (it makes Elena laugh to recall the

towering castles of rejection and abandonment she had
been erecting alone, or her suspicion, sustained until a few
seconds ago, that the genius' affliction, his bitterness, could
be due to a question of love and jealousy, although she is
now sure that later on, some hours or days from now, he'll
ask her with slight annoyance about her relationship with
Arturo, and above all, he'll tell her everything from A to
Z, whether or not she wants to hear, whether it interests or
bores her, about his adventures with the girl) why the success was not in fact as great as it appeared, nor did it come
about in the decisive way of which they had both dreamed,
because in short New York is not what it used to be, and
Times Square even less, and the movie only ran twelve days,
which everyone assured him for a film of this kind was a
success, but he doesn't see it that way at all, and the reviews
were certainly favorable, but not equally or unanimously
so, and in a little town in Oklahoma the local or parish
newspaper said that Julio is basically finished, that he has
nothing or almost nothing new to say, and it's not even
certain that the opinion of students at Columbia and other
universities was radically different, because sure they filled
the halls where the lectures were held, and even clapped
and cheered him on quite a bit, but when you came right
down to it . . . so this voyage which they're all so frivolously
celebrating as a success had at least as much of failure as
of genuine success, and Elena thinks that there's no help
either for Julio Welles, Julio da Vinci, Julio the Marvelous,
Julio the Triumphant, because he will always feel – at least
in his periods of depressive disillusionment – which follow
and precede the periods of wild euphoria, during which
he continues to believe he can devour the world – as defeated as Eduardo, who in the judgment of others, in public
opinion, has come to nothing, or as Arturo, who has not
managed to put down roots in anything or anyone or any
place, or as Andrea, who is setting out on the hard road
to the loss of youth and beauty – so difficult for those who
have been truly beautiful – and may also have lost or be

losing the ability to fall in love over and over and on each occasion abandon herself to the highest pleasure openly and without reserve (in any case Julio less defeated than Elena, all of them less defeated than Elena herself, who has never lost because she's never had the guts to place a bet, to finish her poems and stories and try to publish them, who hasn't had the courage to add her king to the game and thus run the risk of losing him and losing it), so there's no help either for Julio, he will never reach the height of his ambition: although others see him at the top, there will always be some obscure critic in the provinces who maintains he is a sham, or that his creativity is exhausted or spent, there will always exist somewhere, inside or outside the university, groups of young people who perhaps admire him but file him away as an admittedly important figure of the past, his name will always be omitted, out of spite or neglect, from some of the lists of the best films of the year or of the entire history of cinema, and now Julio looks at her expectantly, "So now tell me what you're thinking," and Elena prepares all the mechanisms at her disposal to reassure the genius, to return to him his faith in himself in all its glory, to reaffirm him during moments of doubt and vacillation, like this one perhaps, in the belief that he is the greatest or figures in the short list of the greatest, but first she has a fleeting thought, which she does not tell him, for one thing because in these circumstances nothing can interest Julio that does not relate directly and exclusively to himself, so Elena lines up her instruments, her arms, and she smiles, and does not tell him she's been thinking that tomorrow, when the Wizard opens the door to his consulting room, she'll take the hand he offers her and not let go, she won't let him set out on the winding path to the brothel-sanctuary, but first, on the very threshold, she'll tell him the big news: "You know something, Wizard, I'm going to undergo psychoanalysis."

Afterword

Barbara F. Ichiishi

The Catalan author Esther Tusquets is a well-known figure on the Spanish literary scene. Since the early sixties she has directed the small Barcelona publishing house Editorial Lumen, which has established a solid reputation in contemporary Spanish literature, translations of foreign classics, and children's literature. Tusquets became known as a writer during the late seventies and eighties with the appearance of four novels that are considered by many to constitute a narrative tetralogy: *El mismo mar de todos los veranos* (1978), *El amor es un juego solitario* (1979), *Varada tras el último naufragio* (1980), and *Para no volver* (1985).[1] Each of her novels has received high critical acclaim on both sides of the Atlantic; her second book won the Premio Ciudad de Barcelona in 1979. Her fiction has a wide readership in Spain, especially among women, and her works have been translated into a number of foreign languages. This English translation of her fourth novel completes the above-mentioned series in English, following the works of the original trilogy: *The Same Sea As Every Summer* (1990), *Love Is a Solitary Game* (1985), and *Stranded* (1991).

Although Tusquets has not been directly involved with the feminist movement in Spain, her writing is intricately bound up with recent developments in feminist theory and narrative practice. With the rise of the women's movement in recent decades, questions relating to female psychology and emotional development have emerged as a subject of passionate interest and concern. Women's quest for understanding and self-realization has taken many forms, finding expression notably in the field of psychology and in the arts, especially literature. On the one hand,

173

feminist psychoanalytic thinkers have surpassed the Freudian legacy by formulating theories seeking to explain and validate a somewhat different (rather than inferior) developmental course for women. Recent Anglo-American theory highlights the importance of the mother-daughter bond to the girl child's gender identity and sense of self and believes this intense and prolonged primary bond to be at the root of a deep ongoing desire for the human connection, for close relationships with family, friends, lover, or spouse, a desire that persists throughout life along with the need for autonomous achievement.[2] Over the same period some French feminist theorists have explored the distinctive nature of woman's emotional-erotic experience, grounded in her ability to generate and nurture new life, and believe in the possibility of a "feminine writing" that will express a vision of life as flow and interpenetration between self and other.[3] Meanwhile on both sides of the Atlantic, a growing number of women writers have given voice to their own special forms of experience in their narrative works, works that often depart from the literary models of their male counterparts to define a uniquely female novel of development.[4]

Such is the case of the narrative tetralogy of Esther Tusquets, a daringly innovative series of female novels of development that suggests through narrative structure, voice, and style a distinctive psychic makeup and developmental path for women.[5] While each novel in the series can be read as a separate work having its own characters and plot, the intricate pattern of theme and variations that weaves them all together makes it possible to regard the series on another level as a single extended developmental tale that takes the reader through various phases of the life cycle, a narrative tapestry depicting a story that is at once individual, distinctly feminine, and in the largest sense, universal.

In Tusquets's fictional world the developmental process is deferred until midlife, after societal expectations concerning marriage and family have been fulfilled. Each work repeats the same basic emotional situation: a middle-aged woman, wife and mother, undergoes an emotional crisis that shakes her world to its foundations, a crisis involving the failure of love. This failure serves as the catalyst for an inner journey of discovery, a voyage inward and backward in time to unravel the mystery of the course her life has taken. The journey becomes an unconscious pilgrimage in search of the lost mother and the satisfactory primal bonding she needs in order to live and grow.[6] The ardent quest for love and for union of her past and present selves is apparent both in the subject matter of the texts and in their circular, repetitive structure, in the breakup of chronological time to make the protagonist's emotional life the organizing principle of the narration, and in the musical, dreamlike style that inscribes the endless prolongation and flow of female desire.[7]

In the apparently circular pattern of the four tales is embedded evidence of psychic evolution: as each heroine relives the tragic story of her own past, she arrives at a higher level of understanding in a rising spiral of self-awareness. Taken as a whole the series can be said to define a "midlife apprenticeship" novel that holds out the possibility of growth and development during the middle years, as the author's female personae struggle on to a more mature awareness of self and world in preparation for a fresh start on the rest of their lives. The overall direction is from a stance of deathlike retreat in the first and second novels to a more engaged and realistic outlook in the third and fourth, a change in attitude that parallels a progression through the life cycle from the all-female preoedipal world of *The Same Sea As Every Summer* to the heterosexual (oedipal) worlds of *Stranded* and *Never to Return*. Along with this maturational process comes an evolution in imagery and style from the childlike fantasy idiom of the first book to the more realistic, adult modes of discourse of the third and fourth.

And yet, as the author slowly unfolds a midlife progress narrative that moves her protagonists in the direction of greater autonomy and independence, she also throws into question the very notion of human development in a phallocentric world. As her fictional personae struggle to become individuals and to adapt to the society in which they live, there is a sense in which the growing-up process connotes a moving away from their true selves. They must achieve integration into a world of separateness, of isolation, of unbridgeable gulfs between mind and body, intellect and feeling that cut them off from the emotional core of their being. Tusquets's narrative consciousness seeks to overcome emotional estrangement in two ways: by a gender-marked writing that creates on the level of style the harmonious world of her desire and by narrative strategies designed to challenge and subvert some of the discourses that have formed the female protagonists, thereby implicitly calling into question the developmental norms of a patriarchal world. In incorporating these "alien" idioms into her own, she plays with them in ways that serve to liberate her (and her reader) from their pervasive influence.

Tusquets's fourth novel, *Never to Return* (1985), returns to the themes of her earlier works, now viewed from the vantage point of an older, more mature woman. As in the novels of the trilogy, the narrative inscribes the working-through process of a midlife protagonist who is in the throes of an emotional crisis owing to the real or imagined failure of love. Elena, a woman on the brink of turning fifty, suddenly falls into a deep depression brought on by her husband's odyssey to New York to celebrate the American premiere of his latest film not with his wife but with an unknown lover half her age and by the departure of her grown-up sons to their own lives and relationships. In a state of desperation, fearing aging, loneliness, a failed love, and a failed life, she begins sessions with a reputable Argentine analyst. So here the primary vehicle of development is Elena's experience of psychoanalysis as recounted in her third-person inner monologue over the period of undergoing treatment in her husband's absence. Her narration becomes another intense exploration of self and world, this time in the context of the analytic relationship. The verbal account of her experience brings character and reader face to face with basic issues of female psychology and gender roles as it explores the implications for female development of one of the master discourses of patriarchal society. Situated both outside and inside the analytic experience, Elena's discourse offers a perspective that is complex and ambivalent, at once a sharply satiric view of the analytic endeavor and a consideration of its possible power and effectiveness.

It is interesting to consider why it is in the fourth novel that Tusquets's fictional persona finally turns to analysis. The texts taken both individually and as a series clearly demonstrate the psychic phenomenon identified by Freud as the "repetition compulsion." According to Freud, when a traumatic (often childhood) event that is too painful to bear is repressed into the unconscious, the unresolved emotional conflict continues to make itself felt in the individual's waking life, surfacing repeatedly in disguised form as a physical symptom or mode of behavior that the patient does not understand and cannot control. The purpose of the analysis is to free patients from their obsessive behavior by allowing them to act out (or repeat) the unconscious conflict with the analyst and eventually bring to light the repressed material that has been blocking their progress.[8] In like manner, the narrative voices who speak in the tetralogy appear to have a compulsive need to go over and over the same psychic issue in a working-through process without end. The choice of psychoanalysis as the subject of the fourth book appears to express a firm resolve to tackle and overcome the problem once and for all by the most powerful ("scientific") means available. The narrator who speaks here has decided that the time has come when she *must* grow up: there is no more turning back. Hence the suggestive double thrust of the Spanish title with its

lyrical fragment from Rubén Darío. Darío's haunting refrain, "Juventud, divino tesoro, / ya te vas para no volver"
[Youth, divine treasure, / now you're leaving, never to
return], which serves as the epigraph for Tusquets's book,
expresses a melancholy nostalgia for the passage of time,
the loss of youth and love.[9] Aging, loss, and disillusionment
are central themes of the novel. But interestingly, when
the phrase "para no volver" is taken out of context, the
"para," with its common meaning "in order to," endows
the phrase with a different (yet related) meaning. Along
with Darío's wistful "never to return," it can also signify "*in
order not to* return." Elena is determined not to revert to her
former state of naive innocence or to the dark labyrinths
of a mythical past. Thus, the three-word title condenses the
central conflict of Tusquets's work while pointing the way
to recovery: the emotional pull back to our lost (illusory)
paradises is countered by the strong resolve to move for-
ward, bolstered by a more mature, sober view of life.

While *Never to Return* may be read as a midlife progress narrative that charts a course to inner development,
this elusive text refuses to offer a simple set of answers. The
key to the novel's complexity lies in the interaction between
the narrative voice and the conceptual system of psychoanalysis as embodied in her Argentine analyst. The reader
does not have access to the actual words of Elena's doctor:
we do not witness directly the transactions between the two.
Rather, we experience the analytic dialogue at one remove,
as it has been internalized by one of the participants – the
analysand – as she reviews and meditates on her own experience. Blended into Elena's discourse is a parodic imitation of the language of analysis: its basic beliefs, vocabulary,
methodology, and so on. By filtering the discourse of analysis through the voice of a lay person who is coming to it
for the first time, the author can give us an inside picture
of the therapeutic process while at the same time subject-
ing it to her own intentions. The narrator's monologue
overflows with her ongoing ambivalence toward analysis, an

ambivalence that is never fully resolved. At times she mocks and deflates basic analytic doctrines – the techniques, attitudes, and even physical appearance of her analyst – while at other times she appears to recognize its potential force. What results is a vital encounter between two contrasting points of view, a tense, dynamic, ever changing and evolving conversation that as in life does not lead to final resolution or closure. The text arrives at no final answers but instead challenges the reader by engaging her or him with this open-ended dialogue and demanding her or his active participation in the creation of meaning.[10]

Tusquets's subtle parody of analysis raises important questions about Freudian doctrines and procedures as they pertain to female development and in so doing points to the role played by culture in forming the individual.[11] The main premises of the Freudian system relegate woman to a secondary position by setting up the male developmental model (based on such foundational theories as the Oedipus complex and castration anxiety) as the norm for all human development and regarding female difference as developmental failure. While every analysand is in an inferior position to the analyst in the "asymmetrical" patient-doctor relationship, according to the premises of classical Freudianism woman is doubly diminished since she is defined by what she lacks: the crowning glory of the male phallus. Orthodox analytic procedures accentuate this hierarchization, the (usually male) analyst sitting above with the patient in full view, the (often female) analysand lying down and facing away from him. Moreover, in maintaining the strict rule of silence and sitting outside the patient's range of vision, the analyst denies the patient any kind of warm affective response, verbal or nonverbal: the treatment becomes an arid scientific quest without any appreciation of the basic need for the personal, for an understanding, empathetic human connection.

The discourse of psychoanalysis repeats and reinforces the patterns of male dominance that run through all

179

aspects of patriarchal action and thought: created by and for men, it leaves women no choice but to use a borrowed language that denies their authority to speak with their own voices. The difficulties women have in ascending to the position of subject of their own lives and their own discourse is a central issue in all of Tusquets's work. The women characters tend to play a passive role, their emotional lives revolving around men and finding their purpose in serving others' needs. In *Never to Return* this problem is dramatized in the story of the protagonist, Elena. She is quite literally a woman living in a man's world, since all of the important people in her life are men (with one exception, a character who is almost invisible in the text). And Elena is largely a product of the phallocentric discourses she has absorbed over the course of her life: Francoist propaganda on the role of the good wife and mother, romantic images of women in literature and film, psychoanalytic doctrine, and so on. She behaves in accordance with many of the spoken and unspoken laws of the patriarchal world: both her emotional life and her work center on men (her husband and sons); she is dependent and has difficulty asserting herself as the subject of her own story.

This dynamic is symbolically reenacted in Elena's relationship with her Argentine analyst, a member of the Freudian-Lacanian school. The analyst exudes the mystique of the quintessential male authority figure, a distant sage, presumed repository of all wisdom, whom she simultaneously worships, hates, and adores. Fiercely dependent on him, she is unable to break off treatment even when she consciously thinks it is of no help, hangs on his few words as though they were "judgments of the oracle," and desperately seeks his approval and love as though her life depended on it. And yet, her narration displays her own strategies to resist subjugation to the order of the phallus, to reject the role of passive, obedient daughter. She is an active, impertinent interlocutor who punctures and ridicules, interrogates and challenges the analyst's claims to a higher truth while attempting to expose his own hidden weakness and desire. She submits to the rules of the talking cure while at the same time using language as a weapon to defeat the analyst in his own game, to unravel the thread of insight and mock and deflate his claims to importance. Her behavior can be read in one sense as a manifestation of the transference and resistance, an acting out of her past dependency relationships and conflicts. But it can also be seen as an attempt (albeit unsuccessful) to really engage with the analyst on her own terms, to break out of the rigid rules of a one-sided game to embark on a more genuine encounter between two human beings.

Ironically, both despite and because of all her difficulties, Elena does appear to grow through the analytic experience. She seems to develop through her double posture of being both inside and outside the experience, that is, through the dynamic interaction that unfolds in her third-person discourse. From her perspective within the experience, the transference finally leads her to confront herself, allowing her to see that the conflictual dependency relationship she has established with the Wizard repeats the pattern of earlier attachments, with mother, husband, and others, and to acknowledge her own accountability in past and present failures.

On the other hand, her irreverent challenging and deflating of the Wizard's pompous claims to a higher truth soon extend to a questioning of her relationships with the important men in her life, the "male authority figures" upon whom her emotional (and physical) well-being depends. Suddenly she sees the men who have overawed her with their strength and self-sufficiency in the new light of their own human weakness and vulnerability. By the end of her weeks of self-discovery, Elena finds the giants of her world reduced in size, especially the legendary figure around whom her life revolves: her husband, Julio da Vinci, Julio Welles. She feels a real disillusionment in her perpetual "child genius" husband and in the power of romantic love. Although at the story's end she returns to the pre-ordained female roles, she does so with a secret sense of superiority, borne of the simple fact that she sees herself and the world as they really are, while the men continue to delude themselves about their own importance.

As we close the book, however, we sense that the key questions remain unanswered. Is the analysis really beneficial to Elena, and does it justify her final commitment to treatment? Can an analyst of his ilk further help this kind of woman, or on the contrary would it be essential, as many have come to believe, to find a person who can make up for the deficit in empathic nurturance and understanding she suffered as a child?[12] Is there evidence to suggest that Elena has changed and progressed by the end of the book in a way that will influence her future behavior? Taking a larger view, what can we conclude about the developmental process that unfolds in the tetralogy as a whole? Indeed, what is the nature and significance of psychic maturation in a patriarchal society, in particular as it relates to female development? Does the prevailing male developmental model, with its emphasis on separateness, autonomy, and mastery, lead to a joyous state of plenitude and wholeness, or does it on the contrary tend to diminish us, to impoverish our lives on the imaginary-affective level? The Elena of the final pages of the book has a more mature, realistic outlook than any of her predecessors – but it is left to the reader to assess what has been gained and what lost as Tusquets's female persona has moved away from the emotionalism of youth in the struggle to achieve full adulthood.

The style of discourse in Tusquets's fourth book likewise reflects and fosters a new desire and readiness to "grow up." For the first time the narrative voice adopts a lighter tone that shifts the work from the tragic to the ironic mode, lowering the emotional register and allowing her (and us) to step back and view self and world with greater detachment and objectivity. Ironic humor, including witty wordplay, anecdotes, and jokes, serves as a narrative strategy designed to distance and thereby free herself from the discourses that have hitherto governed her life: in particular, the literary discourse of romanticism and the "scientific" discourse of analysis as representative of the belief systems of her social world. Imagery and style are somewhat drier and less poetic than in the earlier novels, in consonance with the "dry" masculine science of analysis as emblematic of a phallogocentric approach to life. While maintaining Tusquets's stylistic constant of the long, winding sentences that follow the associative flow of the characters' thought, in contrast to the dreamy erotic style of the first book, here the idiom appears more rational and matter-of-fact in tone: Elena is sparring with the analyst and with herself on the intellectual level. But at the same time, the more detached tone attests to progress in individuating, to a moving beyond the regressive urge toward merger between self and world. The text demonstrates a new ability to see the humor in her situation, to loosen up and not take life so seriously, a new openness to the world around her and to her own problems and shortcomings, which signifies the capacity to integrate and better come to terms with the effects of unconscious desire. And this is in turn reflected in a warmer, more sympathetic view of the narrator's social world, featuring a colorful cast of characters whose all too obvious failings only underscore their basic humanity.

Female development has been described as a rising spiral, a continual going over the same ground of concerns each time at a higher level of awareness.[13] The narrative consciousness of *Never to Return* views life from a more mature perspective than that of the earlier works and by the end of the novel has reached a new point of elevation on the spiral. This is attributable not to any one cause but rather to a complex of factors – and the insight gained is on many levels. Elena's intercourse with those of her social background leads her to confront the failure of those of her generation to realize their youthful dreams of changing the world. Her marital story forces her to give up forever her exalted romantic notions in favor of a more enduring form of love, while her experience of analysis implies a questioning of the roles assigned to women in a phallocratic world. Above all, it is her exposure to universal human weakness and vulnerability, to the inescapable facts of aging and death, that yields inner growth. When faced with the rigid boundaries of the human experience, as condensed in Darío's haunting phrase "never to return," she realizes that the time has come to shed her adolescent idealism and adopt a more sober, realistic attitude toward the future. She has learned that, given the short time we have and the limitations that affect us all, we have no choice but to embrace life in its imperfection, to accept ourselves as we are, and as best we can to help each other (man and wife, mother and child, friend and lover) get through.

Tusquets's highly self-conscious texts engage in a shrewd questioning and challenging of some of the discourses that contribute to the socialization process, in particular, as they impact on female development. In *Never to Return*, the subtle parody of psychoanalysis points to woman as the product of a series of alien discourses not of her own making and in so doing appears to raise the problem of the place of woman in a male-centered world. In challenging the claims of analysis to provide a scientific path to man's salvation, the female narrator's irreverent discourse goes further to implicitly question the entire fabric of patriarchal forms of thought, subtly undermining man's teleological belief in a transcendent purpose behind our life on earth, a purpose that is ultimately knowable by dint of his tireless quest for mastery, knowledge, truth. In her fourth book, as in her fictional work as a whole, the author implicitly affirms a different kind of knowledge, the softer, warmer understanding that derives from the body, nature, and the human connection – that is, the wisdom of love, which can uniquely illuminate our vital experience. In suggesting through form and content the lifelong importance of the originary mother-daughter bond, she points to an alternate

developmental path imbued with closeness, interpenetration, and deep human communion. Her writing counters
the prevailing mind-body split with a vision of psychic plenitude and wholeness, of wisdom that flows from body feeling
and from the experience of intimacy itself. In so doing
Tusquets's work offers an alternative model that dissolves
the barriers among diverse modes of sexuality and affirms
love in all its forms as the supreme value of life.

NOTES

1. Since completion of this essay, Tusquets has published
a fifth novel, *Con la miel en los labios* (Barcelona: Editorial Anagrama, 1997). Her new novel is a reworking of the themes of her
earlier works, but they are no longer viewed from the perspective
of a midlife protagonist in the throes of an ardent search for
self. She has also published two collections of short stories, *Siete
miradas en el mismo paisaje* (1981) and *"La niña lunática" y otros
cuentos* (1997); two children's tales, *La conejita Marcela* (1980)
and *La reina de los gatos* (1993); and other short works.

2. See, for example, Nancy Chodorow, *The Reproduction
of Mothering: Psychoanalysis and the Sociology of Gender* (Berkeley:
University of California Press, 1978); Carol Gilligan, *In a Different
Voice: Psychological Theory and Women's Development* (Cambridge MA:
Harvard University Press, 1982); Carol Gilligan, Janie Victoria
Ward, and Jill McLean Taylor, eds., *Mapping the Moral Domain:
A Contribution of Women's Thinking to Psychological Theory and Ed-
ucation* (Cambridge MA: Harvard University Press, 1988); Carol
Gilligan, Annie G. Rogers, and Deborah L. Tolman, eds., *Women,
Girls and Psychotherapy: Reframing Resistance* (New York: Haworth,
1991); Jean Baker Miller, *Toward a New Psychology of Women*, 2d
ed. (Boston: Beacon, 1986); Jean Baker Miller and Irene Pierce
Stiver, *The Healing Connection: How Women Form Relationships in
Therapy and in Life* (Boston: Beacon, 1997); Mary Field Belenky,
Blythe McVicker Clinchy, Nancy Rule Goldberger, and Jill Mattuck
Tarule, *Women's Ways of Knowing: The Development of Self, Voice,*

and Mind (New York: Basic, 1986); and Sara Ruddick, *Maternal Thinking: Toward a Politics of Peace* (Boston: Beacon, 1989).

3. Among the French theorists who have explored these questions, the most familiar to English-speaking readers are perhaps Hélène Cixous and Luce Irigaray. For a basic overview of the French feminist landscape, which discusses the work both of theorists and of contemporary French women writers, see Susan Sellers, *Language and Sexual Difference: Feminist Writing in France* (New York: St. Martin's, 1991).

4. For a seminal study of the female novel of development, see Elizabeth Abel, Marianne Hirsch, and Elizabeth Langland, eds., *The Voyage In: Fictions of Female Development* (Hanover NH: University Press of New England, 1983). See also Carol P. Christ, *Diving Deep and Surfacing: Women Writers on Spiritual Quest* (Boston: Beacon, 1980); Katherine Dalsimer, *Female Adolescence: Psychoanalytic Reflections on Works of Literature* (New Haven: Yale University Press, 1986); Shirley Nelson Garner, Claire Kahane, and Madelon Sprengnether, eds., *The (M)other Tongue: Essays in Feminist Psychoanalytic Interpretation* (Ithaca: Cornell University Press, 1985); Sandra M. Gilbert and Susan Gubar, *The Madwoman in the Attic: The Woman Writer and the Nineteenth-Century Literary Imagination* (New Haven: Yale University Press, 1979); Marianne Hirsch, *The Mother/Daughter Plot: Narrative, Psychoanalysis, Feminism* (Bloomington: Indiana University Press, 1989); Patricia Meyer Spacks, *The Female Imagination* (New York: Alfred A. Knopf, 1975); and Patricia Yaeger, *Honey-Mad Women: Emancipatory Strategies in Women's Writing* (New York: Columbia University Press, 1988).

5. The material in this essay is drawn from Barbara F. Ichiishi, *The Apple of Earthly Love: Female Development in Esther Tusquets' Fiction* (New York: Peter Lang, 1994).

6. The impact of faulty preoedipal mother-daughter bonding in Tusquets's first novel is examined in Mirella Servodidio, "A Case of Pre-oedipal and Narrative Fixation: *El mismo mar de todos los veranos*," *Anales de la literatura española contemporanea* 12, no. 1–2 (1987): 157–74; and Ichiishi, *The Apple of Earthly Love*. Since the publication of her fictional tetralogy, Tusquets has written an autobiographical account of her relationship with

her mother and its profound psychological influence in the short narrative "Carta a la madre," in the collection Laura Freixas, ed., *Madres e hijas* (Barcelona: Editorial Anagrama, S.A., 1996), 75–93.

7. Tusquets's prose style resonates with the French feminist notion of an "écriture féminine" (feminine writing), a writing of the body that would inscribe textually the distinctive nature of woman's erotic-emotional life. This tendency is most pronounced in Tusquets's first novel, although the basic style carries through her narrative cycle. For representative French feminist theory on women's writing, see Hélène Cixous, "The Laugh of the Medusa," in *New French Feminisms*, ed. E. Marks and I. de Courtivron (New York: Schocken, 1981), and "Sorties: Out and Out: Attacks/Ways Out/Forays," in Hélène Cixous and Catherine Clément, *The Newly Born Woman*, tr. Betsy Wing (Minneapolis: University of Minnesota Press, 1986); and Luce Irigaray, "This Sex Which Is Not One," in *New French Feminisms*, and "When Our Lips Speak Together," tr. Carolyn Burke, *Signs* 6, no. 1 (autumn 1980): 69–79. For analyses of Tusquets's prose style, see Catherine G. Bellver, "The Language of Eroticism in the Novels of Esther Tusquets," *Anales de la literatura española contemporanea* 9, no. 1–3 (1984): 13–27; Akiko Tsuchiya, "Theorizing the Feminine: Esther Tusquets' *El mismo mar de todos los veranos* and Hélène Cixous' *écriture féminine*," *Revista de estudios hispánicos* 26, no. 2 (May 1992): 183–99; Mirella Servodidio, "Esther Tusquets's Fiction: The Spinning of a Narrative Web," in *Women Writers in Contemporary Spain: Exiles in the Homeland*, ed. Joan L. Brown (Newark: University of Delaware Press, 1991); and Ichiishi, *The Apple of Earthly Love*.

8. Sigmund Freud, "Remembering, Repeating and Working-through (Further Recommendations on the Technique of Psycho-analysis II)" (1914), *The Standard Edition of the Complete Psychological Works* (London: Hogarth, 1953), 12:147–56.

9. Rubén Darío, "Canción de otoño en primavera," in *Cantos de vida y esperanza* (Barcelona: F. Granada y Ca., Editores, 1907), 85–88.

10. The novel offers a brilliant example of the theory of internal dialogism developed by the Russian sociolinguist Mikhail M. Bakhtin in his essay "Discourse in the Novel," in *The Dialogic*

Imagination, tr. Caryl Emerson and Michael Holquist (Austin: University of Texas Press, 1981), 259–422.

11. Several recent articles explore these connections. See, for example, Catherine G. Bellver, "Assimilation and Confrontation in Esther Tusquets's *Para no volver*," *Romanic Review* 81, no. 3 (May 1990): 368–76; Gonzalo Návajas, "Civilization and Fictions of Love in Esther Tusquets' *Para no volver*," in *The Sea of Becoming: Approaches to the Fiction of Esther Tusquets*, ed. Mary Vásquez (Westport CT: Greenwood, 1991); Mercedes M. de Rodriguez, "*Para no volver*: Humor vs. Phallocentrism," *Letras femeninas* 16, no. 1–2 (1990): 29–35; Mirella Servodidio, "Esther Tusquets' Fiction: The Spinning of a Narrative Web," in Brown, ed., *Women Writers in Contemporary Spain*; and Robert Spires, "The Games Men Play: *Para no volver*," in *Post-Totalitarian Spanish Fiction* (Columbia: University of Missouri Press, 1996). It is also examined from a different perspective in Nina L. Molinaro's intertextual study of power relations in Tusquets's work, *Foucault, Feminism, and Power: Reading Esther Tusquets* (Lewisburg PA: Bucknell University Press, 1991).

12. See, for instance, Heinz Kohut, *The Restoration of the Self* (New York: International Universities Press, 1977); and Alice Miller, *The Drama of the Gifted Child*, tr. Ruth Ward (New York: Basic, 1981), and *Thou Shalt Not Be Aware: Society's Betrayal of the Child*, tr. Hildegarde and Hunter Hannum (New York: Meridian, 1986). For a feminist perspective on this issue, see Annie G. Rogers, "A Feminist Poetics of Psychotherapy," and Catherine Steiner Adair, "When the Body Speaks: Girls, Eating Disorders and Psychotherapy," in Gilligan, Rogers, and Tolman, eds., *Women, Girls and Psychotherapy*; and Miller and Stiver, *The Healing Connection*.

13. See, for example, Christ, *Diving Deep and Surfacing*; and Gilligan, *In a Different Voice*.

Glossary

Spanish and Latin American
Historical and Cultural Terms

bolas (boleadoras): A hunting weapon used by the Argentine gauchos consisting of several ropes tied together with stone or metal balls at the ends.

Falangist party (Falange Española): The primary fascist movement of twentieth-century Spain, founded in 1933 by José Antonio Primo de Rivera. The manifesto of 1934 set forth the basic party doctrine, advocating the creation of a national syndicalist state, a strong government and military, and Spanish imperialist expansion, while repudiating the republican constitution, party politics, Marxism, and capitalism. When General Francisco Franco became dictator in 1937, he announced that the Falange would merge with monarchist and Catholic groups to form a united movement, Falange Española Tradicionalista (FET), to serve as a state party for the new regime. The main functions of the FET were to direct political indoctrination and education for Spaniards, provide reliable personnel for the government and bureaucracy, and conduct the regime's social and labor programs. Membership in the Falange became indispensable for political advancement, but the party gradually distanced itself from its original fascist agenda as Franco's regime evolved during the late forties and fifties. Several months prior to Franco's death in 1975, a law was passed allowing the establishment of other political parties; thereafter, and especially after Franco's death, other parties began to proliferate. By this time the Falange had become moribund; it was formally abolished in 1977.

El Hogar y la Moda: The first woman's home and fashion magazine in Spain. First published in 1909 in Barcelona.

Malinche: Indian mistress and companion of Hernán Cortés. Daughter of an Aztec governor, she was given to Cortés on the Tabasco coast in 1519. She served as interpreter for Cortés in the conquest of Mexico: her knowledge of the Nahuatl and Maya languages enabled her to negotiate successfully for Cortés and to advise him about the intentions of the people with whom he was dealing. In 1522 she gave birth to a son by Cortés. She was later married to Captain Juan Jaramillo, and Cortés endowed their union with a labor grant. She and Jaramillo had a daughter, and she died soon after, in 1527.

Manolete, Manuel Rodríguez Sánchez: Spanish bull-fighter. A great matador, he was the most representative bull-fighter of the forties. He was killed in Linares in 1947, at the age of thirty, by the bull Islero.

maté: An aromatic beverage used in South America, especially Paraguay, that has stimulant properties like tea or coffee and is made by pouring boiling water over the dried leaves and stems of the maté plant. Also, the small gourd used for holding the maté drink.

Primo de Rivera, José Antonio: Son of the dictator Miguel Primo de Rivera and founder of the Spanish fascist party Falange Española. In 1933 he launched the Falangist party, an extreme nationalist political movement that stood for a new authoritarian system, a centralized syndicalist state, and an antiliberal, antimarxist ideology. Soon after the leftist Popular Front came to power in 1936, he was imprisoned and his party dissolved. With the outbreak of the Spanish Civil War he was given a summary trial, found guilty of treason, and executed by firing squad in November 1936. Primo de Rivera's articles and speeches formed the doctrine of Franco's nationalist movement in the years following the civil war.

El ruedo Ibérico (The Iberian wheel): A series of historical novels by the Spanish author Ramón María del Valle-Inclán. In writing a satirical attack on the court of Isabel II preceding the revolution of 1868, the author used the historical setting to evade the censorship of Miguel Primo de Rivera and make oblique comments on the corruption and brutality of his own time, the Spain of the 1920s and 1930s. Only two of the projected nine volumes in the series were completed: *La corte de los milagros* (The court of miracles, 1927) and *Viva mi dueño* (Long live the chief,

1928); the unfinished *Baza de espadas* (The generals' trump suit) appeared in serial form in the newspaper *El Sol* starting in 1932.

Social Service (Servicio social de la mujer): Mandatory community service imposed by Franco's decree of 1937 requiring all Spanish women between the ages of seventeen and thirty to spend six months participating in various social service activities in institutions such as schools, hospitals, and churches. The Social Service was a program organized by the women's branch of the Falangist party (Sección Femenina), which was designed to train Spanish women for their "proper" role through compulsory courses and social work. The "new" Spanish woman was to create an ideal home life: she was to be happy in motherhood, be a teacher to her children, take a proper feminine interest in the affairs of her husband, and provide a tranquil refuge for the man from the uncertainties of public life.

vicuña: The smallest member of the camel family. It lives in the Andes Mountains of Ecuador, Peru, and Bolivia in places from twelve thousand to fifteen thousand feet above sea level. It has finer fleece than any other wool-bearing animal; the inner fleece is used for high-grade worsted.

IN THE EUROPEAN
WOMEN WRITERS SERIES:

Artemisia
By Anna Banti
Translated by Shirley D'Ardia
Caracciolo

Bitter Healing
German Women Writers,
1700–1830
An Anthology
Edited by Jeannine Blackwell
and Susanne Zantop

The Maravillas District
By Rosa Chacel
Translated by d. a. démers

Memoirs of Leticia Valle
By Rosa Chacel
Translated by Carol Maier

The Book of Promethea
By Hélène Cixous
Translated by Betsy Wing

The Terrible but Unfinished Story
of Norodom Sihanouk,
King of Cambodia
By Hélène Cixous
Translated by Juliet Flower
MacCannell, Judith Pike, and
Lollie Groth

The Governor's Daughter
By Paule Constant
Translated by Betsy Wing

Maria Zef
By Paola Drigo
Translated by Blossom
Steinberg Kirschenbaum

Woman to Woman
By Marguerite Duras and
Xavière Gauthier
Translated by Katharine A.
Jensen

Hitchhiking
Twelve German Tales
By Gabriele Eckart
Translated by Wayne Kvam

The South and Bene
By Adelaida García Morales
Translated and with a preface
by Thomas G. Deveny

The Tongue Snatchers
By Claudine Herrmann
Translated by Nancy Kline

The Panther Woman
Five Tales from the Cassette
Recorder
By Sarah Kirsch
Translated by Marion Faber

Concert
By Else Lasker-Schüler
Translated by Jean M. Snook

Slander
By Linda Lê
Translated by Esther Allen

Daughters of Eve
Women's Writing from the
German Democratic Republic
Translated and edited by
Nancy Lukens and Dorothy
Rosenberg

Celebration in the Northwest
By Ana María Matute
Translated by Phoebe Ann
Porter

On Our Own Behalf
Women's Tales from Catalonia
Edited by Kathleen McNerney

Dangerous Virtues
By Ana María Moix
Translated and with an
afterword by Margaret E. W.
Jones

The Forbidden Woman
By Malika Mokeddem
Translated by K. Melissa
Marcus

Absent Love
A Chronicle
By Rosa Montero
Translated by Cristina de la
Torre and Diana Glad

The Delta Function
By Rosa Montero
Translated and with an
afterword by Kari Easton and
Yolanda Molina Gavilán

Nadirs
By Herta Müller
Translated and with an
introduction by Sieglinde Lug

Music from a Blue Well
By Torborg Nedreaas
Translated by Bibbi Lee

Nothing Grows by Moonlight
By Torborg Nedreaas
Translated by Bibbi Lee

Bordeaux
By Soledad Puértolas
Translated by Francisca
González-Arias

Candy Story
By Marie Redonnet
Translated by Alexandra
Quinn

Forever Valley
By Marie Redonnet
Translated by Jordan Stump

Hôtel Splendid
By Marie Redonnet
Translated by Jordan Stump

Nevermore
By Marie Redonnet
Translated by Jordan Stump

Rose Mellie Rose
By Marie Redonnet
Translated by Jordan Stump

The Man in the Pulpit
Questions for a Father
By Ruth Rehmann
Translated by Christoph
Lohmann and Pamela
Lohmann

Abelard's Love
By Luise Rinser
Translated by Jean M. Snook

Why Is There Salt in the Sea?
By Brigitte Schwaiger
Translated by Sieglinde Lug

The Same Sea As Every Summer
By Esther Tusquets
Translated and with an
afterword by Margaret E. W.
Jones

Never to Return
By Esther Tusquets
Translated and with an
afterword by Barbara F.
Ichiishi

*The Life of High Countess Gritta
von Ratsinourhouse*
By Bettine von Arnim and
Gisela von Arnim Grimm
Translated and with an
introduction by Lisa Ohm